Sadie's Story

Sandra Dears

ONE
49 Carver Street - 1910

Sadie Settle groaned quietly as she heard the familiar tapping of the knocker upper on the bedroom window. Micky O'Carrol had been knocking on that window for twenty years, Carver Street was on his round, as were many of the terraced streets in that part of Liverpool. The knocker upper was known as Tappy, that was the only name Sadie had ever heard anyone call him. Since her mother had got too frail to work, it was Sadie who woke to the sound of his tapping on the windowpane. Quarter to six, her time to rise every morning except Sunday. Hurriedly, Sadie threw on a petticoat, an ankle length, black skirt and one of her two white work blouses which she had ironed and hung on the bedpost the night before. She shivered, feeling the chill in the room, unusual this late in May and she reached for her shawl from the top of the bed and wrapped it around her shoulders. Finally, she shook her sleeping sister hoping for a few seconds of sensible communication.

"What?" snapped Gracie and in retaliation, Sadie was equally snappy.

"Don't forget to buy something in for the tea, it's your turn," she replied.

"You'll have to do it," returned Gracie, stretching, "I'm going to the Irish Centre with Jack tonight, it's his friend's birthday, he's picking me up from work."

Gracie worked in Ladies Wear at Bunneys, the biggest and oldest department store in Liverpool as she was so fond of reminding everyone. She fitted in well at Bunneys, she was eighteen, a beauty and at ease with glamour. As sisters go, these two were very different. They both had similar features, thick chestnut hair which curled in all the right places, almond shaped blue eyes and pale complexions, but it was the way their features were put together which made the difference and Gracie wore her beauty as if she deserved her perfectly put together face. Consequently, she turned heads. Sadie struggled to see past her slightly crooked nose and small mouth, so could never admit to her own beauty and anyway, she had always told herself that she had no time for fretting over how she looked.

"Don't forget to make mam's porridge before you leave," Sadie said and then out of sheer exasperation she threw in "and bring a bucket of coal up from the cellar, I can hear our Fred lighting the fire."

Fred was putting a match to the newspaper under the kindling in the grate when his sister came down the staircase into the kitchen. Keeping the cast iron range clean and the fire burning had been Fred's responsibility since he was a boy. Fred was young for his seventeen years. He came into the world the same year as his father prematurely had gone out of it. He had been molded and shaped by his mother and two older sisters and consequently he found some of the male banter that went with his job as a carter on the docks a little intimidating. There were still a few dockers who had worked with his father and they kept a watchful eye on Fred. They remembered the accident. John Settle had been loading barrels onto a cart on the dockside when a rope broke sending a barrel hurtling through the air towards him. He managed to leap out of its path, but the barrel glanced him on the side of the head just above the temple. At first, the damage appeared minimal, a cup of tea in the foreman's hut and an hour's rest and John Settle was back loading the cart. A few days later he woke speaking gibberish and couldn't get out of bed. He died leaving a pregnant wife and two young daughters. The family lived in the Courts in Ashwell Street near the river. They had one room divided for privacy's sake by an old curtain which a previous tenant had hung. Gracie had no memory of the Courts, Sadie could still remember the stench of the open sewer in front of the houses and Fred only knew the Courts by reputation, he was born in Carver Street.

Mary Jane always said that her husband gave his life to get his family out of Ashwell Street. No self-respecting doctor would ever visit the Courts. For one thing, there was no chance that they would be paid for their services and for another the place was rife with disease. But Doctor Angus McKay was different. When he went to see John Settle, he insisted that his patient had died due to the accident and as a result Mary Jane was awarded a small sum in compensation. It was just enough to pay the key money on forty-nine Carver Street and to get her family out of the Courts.

Mary Jane was determined that she and her children would never return to the slums or worse still, be forced into the workhouse. She took in washing, looked after other peoples' children, collected wood from the railway embankments and the dockside and sold it as kindling. As soon as the children were old enough, she did multiple cleaning jobs in the chemist, the Nag's Head and at the tobacco factory. As hard as she tried, Mary Jane could never wash the smell of beer and tobacco from her skin. Sadie became a surrogate mother to her siblings, especially to Fred. She did her best to lighten her mother's load and she was overjoyed when she got a job in the bakery on the day she turned fifteen.

As Fred left the house, he called to his sister, "thanks for the carry-out Sadie, I've lit the fire for Mam, it's a bit chilly down here. See you tonight."

A final shout upstairs to Gracie to make sure she was out of bed and Sadie closed the front door behind her joining all the other early birds on their way to work. She hurried along Carver Street, past the terraced houses, all in various stages of waking up. Sadie hurried along, not so much because she was afraid of being late, although Mrs. Morris was a stickler for time keeping, but because she was feeling the damp chill in the early morning air. She pulled her shawl tightly around her neck, careful not to dislodge the white cap that kept her hair in place.

TWO
The Bakery

The bell clattered as Sadie pushed open the shop door. She hardly noticed the harsh sound after six years of noisy entrances and exits. She saw Mrs. Morris glance at the clock on the wall, it said six twenty-nine, sadly for her there was no reason to complain. Complaining was Mrs M's reason for being.

Beatrice Gray came into the shop from the bakery carrying two wooden trays of individual meat pies which the long-suffering Mr. Morris had just taken out of the ovens. She smiled at Sadie as she placed them carefully on the display counter in neat rows. Sadie rang up "No sale"on the till and counted out copper and silver coins, dropping them expertly into appropriate compartments in the drawer.

By seven o'clock the shop would be heaving and there would be no time for anything but pies, pasties, bread and barms and then laying out cakes and biscuits before the afternoon rush. Trade was brisk. Mr. Morris never left the bake-house, his wife never entered it, not since she had started with her hot flushes. Her preference was to supervise the window display and position herself as near to the window as she could, in order to benefit from the cool breeze each time the door opened. The baker's wife was a small woman, broad at the shoulders and narrow at the hips, she often wore red. She resembled a soldier in his sentry box, a vantage point where she could take note of all the comings and goings of her customers, not to mention the passers-by on the street, whilst at the same time keeping a critical eye on her employees. Notably,

5

her position enabled her to whisper about the latest gossip with certain of her regulars without being overheard.

It was during these gossip sessions that Sadie and Bea were able to chat, free from Mrs. M's scrutiny. Each made the other's day bearable, even happy. Bea was a pretty eighteen-year-old, with bird like features and a full of life personality that went well with her face. She wore an engagement ring round her neck, Mrs. M having ordered its removal from her finger the day Bea came in and announced that she was going to marry Peter. In a tiny act of defiance, she started to wear the ring on a chain like a necklace. Sadie wished the couple well but occasionally when she heard that they had been to the cinema or the Rotunda to see a show, which was not very often, she felt a kind of longing which she couldn't always check before it morphed into jealousy. She didn't like this about herself.

When she could get Mrs. M's attention Sadie took a steak and kidney pie from the shelf, wrapped it, put it to one side and put the right amount of money in the till. No personal transactions were allowed without Mrs. Morris's close supervision. Sadie made a mental note to call at the greengrocers for carrots and potatoes on the way home. She was considering this when the bell clattered and in strode Councillor Braxton. His presence filled the entire shop. Mrs. M leapt out of her sentry box leaving her friend open mouthed and discarded in mid–sentence.

"Councillor Braxton, what can I do for you, how's Mrs Braxton, is she well?"

"We're all well thanks Mrs. Morris. And you and Mr. Morris, well, I hope?" he said, glancing towards the bakehouse door. But for the fact that he and Mr. Morris met regularly at Rotary meetings, Mr. Braxton would have doubted his existence. Front of house was definitely not Mr. M's calling.

Before Mrs. Morris could get into detail with regards to her health issues, Councillor Braxton launched into a hard sell. There were going to be street parties to commemorate the coronation of the new King. The Council had discussed it at length and there would be prizes for the best decorated street. Councillor Braxton felt sure that Mr and Mrs Morris would like to do their bit. After all it wasn't every day a new King was crowned. June 22nd would be the day.

"If we can't join His Majesty King George down in London the least we can do is raise a glass or two to him up here…"

Councillor Braxton continued with his pitch, explaining that as luck would have it, the Olympic would be docking in Liverpool on the very day of the coronation and the captain would be treating his guests, dignitaries, and local residents (of course) to a display of fireworks on the river. Did they know that the Olympic had the title of the largest cruise liner in existence? This was going to be the grand finale to the best street parties ever seen in the neighbourhood.

He didn't stop for breath or more likely he rattled on to stop Mrs. M from interjecting with objections.

"So, as I say, everybody is getting involved, all the shopkeepers are contributing. The butcher is curing a couple of hams, the post office is doing a raffle, Mrs. Johnson the haberdasher is making bunting and her lass works in a florist in town so she's making table decorations. We are having races for the children and

Percy Baines from the dairy has offered to do rides round the streets on his cart. What we thought, that is what the committee thought Mrs. Morris, is that Mr. Morris might be able to make a celebration cake, you know, something a bit special."

Councillor Braxton read all this from a clip board which he held in front of him but the girls could tell he knew the whole thing by heart.

Mrs. M could hold back no longer. "I think you'll find that all our cakes are special Mr. Braxton. What the committee obviously doesn't appreciate is that Mr. Morris and I get up at four thirty every morning, I don't know where we would find the extra time to make cakes." Then for good measure she added "and what with the price of dried fruit and sugar …"

Sadie glanced at Bea, neither of them daring to look at Mrs. Morris never mind proffer any opinions when Councillor Braxton pulled out his trump card.

"Of course, the Council is going to present an award for the best window display Mrs. Morris. Your cake would make a lovely centre piece and after the competition we would take it to the top table, it would have pride of place."

And that was enough to swing it. After assurances that his own wife was taking care of jellies and the council was going to supply free tables, chairs and what he called signage, Mrs. Morris agreed to have a word with her husband to see what sort of cake he could manage.

Councillor Braxton left the shop with a clatter and an "I'll bid you good day then ladies." Six of his strides and he was into the grocery shop next door to continue his mission and Mrs. Morris had returned to her post and re-joined her friend.

All previous conversation now superseded, she said "they think they're somebody these councillors but he's no better than he ought to be he's only on the council because he needed planning permission for some land he bought up near Rimmer Street. Twelve houses he's building up there, a new road and everything going in. I did hear they are going to name the new road after him, Braxton Road! He's sold three houses already and they're nowhere near finished yet. And all his wife can come up with are a few jellies!"

But the acid tongue of their employer couldn't dampen the spirits of the two young shop assistants and the days that followed were full of plans, mounting excitement and ideas. Royal memorabilia started to appear, lots of people put pictures of the new King in their windows. Neighbours got together to come up with party games and street decorations, people offered to wheel out their pianos into the streets. The men had a whip round for casks of ale and in school the children made paper chains and lanterns to hang between lamp posts. Mrs. Johnson, the seamstress and haberdasher had never been so busy. It seemed like every female in the North of Liverpool wanted something new to wear even if it was just a feather or a ribbon to re-vamp a hat.

THREE
William Tierney

Sadie's mother looked forward to hearing news about the street party plans from her elder daughter when she got home from the bakery each evening. For once, it was Sadie not Gracie who was stealing the limelight. Mary Jane was proud of her daughters. Sadie's wage from the bakery was regular and reliable and two years after she started work, sister Gracie was offered a job at Bunneys. With three wages coming in and only Fred at school, life became less hard and for a short time it was almost comfortable. Sadly, it wasn't to last, by the time Fred started his job at the docks, Mary Jane had developed a heart problem which would prevent her from working and eventually confine her to the house. Despite her mother's deteriorating health, Sadie and her siblings were determined to get her to the party, even if it meant carrying her in her chair from the table in the kitchen to the table in the street.

In the Bakery, Mrs. Morris was orchestrating her window display with military precision and mentally making room on her mantel piece for the trophy. Mr. Morris was planning a huge fruit cake, despite his wife's concern about the price of dried fruit. He was determined to make it in the shape of a cruise liner.

"Everyone will be expecting a crown," he said, to which his wife just shook her head.

Sadie was busy serving a couple of railway workers with warm pies when two young men walked into the shop. They were nudging and pushing each other in friendly banter until Mrs. M fixed them with a stare and a slight movement of her eyebrows. Sadie recognised one of them.

"We've been sent to settle Mrs. Carmichael's bill. Number 115 Carver Street. She's our landlady," said the stockier of the two.

They were brothers, though Sadie would never have known until the stocky, chatty one told her.

"I think I have seen you before", he continued, "you live in Carver Street too don't you? I've seen you going into your house, and don't you have a sister, she's a looker too."

Sadie was a little surprised that he knew so much about her, she was taken aback by his attention. She had difficulty in replying, her mouth wouldn't seem to move. Actually, it hardly mattered because his words just rattled on like rifle fire. It seemed that he and his brother were sailors, lodging with Mrs. Carmichael.

"Great landlady, cooked breakfast at the weekends not like some lodgings I could tell you about, we are only here for another couple of weeks, we've signed up for the Olympic back to New York. I'm a steward, I get to hob nob with all the toffs. Paddy here is a stoker in the engine room," and he thumped his brother on the arm. His brother shook his head but said nothing in reply.

"I'm William Tierney by the way," he said holding out his hand.

Sadie hardly knew what to do, she was flustered. Mrs. Morris had let it go so far, but only because she was curious as to who these two were. As for fraternising with her staff that was quite another matter. She moved to a strategic position between William and Sadie but unperturbed, William Tierney withdrew his hand and smiling at Sadie, he said, "I don't suppose you fancy coming for a drink with me tomorrow night do you?"

Mrs. M's face was now purple. Sadie's feet moved but she wasn't sure how. She wanted the ground to swallow her up. She turned, pushed open the door, and stepped into the safety of the bake house. She could hear nothing but the beating of her heart. She reached for Mrs. Carmichael's order, two loaves, four medium pork pies and six scones. Carrying them carefully, Sadie returned to the shop to look for the receipt book which hung from a nail under the counter. Her brain rehearsed her reply.

"I'm sorry my mother's not too well she likes me to sit with her in the evenings."

But what came out of her mouth was a different thing altogether.

"Ok, that would be nice, not too early though I need to settle my mother for the night, eight o'clock."

William's handsome face lit up as he grinned. Sadie noticed his mouth, he had a strong, confident smile. Mrs. M's face was positively puce now. She moved away to re-gain her equilibrium and think through a strategy for a reprimand.

"I thought you were going to refuse him for a minute there," whispered Bea. "He's gorgeous, blonde hair, blue eyes, and those shoulders. I could go for him myself if I didn't have my Pete. It's time you had a bit of fun Sadie but think on, I want all the gossip."

When Sadie told her mother and sister about her date with a sailor, she half expected them to rib her or even talk her out of it but instead, they surprised her.

"It's high time you had a bit of fun my girl," said her

mother, "and if he's lodging with Ruby Carmichael he'll be a nice enough lad. She doesn't let her rooms to riff raff."

Gracie went into action. She brought down a maroon cotton blouse, full sleeve, white lace collar. "I've had it for a couple of years but it's still quite fashionable. I sold one just like it the other day." It was as if Sadie was one of her ladies. "Try it on and I'll bring some stockings home from work tomorrow night. I'll get you ready, you can't be left to your own devices when it comes to what you look like." And the two sisters climbed the staircase to sample Gracie's magic.

She was waiting on the doorstep when William arrived, Sadie had spotted him walking down Carver Street from the bedroom window. He had lost none of his attractiveness and Sadie loved the fact that he was wearing what she assumed to be his best clothes, navy trousers, a pale blue collarless shirt and a waistcoat, left open at the front. He wore a pale grey cap covering his blonde hair. She was mesmerised and she knew that she looked good too. He whistled when he saw her, Sadie coloured a little and shook her head but she took the whistle for a compliment and secretly, she thought that she deserved it.

"I thought we might get the tram into town," he said, "there's a nice, quiet pub I know."

He was full of tales about rich people on cruise liners, what they ate, how they got friendly with the Ship's Captain, how they danced the night away on the top deck under the stars. Sadie was transported to a different world. She could not get enough of his stories, descriptions of candle lit dinners and fabulous ball gowns, music and romance. Before she knew it Sadie was absorbed in him. By comparison, nothing ever seemed to happen in the bakery that was worthy of a story so instead, Sadie recounted some of the tales that Gracie had brought home from work. The things that went on in Ladies wear at Bunneys provided Sadie with more than enough fuel for conversation especially after a couple of port and lemons and William seemed happy enough to listen.

"How about we walk through the park on the way home?" he suggested. "It's a lovely night and there's almost a full moon. We can pretend we're on the top deck!"

So, like a real couple, they strolled the last mile or so together, at times in easy silence. The perfect gentleman, once home, he asked if he could kiss her goodnight. He took her face in his hands and as their lips met it was to Sadie as if some magic had stirred her into life, such was the thrill that she felt in the pit of her stomach. When he suggested that he might call the following evening to meet her family, Sadie thought she might burst. The evening could not come quickly enough.

"So there we were, Mrs. Settle, the whole class full of boys sat on the front pews where the priest could keep his beady eye on us and he walked down from the altar to get the host out of the little cupboard, you know the way they always do. Well, some of the lads had put Ted Murphy's pet rat in the cupboard and when he opened the little door it jumped right out over the priest's shoulder. It was like war broke out, all the owld ladies scrambling onto the pews, skirts up to their bloomers. Father McGuire forgot where he was and started grabbing any lad he could get his hands on to give him a good hiding. He was even chasing us round the altar. Well, naturally, we didn't hang around, there were boys climbing out of windows and running over pews to get out of that church…"

Sadie's mother laughed so hard at William's childhood tales in Kildare that she started to cough and was struggling for breath.

"Breathe slowly there Mrs. S. I'll get you some water shall I? Drink the water, you'll be grand."

Mary Jane Settle had been back in her own childhood in the West of Ireland as she was drawn into this young man's stories. While he spoke, she was picturing her church, her school, the corner shop, her home in Clare, and when she regained her breath she said "you're better than a tonic son, that's for sure."

"I'll see you at the street party then Mrs. S and me and Paddy will tell you some more stories, he tells them better than me," said William before he kissed Sadie goodnight at the door.

Sadie was beyond joy. She wondered if this was what being in love felt like. William took to waiting for Sadie outside the bakery each evening as she finished work. He would make faces through the window whenever Mrs. Morris's back was turned. Sadie and Bea were terrified to look at one another for fear of dissolving into fits of giggles. He would go with Sadie to the butchers or the greengrocers and would carry the shopping basket.

"That's it Sadie," the butcher would say, "start as you mean to go on girl, get your fella to carry the heavy stuff."

Sadie loved the fact that people thought they were a couple, she loved the fact that William was indeed "her fella." She talked about little else.

"It feels like I've known him my whole life," she remarked to Gracie. Her sister said nothing but simply rolled her eyes.

FOUR
The Street Party.

The days leading up to the street parties were a hive of activity. The whole world wanted to be part of the excitement except for a couple of abstainers, the most vociferous being Bert Williams who was going to take himself off fishing for the day.

"Can't abide the Royals, leaches, the lot of em," he would say whether anyone was listening or not.

Mr. Morris's gateau, deemed too good to be called a cake, was, in truth, magnificent. He made a huge ship, iced in white with three red funnels, blue port holes and tiny marzipan figures standing on the top deck. Mrs. Morris added a sparkler in each funnel and lit them as the judges arrived to inspect her window display. She won a disappointing second place. The butcher had done something comical with a couple of pig's heads, a crown and a union jack. No-one thought it was fair but Mrs. M had upset one of the judges' wives over a late payment a couple of weeks before and scuppered her chances of first place despite her husband's herculean efforts to win his wife the trophy. It was never destined for that space she had made on the mantel piece.

The day itself was a huge success. Even Sidney Marston's speech was unable to dampen the atmosphere. No-one ever knew why working in TJ Hughes's shoe department qualified Sidney to make speeches but every time there was a community event he would take up the cudgels when it came time to acknowledge the contributors and the dignitaries. The singing, the warm weather, the food, the ale, the races and the tug o war, Percy Baine's horse and cart and the general feeling of "pulling together" were better than gifts at Christmas. All this was the gist of Sidney's message.

"Today has been almost as good as TJ's annual picnic," he said with pride, just before he launched into a long thank-you list. "And we have still got the fireworks to come, tonight we are guests of the captain of the largest cruise liner in existence."

Mid-speech, Sadie and William slipped away unnoticed to find a quiet place from which to watch the firework display. They walked hand in hand towards the river as darkness fell like a blanket over the warm night. When William began to unbutton Sadie's blouse she thought about resisting but didn't. She loved him and he loved her, she was certain of it. The next few months without him would be agonising, but they were destined to be together, she was sure of that too. The black sky, the moon, the silhouettes of the ships, the fairy lights on the decks of the Olympic, the sounds of the river, the reds and golds and splashes of silver as fireworks tumbled from the sky into the Mersey and the closeness of her man made Sadie complete. She was satisfied, full, for the first time in her life she felt nothing but hope.

"How long will you be in New York?" she asked him. He wasn't sure, he would send a telegram as soon as he signed onto a return voyage. He would be away for about twelve weeks he thought, maybe less with a bit of luck. He would bring Sadie back something beautiful from America.

"You can get stuff that no-one has ever seen in Liverpool," he said.

The weeks would go quickly, he promised, three

months was nothing really. And when he returned, they would make plans so that they could be together, properly together. These had been the best few weeks of his life.

Surprisingly, William had been right. The initial few weeks passed quickly after the Olympic sailed taking William and his brother with her. Tales from the street parties circulated, who had been the worse for wear, the nicest frocks, Aggie Connor's inedible trifles, the butcher's pigs' heads, the firework display which must have cost a fortune. Photos from the Echo appeared in the Post Office window which everyone went to see. The butcher sent for a copy of the trophy presentation, Mrs. Morris declined, it wasn't a good likeness

FIVE
Waiting

Life settled into its usual rhythm of work and home and the summer brought out a cheerfulness in people.

Four weeks went by and Sadie began to hurry home from work in the hope that a telegram would be waiting. Five weeks and still no word, but she had been warned that a return ship might take some time to find. Six weeks and Sadie began to lose a little of the certainty which had made her feel so buoyant. She hesitated each time she put her key in the door, afraid of the disappointment which lay inside. Yet she held on to a thread of hope that she would see a telegram on the table, that her mother might say.

"It came this morning just after you left…"

Instead, each evening, she saw the pity in her mother's eyes and she couldn't handle her sister's criticisms of William and her plenty more fish in the sea comments. So, over the next few weeks all hope faded.

Autumn came and shunted the summer aside. Sadie was quiet, distracted, she felt like she was disappearing. She decided that not knowing was worse than bad news so early on Sunday morning, she left her mother sleeping, slipped out of the house and walked down to Mrs. Carmichael's boarding house. It was a large end terrace with steep steps leading to a red front door.

"I wouldn't bother you Mrs. Carmichael but Mrs. Morris has sent me to ask you if you know when the two Tierney brothers might be returning. They ran up a bit of a bill at the bakery and you know what she's like, a dog with a bone."

"It's not my bill is it luv?" Mrs. Carmichael asked. "Only I gave those scally wags money to pay my bill just days before they left. I hope they brought it into the shop."

"No, no it's nothing like that, it's only a couple of pence, for some pies they bought, nothing really but Mrs. M thought William said that they were going to look for a ship coming back to Liverpool after they docked in New York with the Olympic."

"The Olympic? Only Patrick went off with the Olympic, he looked a right treat in his steward's uniform," returned Mrs. Carmichael.

"And William?" said Sadie softly.

"Oh, there's no way that one would have got taken on a ship as fine as that, even as a stoker. Different kettle of fish to his brother he is. Couldn't trust anything he said, too fond of his own voice. It will be William who's run up the bill and left without paying, you mark my words, I hope he hasn't done the same in all the shops, what will people think of me?"

Sadie felt dizzy. She steadied herself by holding onto the railings at the sides of the steps. Her tongue stuck to the roof of her mouth so that words were impossible. She didn't respond so Mrs. Carmichael pressed on.

"William told me he was going to join a merchant ship in Southampton, he was supposed to be heading down there. But I did hear that he got married a couple of weeks after he left me, to a girl from Seaforth. He went to school with her I believe."

"But I thought he went to school in Ireland," breathed Sadie.

"What luv, no, his mother and father came over from

Ireland but he was born here. You know I only took that pair in because they went to school with my nephew, that's how I know so much about them. Mind you, to be fair, they didn't cause one ounce of trouble when they were with me, I insist on rent in advance you see, except for old Mr. Rawson but he's been with me for years bless him."

She could see Mrs. Carmichael's lips continuing to move but Sadie lost track of what she was saying. She had soaked up William's stories like a dry sponge, not one of them was true. Eventually she managed to move her legs and she thanked Mrs. Carmichael.

"Well say hello to your mother for me Sadie," she said, "we had a good old gossip the day of the street party, it was good to see her out and about, seems a long time ago now all that."

Mrs. Carmichael hesitated for a second as if wondering whether or not to throw in her last piece of news.

"I did hear that the girl he married had a baby a few weeks ago, a little girl, but she died, two days old. No need to pass that on to Mrs. Morris, she'd only say it was God's punishment. I know William Tierney's a bit of a rogue but you can't help but feel for them can you? No-one deserves to bury their child."

With that, Mrs. Carmichael gently closed the door. Sadie walked and walked, anywhere and nowhere until her knees gave way and she dropped like a stone on some slime covered steps beside the canal. Her head in her hands she waited for the nausea and dizziness to pass. Images were raining down on her. Dead babies, her mother's face, William's hands, Mrs. Morris's sneer, couples dancing on top deck, fireworks shooting off in every direction. Finally, she was jolted back into the present by the sound of her own sob. It was a hollow escape of breath that comes with misery and she heard herself say "what's going to become of my baby?"

Sadie felt the lure of the peace beneath the murky water in the canal. It would be so easy to slip away, down to a silent place where none of this was happening. She tried to stand and her foot slipped on the mossy step, she lost balance, fell backwards and the shock wave that shot through her wrist as she broke her fall made her cry out in pain.

Sadie noticed nothing on her journey home, she never saw the landscape, the cats that crossed her path, the people who bid her good morning. Instead, she carried on a conversation with various voices that even the pain in her wrist could not silence.

She heard her mother, "Oh Sadie, luv, not you. I might have expected it from our Gracie but you're the sensible one. What are people going to say?"

She heard Gracie's voice "after the way you've criticised me for bringing problems to the door…"

And Mrs. Morris, "well we make our own beds and then we have to lie in them, you know you won't be able to keep your job."

But worst was the sound of her own voice "another mouth to feed and no job, how will we manage? How am I going to face the shame? How could I be so stupid, how did I imagine he loved me? Oh God, they'll call my baby a bastard."

She had no idea how long she had been out of the house but when Sadie got home, she was faced with a different reality. She opened the door and heard her mother groaning. She raced up the stairs and into the bedroom to find Mary Jane lying on the floor, a strong smell of urine filling the room. Her mother had woken to find no-one in the house and tried to get herself out of bed. She had tumbled onto a chamber pot of her own pee that was waiting to be emptied and it had spilt onto the floorboards at the side of the bed. Sadie got her mother into the bedside chair, gently stripped off her nightdress, took off her own shawl and wrapped it round her mother's frail body. Then she fetched soap and water from the kitchen. Swiftly, Sadie got her mother clean and warm, reassured and back into bed. Mary Jane drank tea while her daughter opened windows and fetched a mop and bucket from the yard. Soon the room was smelling of pine and coal tar and the bluish tint on Mary Jane's lips was slowly turning pink.

"Did you go for a walk?" her mother asked. Then she listened without moving as Sadie told her the whole sorry story. Only now did Sadie become conscious of the throbbing pain in her wrist.

"You're not the first darlin, you certainly won't be the last, and I fell for his charms too! All that stuff about when he lived in Ireland and he never lived there at all," consoled Mary Jane.

There were no words of condemnation, no talk of disgrace. She simply held open her arms to her eldest child, drew her into her chest and kissed the top of her head as if Sadie was still six years old.

Minutes later, Gracie crashed into the room explaining that she had stayed at Jacks overnight. "It turned out to be a late one and I missed the last tram so …" She finally took in the scene and sensed the charged atmosphere and her mother interjected.

"Your sister's going to have a baby, we all need to focus on her now Gracie."

Gracie ran a cloth under the tap and placed it on Sadie's wrist which was now shades of yellow and blue. They talked and cried and Gracie made a speech about bloody men getting away with murder but having got that out of her system, she swiftly went into planning mode.

"Jack's cousin has just finished with her pram, it'll need some fixing up, she's had four of them in it but our Fred can do that. Wear Mam's big apron for work, the one with the bib. That old witch at the bakery will sack you as soon as you are showing, the pinny might get you a bit more time. We've got a big stock-take coming up in work, I'll ask for some more overtime. We will be ok you know Sadie."

Gracie wanted to help, she was a natural rescuer and she hated to see her sister suffer but Sadie wasn't ready to think about prams. She was grateful however that her sister was in her corner and had come out fighting she wished that she had even a little of Gracie's spirit. As for Fred, he reckoned that he hadn't trusted William Tierney from the start.

"That type don't care who they trample on, if I ever see him I'll knock his bleedin' head off his shoulders."

They all knew that would never happen, Jack was famously unable to kill the chickens that they kept in the yard, even when they stopped laying eggs. When his mother got too frail to do the slaughtering, Fred was meant to fill her shoes. But he didn't have the stomach for the killing so he recruited Richie, his friend who was happy to do it for a couple of fresh eggs. Fred blamed his sisters for giving the chickens names.

"How can I go out there and kill Doris or Minnie?" he would say.

Besides, they would never see William Tierney again, he had disappeared from their lives as spontaneously as he had entered. Sadie never told anyone that her heart missed a beat every time the bell over shop door clanged because she expected him to walk in and only she knew that each time her baby kicked inside her, it was William Tierney she wanted to tell.

SIX
Life And Death

The over-sized apron turned out to be a good idea. Sadie managed another few weeks in the bakery and then on Gracie's advice she worked a week's notice and left.

"Tell the old witch you are leaving before she has the pleasure of throwing you out, that way you won't have to listen to her gossiping behind your back," Gracie had said.

Sadie was surprised to find that she missed the bakery. She missed the general hub-bub of customers chatting and she missed her friend Bea, she missed the accomplishment of having done a good day's work and most of all, she missed the money. Sadie tried to make up for it by cooking and cleaning and caring for her mother. Mary Jane had regular visitors, old friends, neighbours who would pop in, sometimes bringing a teaspoon of tea mixed with sugar. But these weeks at the end of her pregnancy brought time for Sadie and her mother to re-discover a closeness, a bond between them which had got lost in Sadie's grown-up years.

"I don't think I've been fair to you Sadie," said Mary Jane one day.

"I've expected much more out of you than the other two. It's hard being the oldest child and after your Da died I made you grow up too quickly."

"You had no choice Mam," replied Sadie, "and anyway we did alright in the end didn't we?"

"I just need you to know how proud I am of you Sadie," her mother would not let go of the conversation.

"I know Mam," said Sadie, stroking her mother's hand, "I know."

The baby came on Saint Patrick's Day. Gracie came home from work to find a bicycle leaning against the house wall and Cissie Donovan, the midwife was standing at the sink in the kitchen.

"She's in your mum's room pet, a little boy, they are both fine. A bit early I'd say but everything was straight forward. He's got a good pair of lungs on him anyway. Your sister's a trooper."

Gracie took the stairs two at a time and burst into the bedroom. Sadie was dozing in her mother's bed and Mary Jane was sat in her chair holding her grandson, wrapped in a bundle of blankets against the chill in the room. Mary Jane put her finger on her lips.

"Shush, the pair of them are just going off..." and Gracie had never seen her mother look so content, so complete.

"He's the image of your father," her mother said, "I can see your Da in his little face, he'll be a handsome divil this one."

Gracie took the child from Mary Jane's arms and lay him next to his sleeping mother and she dried her own tears which had sprung from nowhere.

"It looks like you're sleeping with me tonight then Mam, don't want you snoring the whole night. Come on then Granny, let's get you settled."

Even though she was struggling to breathe there was no denying the pride and delight in her mother's eyes, Gracie couldn't remember ever seeing her so happy. Mary Jane safely in bed, Gracie went downstairs to warm up some of Sadie's soup. By the time she returned, her mother was sound asleep, peacefully exhausted by the efforts of the day and clearly content with the results.

That night, Mary Jane died in her sleep. In the morning, Gracie surprised everyone, not least herself. She woke beside her mother lying next to her in the bed. She was too still. She tried to wake her but got no response. Quietly and stoically, she checked her mother for signs of life, found none and gently woke Fred with the news.

"Mammy's passed in the night. She's peaceful, she must have died in her sleep, her eyes were closed. I found her when I woke up."

Fred followed his sister into the bedroom and they knelt, each of them holding her hands. There were silent tears and quiet thoughts but no drama, just a sense of relief that in the end, death had come quietly to Mary Jane.

"After all that struggling her life's over, just like that," sighed Fred.

And from the bedroom doorway, Sadie replied, "No Fred, her life's not over it's complete."

Together, Mary Jane's children stood at the bedside and sobbed.

The days between Mary Jane's death and her funeral were hard. Curtains were closed, the house was dark. Despite it being the middle of March, the winter was dragging on and a damp fog was blowing up from the river.

"You know what they'll say don't you?" said Sadie one evening as they sat in front of the range in the kitchen. "They'll say I brought this on her. They'll say that God gives with one hand and takes with the other and when one comes into this world another one has to leave it."

Fred shot out of his chair. Uncharacteristically, he raised his voice.

"Don't start with that shite Sadie, Mam gave up on all that years ago. You know she did. That baby is the best thing that's happened to this family in years."

Then as if tackling Everest, he strode up the stairs and tunes could be heard from his mouth organ.

Sadie was right of course; people did say those things. When she took her baby out in his pram, a couple of women crossed the street to avoid her and she couldn't be sure but there seemed to be more curtain twitching than was usual. She felt a physical pain in her chest the first time it happened. She had no idea why she couldn't muster more resilience. These people meant nothing to her. Defiance was a characteristic that was unfamiliar to her, she knew how to be determined, and stoic in adversity, but she had always been a good girl so to be the accused, to be the subject of the finger wagging, to be the one they pointed at was alien to Sadie and it made her fragile.

Work life resumed for Fred and Gracie and Sadie's days became consumed with feeds and nappies and the minutiae of motherhood and keeping their home. Her baby quickly became the centre of her world but grief, fatigue, broken nights and money worries took their toll. Sadie wasn't coping. She had no-one to blame but herself, she had brought an illegitimate child into the world and she had no idea how she was going to raise him. She could name a dozen families who had ended up in the workhouse. It was her worst nightmare.

"Come in," said Sadie, "the baby's asleep in the kitchen."

She was astonished to see Mrs. Johnson, the dressmaker at the door. Eva Johnson was striking rather than pretty. She was a tall, slim woman with sallow skin and dark eyes and a mane of black hair which always looked like it had a life of its own. She was a few years older than Sadie and she had a presence which made Sadie think that she did not suffer fools gladly. Sadie half expected her to say that Gracie had ordered some ribbon or feathers for a hat she was altering. Instead, Mrs. Johnson thrust a parcel into Sadie's hands, a little gift that she had made for the baby. It was wrapped in snow white tissue paper and tied with the thinnest blue ribbon. Mrs. Johnson cooed over the child and Sadie unwrapped the gift as though it might vanish once exposed to the air. Inside, she found a small quilt, exquisitely stitched, in a dozen shades of blue.

"It's only made of off cuts I had lying round the workshop," explained her visitor.

Tears welled up in Sadie's eyes that could not be stopped. She had learned to cope with the stares, the whispers and the snubs over the last few weeks but kindness overwhelmed her.

"Has this little fella got a name yet?" asked her visitor, as much to spare Sadie's embarrassment as anything.

Sadie had been toying with a few names but hadn't settled on any yet. With that, Eva Johnson drew Sadie into her life in a way that nobody but close family ever did. In those streets the unwritten rule was "tell no-one anything" and although front doors were never closed and hard times were common to every family, there was still that air of respectability to keep up. All this served to maintain the status quo but also it made for the kind of loneliness that comes with keeping secrets. Sadie was lonely.

It turned out that Eva Johnson called herself Mrs., but in fact, she had never been married. She had arrived in Liverpool with a daughter only weeks old claiming that her husband had died in a mining accident in Nottingham.

"I'm not a widow, Sadie," she admitted, "let's just say my baby's dad and I never got as far as the altar."

Eva's father had been in the rag trade in Manchester, he bought and sold fabrics. He had thrown her out when he discovered his daughter was pregnant. Her mother was too afraid of him to put up much of a fight so instead she had given her daughter the savings that she had put away for a rainy day along with her sewing machine. Eva gave birth to her baby in a mother and baby home in Cheshire and somehow she found her way to Liverpool. She found a room for herself and her baby daughter and started sewing. At first she took in work making corsets for a meagre amount, but word got round that she was a good needlewoman and had an eye for what was fashionable and the rest was history, her business was healthy and fifteen years on, her daughter, Francesca was training to be a florist.

"I can't pretend it has been easy, Sadie, sometimes I haven't known where the next meal would come from and believe me the attitude to widows isn't much better than the way they are with unmarried mothers. You've just got to keep going. Your little one will do that for you, he'll keep you going, you'll see."

There was a subtle change in Sadie as she listened to Eva Johnson's story. She could see a shaft of light, too distant to grasp but light, nevertheless.

"But at least you could sew for a living," said Sadie, "What can I do?"

Mrs. Johnson had a client, an Emma Moran, who was looking for a daily. She was sure that she could persuade her to give Sadie the job.

"She won't mind if you take the little one with you, at least until he starts toddling, by then she won't want to let you go. She's hardly ever at home anyway, she's on loads of those voluntary committees at the Town Hall. Her husband had something to do with designing the overhead railway. I know it's not much, a few mornings a week but it's a start."

It was music to Sadie's ears but Mrs. Johnson didn't give her chance to reply before she continued with "but you must have learned some skills working for that gossiping old bitch down at the bakery."

"I can make a good meat pie," Sadie laughed, and a germ of an idea was already stirring in her mind.

When Eva Johnson got up to go, she said thoughtfully, "I named my girl after her father. He was Francis, she's Francesca. We used to talk about getting married and having children and I always loved the idea of calling a little girl Francesca after him. I thought, I'll be damned if I'm giving up my dream so that's what I called her."

For the first time in months, Sadie could see a way forward. She hadn't told anyone that she had had a visit from the rent man who wanted reassurances that she would not fall behind with the rent. Without some proof of her ability to pay, he would not transfer the tenancy into her name. She was terrified of being evicted.

"I was sorry to hear about your mother luv, she was a nice woman, always respectful. But Mr. Reid is a businessman and he's a stickler for the rules. I know you've had the funeral and everything," the rent man said, glancing at the baby in Sadie's arms, "but there's no sense letting you run up debts is there?"

Mr. Reid's agent was known to everyone as The Snide. Sadie had wondered over the years how it must feel to have a job which caused people to pretend not to be in when you knocked on their doors. In the event, the Snide agreed to a three-month trial period. If she could pay the rent on the nail for the next twelve weeks, he would sign over the tenancy. It would be easier said than done, but spurred on by the visit from Eva Johnson and the need to do her best for her son, Sadie grew in confidence and resolve

EIGHT
Sadie's Resolve

The register office at Brougham Terrace was imposing, high ceilings, molded plaster covings, a huge chandelier, but Sadie with her new-found determination refused to be intimidated.

"What do you wish me to write in the Father's Name column Miss Settle?" asked the registrar. "Is it father unknown?"

Just at that moment, the baby started to stir and Sadie made a thing of shushing him while she responded with "Yes please!" Unwavering in her determination, she left the Registrar's office clutching her son's birth certificate which stated that his name was William Tierney Settle. She laid him in his pram which she had parked under the mahogany staircase on the ground floor and said "we need to get a move on William Tierney Settle, those pies won't bake themselves."

It was hard work, but when Fred took the first batch of pies in his mother's old basket and sold them to his mates on the docks Sadie felt a satisfaction that spurred her on. Soon, other men started to ask for them and Fred started to bring his hand cart home from work to transport a palate of pies every morning to the dockside. It felt good to be able to help herself and Sadie was just about able to make ends meet. Cleaning for Emma Moran, baking pies and caring for William became her life. Some days the work seemed never ending but her name was on the rent book, her son was healthy, the family was pulling together and she had her self-respect.

Weeks rolled into months and before Sadie knew it, William was no longer a baby. William flourished in the care of his mother, his Aunty Gracie and his Uncle Fred. He was seldom short of attention and never short of love. When Gracie married Jack and moved out to live in the Dingle, her nephew missed her but compensation came in the fact that his mother would drop him at Gracie's house while Sadie went to work. He loved his visits to see Gracie, he was proud of his little cousin, Ivy Rose and best of all were the times when Uncle Jack happened to be home. Sometimes, Gracie would put the two children in the pram and walk into the City Centre to visit her mother-in-law. Gracie often said that she didn't know what she would do without her husband's parents.

Jack's mother, Dilys and his father Alun had come to Liverpool from North Wales. They were both from farming families. They started Evans dairy at the bottom of Knight Street with six cows and a horse and cart. Dilys ran the business, looked after the cows and the horse and did the milking. Alun worked on the gardens in two of the city's parks after he had finished his early morning milk round. They talked about having a large family but in the end, their daughter, Bronwen arrived after a year of marriage and Jack came along six years later. Sadly, Bronwen died before her first birthday of a bronchial condition which had stalked her since her birth. Dilys and Alun always joked that they were like ships in the night and didn't have the time to make more babies, in the end, Jack was their only one.

Their son worked in the dairy when he was not in school and Jack turned out to be a bright lad, handling the book-keeping in the dairy almost as soon as he could add up. His mother was determined that her son should reach the potential that she saw in him and she made sure that he made the most of his education. Consequently, when he left school, Jack was employed by Jones and Owen, a firm of accountants in Dale Street. His education continued at night school, paid for by Jones and Owen. He made quick progress, his talents earned him promotion and Dilys was delighted with her son.

The years passed and nowadays Dilys spent as much time as she could with her granddaughter, Ivy Rose. When Gracie brought William to the diary, Dilys welcomed him with open arms. If asked, he would say that days in the dairy came second best to his beloved football. Ivy Rose was much too small to kick a ball but if Uncle Jack was there, he was always happy to stand in goal against the yard wall and kick the ball back to his nephew.

"I'll swear that lad will end up playing for Everton Gracie," he would say. "He's not three yet and he's better than me. Proper little Tommy Browell he is."

Sadie never failed to remind her sister that she was lucky to have in-laws like Dilys and Alun.

"Well they do have a wonderful daughter-in-law," Gracie would laugh but both sisters were grateful for the welcome they found at the dairy.

NINE
The Admiral

Emma Moran and Sadie enjoyed a very good relationship as employer and employee. There had never been so much as a misunderstanding or a cross word, however Sadie was finding it impossible to keep up with her growing business as well as her cleaning job. Sadie found it hard to tell Mrs. Moran that she would like to leave her employ. Her employer made it clear she didn't want to lose her. Sadie would be missed. Was she sure she couldn't manage to stay in her job as well as run her little business? But Sadie was convinced the time was right to invest all her energy into her pie business.

The landlord at the Anchor, a pub on the Dock Road had been replaced. The new chap was young and open to anything that might bring in the punters. He had had a word with Fred who drank in the Anchor on Friday evenings after work. Consequently, Sadie was now supplying the pub with pies and pasties every day, money up front, no returns. The landlord's brother had a horse and cart which he stabled in the funeral director's premises not far from Carver Street. He would call at her home every morning, load up the pies and make his way to the pub on route to his day job at the docks.

"A damn sight less trouble than selling them through your Fred," the landlord had said when Sadie went to check out his suggestion. Sadie knew that he was right and she made plans to do most of her baking during the night, sleeping during the day when William had his nap. She could see no possibility of continuing her work for

Mrs. Moran. She liked her and had enjoyed many a cup of tea with her but it would be a relief not to have to clean her brasses and iron her husband's shirts.

"Don't forget Sadie, if you ever need a reference you just need to ask," Emma Moran had said as she gave Sadie an envelope with an extra week's wages inside. When Sadie thanked her she shushed her with "you have earned that many times over Sadie," and added "do you think if we meet by chance in town you could call me Emma?"

Sadie smiled and nodded but she knew that Mrs. Moran would always be Mrs. Moran.

The landlord at the Anchor was the sort that people called a lively lad but he turned out to be as good as his word. Sadie's income was now stable and predictable, she could even put a bit by for shoes for William and there was less pressure on Fred who was now enjoying the odd night out with his girlfriend, a young woman called Frieda.

Frieda was in service. She was a housemaid in one of the large houses in Shaw Street owned by a German family called Schneider who also owned a couple of furniture shops in Bold Street. On Friday evenings, Frieda would happily get the tram and the overhead railway to join Fred in the Anchor. Sadie, on the other hand, found it excruciating every Monday morning to have to walk into the pub to settle her weekly invoice with the landlord who insisted on doing business from behind the bar. If there were customers at the bar she would sit at a small table near the door and try to attract his attention with a discreet wave of her hand. He enjoyed the game and would pretend he hadn't seen her, serving every customer before acknowledging Sadie. It wasn't long before Jessie, the landlord's wife, sensing Sadie's discomfort began the ritual of bringing over a small port to Sadie. Jessie would hand it to her with a conspiratorial raising of her eyes in the air. Sadie was glad of something to hold in her hands as she sat waiting and sipping the warm liquid until the landlord motioned her to approach the bar where he would make a great show of checking her figures. Finally, invoice checked, signed and thrust onto a spike, the payment was made and Sadie would leave the Anchor to go and pick up her son from her sister's house.

On one such Monday, there were four soldiers in uniform in the Anchor. They were finishing their pies and drinking ale. Sadie sat at her usual table near the door. The men were boisterous, a bit the worse for wear, she was cautious but they paid her no attention, too busy with their banter. One of them approached the bar.

"Lovely pies these mate," he said, as he placed four empty plates on the bar.

"Well, there's the girl to thank," replied the landlord. "She's the cook. Makes all my pies." He nodded in Sadie's direction.

Frank Jordan re-joined his friends, four more pints in his hands. They were on a pub crawl along the Dock Road, beer money in their pockets, weary of army life and determined to make the most of their ten days leave. By the time Frank had deposited the pints on the table and settled in his chair, Sadie had completed her transaction with the landlord and left. Her empty glass was still on the table.

Private Frank Jordan wasn't one to give up easily. He pressed the landlord for more information about the attractive young woman who had caught his attention as soon as she had entered the pub.

"Her brother will be in on Friday night with his girlfriend and his pals from the docks. Best talk to him but I don't fancy your chances with that one mate," laughed the landlord.

Private Jordan was not about to be put off by the scepticism of the landlord, he returned to the Anchor on Friday evening and was soon in conversation with Fred about football and in particular the following day's Everton match against Burnley. Saturday could not come quickly enough!

Saturdays were special for Sadie and William. For one thing, Fred was out so they had the house to themselves. Secondly, Saturday was a none baking day. Thirdly, it was the day they scrubbed the kitchen floor. First, they lifted the chairs on to the kitchen table and brushed up all the crumbs and scraps. Then Sadie fetched her mop and bucket from the yard and William brought in his own bucket which, on other days, he used to go crabbing in New Brighton with Uncle Fred. Together, they sloshed soapy water on to the quarry tiles and Sadie ceremoniously took a sharp knife, never to be touched by her son, and cut off the last inch from her block of soap. This became their pencil as William and Sadie played their Saturday game of "Name That Thing".

William would draw an object, a house, a cat, a dog and his mother would guess what he was drawing. Then it was Sadie's turn, a tree, a sun, a star until the canvass that was the kitchen floor was filled with pictures. More sloshing and the pair would laugh out loud as the house lost its chimney, the dog lost its tail and the sun shone no more. The happy time always ended when their knees were sore and sopping and William asked his mother to tell him the same story about the boy who dreamed of catching his own star. Their game was coming to an end when there was a rapping at the front door. It was open because Fred was due home any minute to get ready for the match. Only a stranger would knock. Wiping her hands on her apron and hooking up a stray strand of hair Sadie arrived at the door to find a young man in khaki uniform standing on the step.

"Hello, you must be Sadie," he said. He waited for an answer but when none came, he pressed on.

"Your Fred told me to give him a knock. I am going to the game with him. We are meeting a few of his mates in the pub at two o'clock."

Sadie was confused. She half recognised the soldier from the Anchor but how had he turned up on her doorstep? Fred hadn't mentioned a new friend.

In the absence of any direction from Sadie, he added, "If Fred isn't home I can just wait here for him. By the way I'm Frank, Frank Jordan."

At last, Sadie gathered her thoughts and led Frank through the parlour into the kitchen.

"And this little'un must be William," he said, ruffling the boy's hair and turning to Sadie he asked, "shall I call him William or Billy?"

"He's always been William," asserted Sadie. And then she added "after his father."

Frank knelt on the tiles next to the boy and before long the two of them were drawing train tracks complete with signals and William had fetched the wooden engine that Fred had made for him and was pushing it along the railway line. Sadie couldn't help smiling but she was aware that not only was the room in complete disarray but she was too.

"We need to dry the floor now William," she said "let's empty the buckets down the yard."

Frank took both buckets through the back door into the yard and Sadie heard squeals of delight from her son when Frank spotted a ball and suggested a kick about.

Minutes later and kitchen reinstated, Fred came crashing through the door ready to take the stairs three at a time to fetch his lucky blue and white scarf that his mother had knitted. He stopped in his tracks when he spotted Frank and William in the yard.

"You're right," shouted Frank to Fred through the open door. "The little fella has got real talent, he's winning five – two."

As the two men were about to leave for their beloved Everton, William began to complain about losing his playmate and Fred distracted him with the familiar ritual.

"So what's the score going to be today William?"

William predicted six – one, his habitual response and his uncle bent low so that his nephew could touch the ends of the lucky scarf.

Sensing that this would probably be his only chance, Frank Jordan turned to Sadie and said, "I don't suppose you would like to come for a walk in Stanley Park tomorrow. We could take the football and he can teach me a few moves?"

Sadie hesitated. She looked at this affable stranger and then at her son and finally she said, "I'll make up a picnic if the weather holds. Twelve o'clock?"

There were several such excursions during that week, Sefton Park, New Brighton, Southport. Naturally enough, people assumed they were a family.

"Is the missus having a cornet?"

"The little one's a chip off the old block isn't he pal?"

They were easy companions, the three of them content to share a thin slice of the Indian summer together. The week they spent was intense but not in the way that it had been with William Tierney. There was none of the passion that Sadie had felt with him, it was more that she and Frank were happy, contented and because she instinctively trusted him, they shared their stories without reserve.

Frank lived in Toxteth with his widowed grandmother Ruby, whom everyone called Nan. She cleaned the trams for a living, her days began at five in the morning. He had six siblings but as fate would have it, since he had been William's age, he had grown up as an only child in the care of his grandparents. It wasn't that his parents had abandoned him, it was more like an oversight. He and his siblings would visit their grandparents and frequently one or other of them would stay for a night or two. On one of these occasions, nobody told Frank to go home. There were consequences of course. His six siblings saw the privileges that their brother got, more food, shoes that fitted, new clothes and they were jealous. For his part, Frank was a lonely child, and occasionally he wondered why his parents had never asked for him back. In the army, he had found friendship and a sense of family. He found taking orders easy, even the constant drilling and repetitive chores appealed to his personality. The rhythm and routine of army life suited him, he liked the consistency. So, when his mates complained and shirked, Frank never did, he was what his sergeant called "a natural soldier".

Sadie could sense Frank's commitment, his loyalty, they were qualities in his character. She was aware that he respected her and she was grateful for the growing friendship that she was witnessing between Frank and her son. Private Jordan was good for all of them, especially for William.

He never actually proposed to Sadie, it happened by default like other things in Frank's life. "I've got three days leave at Christmas," he said, "Christmas Eve would be a good time for the wedding." That was it. And Sadie just slipped into the idea of marriage as easily as Cinderella slipped into her shoe.

TEN
Frieda and Fred

Frank returned to his army life and left Sadie to break the good news of their wedding to her family. She was mulling over how to tell her brother as she peeled potatoes and carrots for their evening meal. Sadie knew he would be pleased for her but inevitably it would change his life as well as hers. Sometimes life gets in the way of our plans and as it happened, her brother spoke first.

"There's something I need to tell you Sadie," he began. Fred sounded serious and a little agitated and Sadie's first thought was that work on the docks was drying up. There had been a couple of strikes recently which meant that even regulars like Fred were being laid off for days at a time.

"Frieda's going to have a baby, we're getting married in a couple of weeks," he said, glancing at his sister then swiftly turning his attentions to William, helping him to cut up the food in his dish. Sadie was doling out scouse from a saucepan onto plates, the smell of the scouse was making her hungry. Her first thought was how young her brother was and his news stopped her in her tracks for a second while she caught her breath. She managed not to give voice to her concern, instead she replied "That's good news Fred, Frieda's a lovely girl, Mam would have loved her. How far gone is she?"

"She's about three months, the thing is, we are going to live with her granddad, he lives over the pork butchers in Ray Street, the one on the corner, the German one. He's got two rooms he doesn't use, it needs a lot of fixing up but we can do that, it's just till we get on our feet. He's a nice old fella, a bit blunt but his bark's worse than his bite. You'll like him, everyone calls him Opa, that's Granddad in German. Frieda will have to leave her job at the Schneiders in a few weeks but the butcher said he'll give her a little job cleaning the shop, just a few hours, but it's something."

"Sounds like her family are going to support her Fred, that's the main thing. You are going to need them."

"You'll like them when you meet them Sadie," he said, I know they are German and Opa is a bit hard to understand but he's looking forward to us moving in and they don't half know how to stick together."

Over the meal, brother and sister discussed arrangements which had been made for a wedding at the German Lutheran Church and Fred talked about Frieda's family.

"Opa came here from Hamburg with his brother," began Fred. They started off in Scotland and he met his wife, Mary. They moved here to Liverpool for work at Tate and Lyle, he was a sugar boiler Sadie, it's a terrible job, stirring boiling sugar in sweltering heat, the money wasn't bad because no-one wanted the jobs. He stuck it till he was sixty-five, they're all hard workers, the lot of them."

"Frieda's dad was from Manchester, but he died when Frieda was sixteen. She lives with her mam and her brother in one of the old tenements in Netherfield Road. They're just a nice quiet family."

Fred went on as if he needed to convince his sister of Frieda's provenance. He so wanted the two women in his life to get along.

"But you don't seem happy Fred," interjected Sadie, "what's worrying you?"

"I'm worried about you and William. How are you going to manage to pay the rent when I move out?" replied Fred.

Sadie assured her brother that his job was to look after Frieda and their unborn child and Fred's relief was palpable when she explained that coincidentally, that very day, she and Frank had made plans to marry at Christmas.

"Makes you believe in Angels doesn't it Fred?" said his sister.

"Maybe Mam's looking out for both of us," he replied.

The months until Christmas flew by. First there was Fred's wedding. Frank managed to wangle a thirty-six-hour pass and got home just in time. His pals called it timeout for good behaviour. Fred had been right, Sadie and Gracie got on well with the Beckers. Frieda's mother was called Laura. Apart from her red hair, which she got from her mother, Frieda resembled her father. Everyone said she had his confidence. She looked striking in a pale blue coat and matching hat. Sadie and Gracie shed a few tears during the service in the German Church mainly because they were remembering their mother but also because the service, spoken half in German and half in English, was unexpectedly beautiful.

The little party celebrated with a home-made buffet with plenty of pork supplied by the butcher and a barrel of beer back at the Becker's house. It turned out Opa was a good pianist and he led the singing. All too soon, it was over and the happy couple left for their new home. Opa agreed to stay with his daughter for a night or two to give Frieda and Fred a bit of a honeymoon. Gracie and Jack got the late tram to Jack's parent's dairy, in town, where his mother was looking after William and Ivy Rose. Frank and Sadie walked home, hand in hand intent on enjoying the rest of Frank's hours of freedom.

The walk to Carver Street was companionable rather than romantic. Any stars were hidden by low cloud, Sadie could feel a very fine rain which dampened her coat and hair. Yet she and Frank chatted, happily, about the events of the day and neither was in a hurry to say goodbye. Talk about Fred's new in-laws, Frieda's outfit and Jack's speech naturally led them to discuss their own impending wedding, just weeks away. It was to be at the Register office in Brougham Terrace where Sadie had taken William to register his birth. Fred had persuaded the landlord at the Anchor to let them have his back room for the wedding breakfast. Frank's younger brother, Mattie would be his best man, he wasn't much good at making speeches but he had been delighted to be asked and it felt important to have at least one or two of Frank's siblings there. His grandmother had bought a new hat and as for Frank, he was easily sorted, he would wear his uniform. Gracie would be the other witness and she had seen a pattern for a matching coat and dress for the bride which she was sure Mrs. Johnson could run up with her eyes shut. All Sadie had to do was choose the material, maybe a heavy crepe, and go for a couple of fittings. Sadie had been putting a little aside to pay for food for the buffet but Frank told her to stop worrying about that, he had a bit saved. William would need a new outfit but his shoes would polish up nicely. And so, buoyed up by memories of a lovely day and excited about the celebration still to come, Frank and Sadie reached Carver Street in what seemed like seconds.

It was gone midnight when they entered the house. It was dark and Sadie felt for the candle which lived conveniently on a stool at the foot of the stairs. The match flared and she held it to the candle until the wick caught and the room was filled with a soft yellow glow. Frank was about to kiss her goodnight, but she took off her damp coat and hung it behind the door. In silence, she took his hand and with the candle in the other, she led him gently up the stairs. On the landing, Frank hesitated, shadows danced on the walls and he whispered, "are you sure?"

Sadie led Frank into her bedroom at the front of the house and placed the candle on the chest of drawers. He held her face in his hands and kissed her so tenderly she nearly cried. She had not realised how much she needed to be touched like this, how much she wanted to be loved, how good it felt to be desired. Frank unbuttoned her dress at the neck and Sadie left it on the floor where it fell. He turned his back while they both undressed and blew out the candle. Only when she lay with her head nestled into his neck and he had folded her, safely into his arms did she hear the words "I love you Sadie Settle," for the first time. Sleep came easily.

"No, don't get up," he said, "it's still early, I'll make you a cup of tea. I need to get to Lime Street to catch the nine o'clock. I can't miss the train or they'll stop my Christmas leave and the wedding will be off and then what's my nan going to do with her hat?"

Frank was beyond happiness, he had thought about little else but making love to Sadie since the day he had seen her in the Anchor. She was everything he could want, she was the one, she was the girl with whom he would grow old.

Sadie couldn't let him leave without sending him off with sandwiches and scones. Despite the tenderness of the night, she couldn't find it in herself to reciprocate his declarations of love. Instead, she hoped the food and the farewell kiss would show Frank how much she cared. It had drizzled all night, the streets outside were wet and the slate roofs were a glossy silver grey. Frank waved as he turned the corner at the end of the street, bells were calling people to early mass at St. Saviors and as Sadie closed the door, she realized that she was smiling, she considered herself one of the luckiest women on earth.

"Sadie Settle," she said to herself, "you've got a son to fetch home and a mountain of work to do, there's no time for daydreaming."

ELEVEN
Ivy Rose

When Sadie got to the dairy to pick up William she expected to see Gracie and Jack who had stayed the night. Instead, she went into the kitchen to find William sitting at the table dipping toast soldiers into a boiled egg. He was delighted to see her and Sadie turned to Dilys, Jack's mother, to thank her for looking after her son. Dilys waved away her attempts to show her gratitude but Sadie thought she looked troubled.

"What is it Dilys, where are Jack and our Gracie?"

Now Sadie could see the strain in Dily's face and she could feel her own anxiety rising.

"Little Ivy woke up covered in a rash this morning, I swear she was ok when I put her down last night. Gracie thinks it could be measles, there's a bit of an outbreak in the schools. Sinead Rogers has just come back from visiting her mother in Dublin and she said they've closed the schools over there, children have died."

Sadie's heart sank, she fought to hold back her tears but Dilys, relieved to be sharing her anxiety with someone who cared, let go and sobbed. William left his place at the table, climbed onto his mother's knee and buried his face in her shoulder. Sadie hardly noticed but instinctively she wrapped her arms around him.

"They took her back to their place, early this morning and Jack was going to fetch the doctor but it's Sunday so I don't know if the doctor would even be at home. The thing is Sadie, Ivy and William slept in the same bed last night." With that, the tears welled up again and Sadie held her son so close to her body she didn't know whether it was his heart or hers that she could hear.

"I've checked him three times all over for spots, there are none," said Dilys, making a great effort to calm herself. She was a pragmatic woman, known for her common sense but when it came to her family, Dilys was all emotion.

Sadie lifted her son's clothes and found no sign of a rash, he wasn't hot or flushed and he had finished his meal. She left him with Dilys and set off for her sister's house promising to bring back news of Ivy as soon as she could.

The doctor confirmed what they suspected. It was the second case of measles he had attended that week. Ivy Rose was in her cot, curtains had been drawn to keep out the light and they were doing their best to cool her down with a soft piece of muslin soaked in tepid water. The doctor had left medicine but it was a case of watching and waiting, hoping that the little girl could fight off the disease. Gracie threw her arms around her sister, who wasn't surprised to see her.

"Is William ok?" she asked, "Jack's mother thinks it's all her fault. The doctor says with the right care she should be fine but measles can have complications Sadie, I can't even bear to think about it."

Sadie took the muslin from Gracie's hand and ordered her sister to go downstairs and drink a cup of tea with her husband who was sitting at the kitchen table still reeling from the shock. She sat beside the bed and gently dabbed her niece's little body with the cooling cloth and finally Ivy fell asleep.

When Jack and Gracie returned to the bedroom they were calmer, more ready to face the fight that was ahead of them. Sadie hugged them both, picked up her bag and coat, reassured them that she would let Dilys know how things were progressing and quietly left the little family to find the strength to do battle.

The dairy was quiet, Dilys was calmer now that Alun was back from his rounds, he sat with William on the floor in the kitchen playing snakes and ladders. All three of them looked up at Sadie with anxious expectation as she entered through the back door.

"The doctor said it is measles," she said and Dilys stifled a sob. William came and stood next to his mother's leg. "She's comfortable now, I think the medicine is helping. It might not be a serious case. Jack and Gracie are strong, they'll see her through it."

"I've checked William again Sadie, and he doesn't have any spots, I promise you…"

"None of this is your fault Dilys, it's just bad luck that's all and you are always so willing to help us out looking after the children. Gracie is always telling me how good you are, she couldn't wish for a better mother-in-law."

"I'll make a detour and call at their house on my early round tomorrow," said Alun, "we'll see how things are in the morning."

"And I'll ask my neighbour to have William so I can go and help out for an hour or so in the afternoons, Ivy Rose will get through this you'll see. And as for this fella, our William doesn't even catch colds, he won't get measles," added Sadie.

Declining their invitation to have a cup of tea, Sadie and William started for home where Sadie was glad to focus on the mountain of baking she had to do before morning. Despite her ebullience in front of Dilys, she kept a vigilant eye on her son, checking him as she put him to bed that night and again when he woke in the morning.

The following days were hard, happy thoughts about weddings and Frank deserted her and Sadie changed her routine, recruiting her neighbour's help so that she could be with Gracie at Ivy's bedside for the next four afternoons. It wasn't easy for Sadie to ask her neighbour for help. Despite their boys being such good friends, the relationship between the two mothers had always been strained. Perhaps it was because Maggie was older than Sadie. Maggie gave Sadie the impression that she disapproved of William, not enough to stop him from playing with her son, in any case that would have been almost impossible, but enough to make Sadie feel judged.

Tommy was the younger of the children next door, Maggie and George had a daughter. She was thirteen. Their father, George was a seasoned soldier, he had served in the Boar War, distinguished himself and was one of the small number of soldiers who stayed on in South Africa. Consequently, he would arrive home for a visit infrequently. The arrangement seemed to suit the couple.

William did not mind at all about the disruption to his week. Each afternoon he was passed next door into Maggie's house, to play with Tommy until Sadie came to retrieve him a few hours later. Tommy had a red fire engine that the boys would sit on and push along with their feet. Maggie let them take it outside to play on the York stone pavement. On the Thursday afternoon the boys had been playing on the engine when Tommy heard his name being called from the other side of the street. He let out a piercing cry "Dad" and ran into his father's arms as he strode up the street, dressed in army uniform and carrying a kit bag on his shoulder. As George scooped up his son, his kit bag rolled onto the cobbles. He carried Tommy to the front door where the boy wriggled free and ran through the house to fetch his mother who was folding washing that had been airing on the pulley in the kitchen. William followed them into the house, just about managing to drag the kit bag behind him. Tommy forgot about William and the engine in favour of sitting on his dad's lap. George's regiment was now stationed in India and his last leave had been ten months ago. He wasn't sure that Tommy would even recognise him, but he needn't have worried. George fished in his tunic and found two lollipops which he had bought, along with his cigarettes, from a sweet shop on his way up from the docks. He gave one to each boy and simultaneously perched William on the edge of the kitchen table. This was enough to compensate for losing his playmate and both boys were happy.

A little later when Sadie had collected her son and they were together in their own house, William asked a question for which she was totally unprepared.

"When is my dad coming home Mam?" he asked.

Sadie was filling the kettle, she dropped it with a clatter into the sink, it startled her but she was glad of the diversion. Hoping that William would be distracted she said nothing.

"Is he a soldier like Tommy's dad?" her son persisted.

This was the moment she might have told William the truth. But Sadie found her truth was too hard to tell.

Instead, exhausted and emotionally drained by the events of the week, Sadie embarked on a lie which she hoped would bide her some time.

She continued filling the kettle, eyes fixed on the water as it ran out of the tap.

"Frank's your dad, William, he's coming home again at Christmas. We are going to have a Christmas party with Fred and Gracie, it'll be grand. Frank's a soldier just like Tommy's dad but his army camp isn't very far away so he can come home more often. I tell you what, when I write to him I'll ask him to bring lollipops for you and Tommy, just like Tommy's dad did."

Content with his mother's explanation and the promise of lollipops, William added, "and one for Ivy Rose."

At five thirty on Friday morning, Sadie heard the rattle of the milk cart on the cobbles. She had only had snatches of sleep for a week. It was Alun bringing good news. She managed to slide up the sash window in the bedroom and he called to her from the cart, "she's going to be ok, Sadie, she's a little fighter that one. I can't stop, I need to tell Dilys and get back to my round," and punching the air, he turned his horse and cart around and set off back down the street.

Sadie wrote to Frank that night, telling him how much she and William missed him. She wrote about Ivy, how ill she had been, how hard she had fought to get better, she said that she was still a little worried that William might catch measles but that she was keeping a close eye on him. She talked about their forthcoming wedding, how Eva Johnson was making her an outfit, how the landlord's wife at the Anchor had taken her into the back room to show her how she could dress the table.

"We miss you Frank," wrote Sadie, "but we have plenty to do, Christmas will be here before we know it."

Still anxious, Sadie watched her son for signs of a rash, day and night for the next few weeks until gradually her fears subsided. Routine restored, Sadie and William settled into a pattern of work and play. She pickled onions and made jam and started work on a Christmas pudding. She baked and made her weekly visit to the Anchor. She took her son to visit Frieda and Fred over at the pork butchers. William wanted to know why Opa had a funny voice which made the old man laugh. It took some time to get used to the idea that Fred was now settling into married life and would not be coming home to Carver Street each evening. Sadie would not need to make up his carry-out and she would not be cooking his evening meal. She looked forward to getting Frank's letters which came regularly. He would describe life in the barracks, scrapes his mates got into, banter that passed between them, details about their families and girlfriends. He was excited about their future together and for the first time in a long time Sadie was beginning to believe that all would be well.

She walked down to the bakery with William. There was the familiar clatter of the bell over the door and Sadie noticed that Mrs. Morris wasn't in her usual place by the window. She was relieved and she asked one of the girls behind the counter for a loaf, pointing to one on the shelf behind her. Mr. Morris made a rare appearance. Sadie was surprised to see him. He was carrying a box, tied with string.

"I've been waiting for you to call in Sadie, I made this for you," he said quietly.

He put the box into her hands and turned to go back into the bakery, a little flushed. She tried to thank him but she had no idea what the box contained or why he had given it to her, she was confused.

Mr. Morris hesitated and half turned to look at her and she thought an explanation was coming but all he said was "there's no need to bother my wife with this, Sadie, it would only worry her."

William wanted to open the box as soon as they were in the street but Sadie overruled him insisting they wait until the two of them were safely back in the house. Once in the kitchen, she loosened the string and eased it from the box and William lifted the lid. Inside was a crystal white wedding cake complete with silver horseshoes and tiny roses made of pale pink icing which covered the whole surface.

"What's it for Mam?" asked William.

"It's for our Christmas party luv," said Sadie.

She had seen many of Mr. Morris's creations but she couldn't remember seeing anything quite so beautiful as this one. What she couldn't understand was why.

TWELVE
The Wedding

The second week in December brought snow, the snow turned to ice of the sort which lay there for weeks. Pipes froze, the trams stopped, people threw coats on the tops of beds and Sadie took the iron shelves out of oven in the range, wrapped them in newspaper and placed them in the bed. William slept with her to share body heat. The windowpanes were frozen inside and out, it was impossible to negotiate the pavements. Sadie began to worry that Frank would not get home in time for Christmas Eve. Then at the start of Christmas week, the temperature rose, trees dripped, pipes burst, the ice melted away and people started to venture into the streets and shops. Life began again.

By Christmas Eve. There was no sign of the grey slush which had dressed the kerbs like dirty petticoats. It was like the big freeze had never happened and though it was cold, the sky was blue and bright. Frank and his brother Matty arrived at the register office a full hour early. They stood outside on the steps smoking and chatted nervously about Frank's life in the army and Matty shared news of their siblings. Dora, their sister would be arriving with their grandmother, completing Frank's side of the wedding party. Fred arrived with Frieda on his arm, Opa came with Frieda's mother, Laura. The old man had been delighted to be asked to the wedding and there had been speculation among the younger generation.

"You never know," said Gracie, "Nan and Opa might

just hit it off and it could be the start of a beautiful relationship."

"You're joking," Frieda had said, "she won't be able to understand a word he says."

"That sounds like a good start for any relationship," Gracie had replied, laughing.

Nan and Dora arrived, wearing very smart new hats followed by Jack who arrived just a fraction before Gracie, William and the bride. Matty ushered them all to the top of the steps and into the imposing entrance hall where, in honour of it being Christmas Eve, someone had lit a blazing coal fire in the huge marble hearth.

Another wedding party was emerging from a room down the corridor and they were assembling in front of the fire, exchanging kisses and congratulations. An usher appeared, gently calling Frank and Sadie's names. Matty led the little group into a splendid meeting room which had a high ceiling, carved plaster covings and a huge chandelier in the centre of the ceiling. They were ushered to the front of the room where they each stood in front of one of the red, plush chairs, trimmed with gold, which were placed in neat rows facing a huge mahogany desk. Sensing that they were unsure whether to sit, the usher invited them to take a seat.

A door opened in the wall behind the desk and the registrar took his place and shuffled some papers on the desktop. He invited Sadie and Frank to stand and for the first time, Frank was able to take a long look at his bride. He told her afterwards that at that moment, his heart had skipped a beat. She wore an ankle length dress in midnight blue with a matching three quarter jacket which had a large velvet collar that buttoned on the shoulder.

Sadie couldn't afford the crepe material that Gracie recommended but this was equally lovely in her eyes. She carried a tiny bouquet of pale pink roses which Mrs. Johnson had pressed into her hand as she exited the house. Eva Johnson was fast becoming a great friend.

"Francesca has made you a little bouquet," she had said.

Sadie had been surprised and delighted to think that Eva's daughter had made such a beautiful thing with her own hands and when several of her neighbours gathered in front of the house to watch her leave for her wedding and to wish her well , she had been visibly moved.

Vows were exchanged, Matty produced the ring on cue, the register was signed and the registrar pronounced them husband and wife. When he said, "you may kiss the bride," everyone cheered including William who was slightly bemused by the whole affair and was complaining to Uncle Fred about the stiff collar he had been made to wear.

The Registrar shook their hands and signalled to the usher who led them along the corridor and back into the reception hall where the previous party had vacated the fireplace and everyone relaxed. For a small group, they made a good deal of noise. They talked over each other, there were hugs and pats on the back, handshakes and banter, the sort of thing Mary Jane would have called "good craick." Then Matty, anxious to light up a cigarette but not liking to do so in the building, suddenly produced an envelope from his pocket and insisted that the bride and groom should open it together. To their absolute amazement, the envelope contained an invitation to rooms in Rodney Street at eleven o'clock on Boxing Day to have their wedding photograph taken. It had been Gracie's idea of course and the two families had contributed to the gift. Sadie, Frank and William simply needed to present themselves at the address on the card, dressed to the nines and pose in front of the camera.

"Chance to wear your wedding clothes again," said Gracie.

Sadie and Frank weren't at all sure they would enjoy their photographic experience and William made his feelings clear about the prospect of having to wear his collar again. Everyone laughed and Jack undid the offending collar saying, "I don't blame you pal, it's as stiff as a board."

When they arrived at the Anchor there was a tray of hot toddies and a ginger beer for William waiting on the bar. "On the house," called the landlord as he and his wife, Jessie joined the wedding party. There was a great chinking of glasses and a toast to the happy couple before the landlord led everyone into his back room where there was an impressive fire blazing in the hearth.

Sadie had left holly and bunches of mistletoe at the Anchor and Jessie had placed them around the room and on the table.

"Send all your food over with his brother on the cart," Jessie had offered, "I'll lay it out for you, leave it to me, I'll make it look nice." And she had, Sadie hugged her in gratitude. The table was covered in a rich red chenille cloth overlaid with a white lace square which Jessie had kept the colour of fresh snow since her grandmother had given it to her. Sadie placed her little bouquet in the centre of the table and the red of the holly berries, the blue glow of the fire the yellow tinge from the gas lights gave the overall impression of cosy festivity.

As for Opa and Nan, they found plenty to talk about and if she did find him hard to understand, he wasn't aware of it. Frieda chatted to the other women about her pregnancy.

"When is it due Frieda?" asked Doris

"I'm six months now," she replied and everyone agreed that she didn't look six months pregnant.

"I was like the side of a house when I had our Ada," said Frank's sister Doris, "you're one of the lucky ones alright."

The men enjoyed their usual football banter, how Everton were having a better season than the previous year when they could only finish mid-table on the same points as Liverpool, the only consolation being a better goal difference. This year they looked like contenders for the title.

"So long as Bobby Parker doesn't get injured I reckon we'll do it," Jack speculated.

"Are you trying to jinx us?" said Fred, "we've already got Browell on the injury list…"

They took their analysis into the bar where the landlord started a debate about tactics and Fred reminded him he hadn't been to a match in three seasons.

"I can read," he retorted, by which he meant the match reports in his daily paper. Frank was settling the bar bill when the landlord asked him if he had heard anything about the rumours that were circulating amongst the dockers.

"What rumours?" replied Fred.

"It looks like the bloody Germans are spoiling for a fight," he said "some of the sailors have told the dock hands that we are stock piling weapons and food."

"I wouldn't know," replied Frank "we've had a great day, let's not spoil it with talk of war."

"I was just wondering if your army pals were being posted abroad, that's all," the landlord pressed on with his questions.

"No, I don't think so, and anyway, we are always the last to be told anything, I'm a bloody Private not a General."

"Thanks for a great do," added Matty protecting his brother. "Let's not upset the women, eh, it's a wedding!"

With that, Sadie and the others appeared from the back room to shouts of congratulations from the regulars at the bar and the wedding party spilled out onto the street.

Night had fallen over the city. It was clear and a frost had just begun to show itself on the pavements. Lights twinkled from the boats and buoys on the river and everyone started for home in their different directions.

"Don't forget your date with the photographer," shouted Gracie, "you never know you might even enjoy it Sadie."

It took some cajoling to keep William from falling asleep on the journey home and once there, Sadie just about managed to retrieve his new clothes before he fell into bed, exhausted. Suddenly Sadie felt shy. It wasn't as if she and Frank had never shared a bed but now she wasn't quite sure what she was supposed to do or who she was supposed to be. What was he expecting of his wife? She called down the stairs to let Frank know that William was fast asleep and that she was getting ready for bed. She was relieved to hear that he would follow her up in a few minutes.

Sadie took off her coat and dress and hung them carefully in the wardrobe. She had never owned what you might call an outfit before, the odd pretty blouse and good skirt, a coat that she had inherited from her mother, a warm shawl which doubled as a blanket in the winter but nothing like the clothes she was presently taking off. She ran her fingertips along the velvet collar on her jacket, took the pins out of her hair, let it fall onto her shoulders, pulled a nightdress over her head and got into bed. It was icy. Should she call down and let Frank know she was ready? She waited and minutes later she heard him making his way up the stairs. There was no need for Sadie to worry, Frank was more nervous than she was.

"He was out like a light before I could get him into bed," Sadie babbled while Frank undressed and slipped into bed beside her.

"Bloody Hell you're freezing," he shouted as she put her ice-cold feet against his shins. And the two of them laughed as she called him a wimp.

"William never complains," she said.

Sadie laid her head on Frank's chest and whispered, "I love you Frank," and the tension melted from her body as he replied, "me too, Mrs. Jordan, me too."

When William woke on Christmas morning there was a stocking at the foot of his bed. The little boy told a very convincing tale about how he had seen Father

Christmas on the roof during the night. The stocking contained an apple, an orange, a chocolate sovereign, a lollipop, a bag of marbles, a blue and white scarf that Sadie had knitted and favourite of all, a miniature football rattle which, for everyone's sake found its way into a high cupboard by lunch time.

Christmas day was the only day in the year when Sadie lit two fires, one in the kitchen and one in the parlour. Outside, the frost clung on until early afternoon when a winter sun made a brave appearance for a couple of hours. When the sun came out, so did Tommy. He was trying to push a hoop along the pavement with a stick. The hoop used to belong to his cousin and had laid in the yard for years until his sister spotted it and made it look like new again. Tommy was clearly delighted with his gift and William was allowed out into Carver Street to play with him.

"But I want you in as soon as the dinner's ready and no complaints," warned Sadie. Frank stood watching the two boys from the parlour window. They soon abandoned the hoop in favour of a game of marbles and when that was over Tommy ran in to fetch his football which they happily kicked back and forth across the street from kerb to kerb.

"They watch the older boys," shouted Sadie as she set the table in the kitchen. "That's how they learn all that stuff. Mind you they learn all the bad stuff too."

She described to Frank how during the summer a handful of the older boys had got hold of some of their mother's dolly blue, sneaked into St. Saviors and poured half a bottle into the holy water. It turned the water the colour of ink. Father Reilly had just laughed it off but the young priest who assisted him didn't see the funny side and treated it like a mortal sin.

"He came bouncing down the street looking for their mothers, going on about Correction Schools and having no respect for themselves or for God. He dragged them all in for confession," explained Sadie, even the Protestants!

Frank laughed out loud at the story and added, "if our William turns out anything like me, he'll get up to a lot worse than contaminating the holy water before he's finished."

When Frank said those kinds of things, claiming her son as his own, Sadie felt like the luckiest mother on earth.

They sat down to the happiest Christmas dinner any of them could ever remember. Afterwards Frank produced a box of toy soldiers for his son and for Sadie, a slim rectangular tin box with a village scene on the lid.

"It's for your hair pins," he said.

Sadie gave Frank the blue and white scarf she had just finished knitting and for the rest of Christmas day he and William wore their scarves and the football rattle was rescued from the cupboard. None of them wanted Christmas day to end.

On Boxing Day, the three of them made their way down Rodney Street, scouring all the brass plaques for one which said "Clifford Photography." Sadie had the impression she should talk in whispers such was the grandeur of the street. They climbed the steps of the Georgian house and rang the bell. A tall, blonde man opened the door, he was much younger than Sadie had imagined a photographer to be. He was wearing a cream, woollen jacket belted around the waist. Frank thought he looked more like he was ready to play cricket than take photographs. The young man led them into a huge square hallway and up a beautiful oak staircase decorated for Christmas with twisted garlands dripping with different fruits, baubles and spices.

"Be careful William don't go touching anything," warned Sadie.

"Don't worry about the child," came the response, "the house belongs to my parents but they are abroad for Christmas, I like to use their drawing room for a studio while they are away. It has three windows so there's plenty of light."

"What does he do?" asked Frank and Sadie threw him a warning look.

"Who?" replied their host.

"Your father," said Frank.

"Oh, he's a merchant, he's in the fruit importing business. If he had his way that's what I would be doing too but I'd rather try my hand at photography, see if I can make a living at it."

His response didn't exactly fill them with confidence.

"Now, I understand this is a wedding photograph, congratulations."

As he spoke, the photographer placed a high-backed mahogany chair next to the Adam style fireplace which was decorated with the same evergreen garlands as the staircase. He invited his clients to remove their coats and scarves and looked at Sadie as if he wasn't exactly sure what he could do with her.

"I think we'll have your hat off," he said at last, "its

casting a shadow across your face."

He passed her a hand-mirror and she hastily removed the offending garment and checked her hair. He sat Frank in the chair, put William on his left and Sadie stood on the right slightly behind her husband. It seemed to take an age to get the positioning right and from the look on William's face, he was overawed or bored. Noticing the blue and white scarves the photographer said, "I think your team is in with a chance of the title this year, what do you think young man?" Before William could reply, there was a flash and the photographer seemed happy enough with his efforts. He handed Sadie a card which had on it an altogether less prestigious address and a date and time to collect the photograph and the three of them were on their way to Nan's house where they were given a royal welcome and slices of cold ham and home - made chutney. There was a teary-eyed farewell between Frank and his grandmother, promises of visits from William and Sadie and the three of them were heading home on a very quiet tram. William took himself off to the front of the tram where, for the twenty-minute journey, he became the driver.

THIRTEEN
Rumours

"I don't want you to worry about money Sadie," said Frank. He told her that the army would send her a separation allowance deducted from his pay every month.

"You'll need to collect it at the Post Office every Tuesday. I'll still be able to save a bit from what's left. The only thing I need money for is my tobacco." Although Frank had found most of the money for their wedding, Sadie had all but depleted her meagre savings and the prospect of not being able to pay Snide when he came for the rent was a constant worry. Sadie squeezed Frank's hand and said nothing.

By the time William woke the next morning, Frank was on the train, half-way to Aldershot and Sadie had cooked and despatched her daily quota of pies. Wearily, she was washing pans and utensils at the sink when she heard her son padding down the stairs. He appeared in the kitchen, bleary eyed. He must have been cold, he was wearing his jumper over his pyjamas, it was back to front.

"Where's me dad Mam?" he asked.

Sadie explained that Frank had gone back to his barracks but that he would be home in a few weeks in time for Easter. The boy was happy enough with her explanation and he was soon tucking into a bowl of porridge and a spoonful of jam. The winter weeks which followed were routine, cooking, cleaning, weekly trips to the Anchor and visits to see Gracie and little Ivy. She called on Nan and went to see Frieda and Opa to check on Frieda's pregnancy and Fred made it his business to call at Sadie's house on match days for a pre-match kick about with his nephew in the yard.

Everton were at home to Sunderland. It was a big match, a sell-out. The Blues were well on course to win the championship and Sunderland were the current title holders. Fred should have been more excited than he seemed.

"What's wrong Fred?" asked Sadie. "It's not the baby is it?"

"No," he answered, "It's nothing like that, Frieda's fine. It's her brother, Michael, he's joined the Royal Navy, they are sending him to Dartmouth to train."

"Is that a bad thing, how old is he now?" she said.

"He's nineteen, no it's not a bad thing. It's the reason he's joined up that's bothering us all. It's all these rumours about us heading into a war with the Germans. It's looking like it could be true Sadie. The lads on the docks are saying we are getting ship after ship from America and Mexico full of oil. We are stock piling all sorts of stuff."

"But I thought her brother was apprenticed at Cammel Lairds," said Sadie. "Why did he suddenly join the navy?"

"He's part German Sadie, he's had to put up with a load of abuse, when the idiots are not calling him names, they are ignoring him as if he's invisible. He must have told them that his mother's family came over from Germany when he started at Lairds I don't suppose it ever crossed his mind he should keep it quiet. Frieda thinks he's joined up to prove he's loyal to Great Britain. To be honest, I'm getting a bit of ribbing myself at work."

"What sort of ribbing?" she asked.

"Oh, just the usual half-wits calling things out. Couldn't I find a Scouse girl to marry, don't talk to him he might be a spy, that sort of thing. It's nothing I can't handle but her brother's just a lad and he's had a lot worse than I have."

Sadie was disturbed by what her brother had shared. Frank's letters didn't even hint at the possibility of war. She thought of asking him directly in her next letter but it occurred to her that serving soldiers may have been ordered to stay tight lipped. The idea that a war was coming seemed so improbable to Sadie. Surely Jessie would have mentioned the rumours when they met at the Anchor or the women in the Tuesday Post Office queue might have mentioned something. There were Easter bunnies in the shop windows, Mrs. Morris was doing a good trade in Simnel cakes, the park was swathed in yellow daffodils, there were signs of spring everywhere. Everything was normal and the more she thought about it, the more improbable war seemed.

William and Sadie made a calendar out of a piece of card that she salvaged from her wedding cake box. They drew squares, coloured them in and marked each one with a date and a day. They counted down the days until Frank's return, crossing out a square every morning. The last day of March was coloured blue and William had drawn a football in the corner. William counted six squares still to be crossed out.

"There you are," said Sadie," we've only got six sleeps and your dad will be home for a whole week."

At long last, the day came. The train squealed and

hissed its way into Lime Street Station, shrouded in steam. William stood behind his mother, stealing a glance at the monster from the safety of her skirt. As the steam evaporated up into the roof, the platform exploded into life. Every carriage door sprang open, porters rushed along the platform pulling trollies, people meeting and greeting appeared from nowhere and pushed towards the carriages, passengers hauled heavy luggage down from the train, guards shouted instructions, people got off the train and others waited to board. All the time, Sadie strained to get sight of her husband. There were several soldiers on the platform but from where she stood, she couldn't distinguish between them. Suddenly William shot from his place of safety and before Sadie knew it, he was racing down the platform towards Frank who had spotted his son and was waiting with open arms. Sadie felt self-conscious. She had no experience of railway stations and hadn't expected their reunion to be quite so public. Frank, on the other hand had no such reservations. He hugged and kissed his wife and didn't mind a bit who was watching.

"Why don't we walk home?" he suggested as the three of them started down the station steps into Lime Street. There were complaints about tired legs from William but nothing that the promise of a lollipop from the kiosk and a kick about in the yard couldn't fix.

The days flew by. It was Saturday and to say that William was excited was a complete understatement. Sadie had not told him that he would be going to his first ever Everton game with Frank and Uncle Fred until the moment Fred arrived at the house on the day of the game. Two minutes later, her son was dressed in his coat and scarf and was waiting on the pavement in front of the house for his two companions. She watched their backs as they walked down the street and then Sadie set off in the opposite direction to take the tram to visit Frieda and Opa at their flat over the Butcher's shop. Opa was just leaving the shop when she arrived.

"Thank goodness," said Opa, "Frieda's pains have started, I'm just going to tell the midwife and fetch her mother."

Sadie could see how anxious he was so she didn't delay Frieda's grandfather with questions, instead, she swiftly climbed the stairs at the back of the shop which led to the rooms on the first floor. Frieda was stood in front of the window overlooking the street from where she had seen Sadie alighting the tram. She was holding onto the window frame, arms stretched above her head to get some relief from the pain in her back.

"How long since the pains started?" asked Sadie.

"Not long, my waters broke a couple of hours ago, just after Fred left," replied her sister-in-law. "Sadie, it's a couple of weeks early, do you think everything will be ok?"

"Loads of babies come early," replied Sadie as confidently as she could manage, "it doesn't mean there's anything wrong, anyway, the midwife will be here soon and if she thinks we should send for the doctor, we will."

"We can't afford the doctor, Sadie," groaned Frieda, the midwife will know what to do."

Frieda had a nagging ache in her lower back which brought from her an occasional low moan but the pain did not stop her from fretting that the bedroom wasn't fit for visitors. She gave instructions and drank sweet tea while Sadie hung up Fred's work clothes, changed the bedding and mopped the floor. The midwife, Frieda's mother and Opa arrived at the same time and suddenly the little flat was all noise and bustle. Sadie went into the tiny kitchen to put the kettle on and she peeled carrots, onions, leeks and potatoes, added some herbs from pots outside the window and put a pan of soup on a low light to simmer. It had occurred to her that Fred, Frank and William would return to her house in Carver Street after the game and that Fred would not suspect that his wife was in labour. She took three cups of tea into the bedroom, checked with the midwife that things were as they should be, put Opa in charge of the pot of soup and left for home.

In Carver Street, the house was empty but the first of the fans were making their way up the street, in celebratory mood. It was no time at all before William came bursting in through the open door waving his scarf in the air singing "two–nil, two-nil". A minute later, the men arrived and Sadie gave Fred the news.

"The trams will be full, it'll be quicker to walk home," said Fred.

"I've been thinking," said Sadie, "why don't you run down to Joey Carters and ask if you can borrow the bike?"

Mildred Carter had eight sons, Joey, the eldest worked on the docks with Fred. He would bring home tea in a cotton bag that his mother had made which he wore round his waist under his coat, away from prying eyes. On the kitchen table, Mildred would divide up the tea into heaps on pieces of newspaper, twist the tops and sell the little packets to her neighbours. Richie, his younger brother by a few years, was a delivery boy for the greengrocer. Unknown to the greengrocer, when he wasn't delivering, Mildred would hire out Richie's bicycle to anyone who could pay her a few pence. These little transactions supplemented the money that Mildred made by taking in washing which she would hang in every room in the house. Her biggest asset was a mangle which she kept in the yard. She had little choice about how she made ends meet in the absence of her husband whom she threw out upon discovering that he had a second family in St. Helens, with whom he now lived. She never mentioned his name referring to him always as "Good for Nothing" and to his partner as "The Trollop."

Luckily, the bike was available for hire and Fred made his way through a maze of wet washing and scrapping children to the yard at the back of the house.

"Will you tell your Sadie there'll be no more tea for a while Fred?" said Mildred, "with all this talk of war with the Germans, they have sent inspectors into the docks, our Joey says they are worried about the oil getting pilfered so he's laying off with the tea for a bit, it's too bloody risky. Our Richie doesn't need the bike till first thing Monday morning, I hope your lass is ok with the birth."

Sadie was waiting with bread and milk and six scones which she placed in the basket on the front of the bicycle and Fred rode up the cobbled street as fast as his legs could turn the pedals.

This wasn't how Sadie and Frank had envisaged the end of Frank's leave. They had been planning a ferry crossing to Birkenhead Park and a picnic on the Sunday but Frank didn't hesitate to offer to catch an early tram on Sunday morning to check on Frieda and the baby.

"It's a boy, he's going to be fine," said Fred as he opened the door of the shop to find Frank on the doorstep. "It's been a long night, the midwife told me to go for the doctor just to be on the safe side but he's a tough little fella Frank, like his mother."

Frank stepped into the bedroom to see Frieda fast asleep, exhausted, with her son tucked into the crook of her arm.

"He's a bobby dazzler alright," said Frank but in truth he could hardly make out the tiny face inside the bundle of blankets.

He crept out again and asked Fred if he could borrow the bicycle so that he could deliver the good news to Gracie and Jack.

"Thanks Frank," said Fred, "that would be great. Tell them we are calling him Henry after Opa. We couldn't name him Fred, we've already got Fred and Frieda," he laughed.

"Will you take the bike back to Mildred Carter for me? She reckons there are inspectors at the docks, we are getting loads of oil and munition parts coming in. Some of the fellas at Cammell Lairds told me they are going to requisition the Iris and the Daffodil from the Ferry Company to fit them out as war ships. I think we're in for a fight Frank. It might be time for you to talk to our Sadie. Don't worry we will make sure the two of them are ok till you get some more leave."

Frank honoured his promise to get news to Gracie and returned the bicycle.

"You've got another cousin William," he announced

to his son and wife, "and this time it's a boy, your mam will have to get knitting another blue and white scarf."

That evening the atmosphere in the house was a mixture of relief and baby talk on the one hand and sadness at Frank's departure on the other.

"But why do you have to go away again?" complained William as Frank helped to get him into bed. "I don't want to say goodbye now, I want to say goodbye in the morning and come with you to the end of the street like Tommy does when his dad goes away."

"Alright", said Sadie, you can wave him off in the morning, now settle down and get some rest."

Frank ruffled his son's hair and went down into the kitchen to stoke up the fire. Sadie lay on William's bed for a few minutes then joined her husband in front of the fire. Frank sat in the armchair and Sadie sat on the floor between his legs, her head on his knee. He loosened her hair and ran his fingers through the curls. He traced the contours of her face with his fingertips as if memorising her features. Sadie felt safe. She refused to let talk of war spoil the moment and when Frank attempted to talk seriously about the possibilities of a posting abroad, she stopped his words with a kiss.

They were both awake before the knocker-upper rapped on the window. Darkness was slowly giving way to a pale light. William was sleeping soundly in the next room and Sadie decided not to wake him despite her promise the night before that he could wave a final goodbye to Frank. They didn't linger in a last embrace, instead, Sadie watched from the doorway as Frank walked slowly to the top of the street. Once there, he turned, waved and disappeared around the corner. Sadie closed the door softly and made her way into the kitchen to distract herself with a new batch of pies.

The Following day when Sadie got to the Anchor to conduct her Monday transaction the Landlord was in animated conversation with one of his customers at the bar. They were talking about a cartoon which appeared showing the German Keiser trampling all over a map of Europe in huge boots.

"I'm telling you," the landlord was saying, "those bloody Germans are just waiting for an excuse to start a war, the Government knows it and so do the newspapers."

A regular at the bar had other ideas, "Nah, everybody's saying it's just rumours, a few German officers thinking out loud."

"Yeh," replied the landlord, "just like they said the Titanic would never sink, look what happened there! Why else are the Iris and the Daffodil being fitted out as fighting ships?"

Sadie concluded her business in the pub as swiftly as she could, she couldn't face more talk of war and anyway, she was anxious to see the new baby and her sister-in-law.

FOURTEEN
A Worrying Time.

Sadie and William arrived at the rooms over the butchers bringing gifts of freshly baked pies and bread and a small bottle of Navy rum from the Landlord by way of congratulations. What confronted Sadie was not what she expected. Opa was there all alone. It seemed that the doctor had returned early that morning and was concerned when he listened to the baby's lungs. He looked at Frieda and declared her to be severely anaemic and the two of them were now in the Northern Hospital. Poor Opa was distraught. People died when they went into hospitals, everybody knew that and surely his granddaughter and his great grandson would get better care from their family at home. And then there was the cost, how could they afford the charges? That very question was occurring to Sadie too.

"The doctor said there were charities who would pay the hospital bill," said Opa, "he said the hospital almoner would sort it out, I paid him his sixpence for coming out to see them. He said he would wave his fee but I told him I didn't want handouts and he took it in the end."

Opa told Sadie that Fred had been to the hospital and from there, had gone to work. The family needed his wages more than ever but that wasn't Fred's only concern. He was one of the lucky ones, he had regular employment, he didn't have to stand on the dockside every day like so many men, waiting for the foreman to take him on. But, security at the docks had been tightened and as a result there was unrest amongst the dockers and disputes between them and the bosses. There was even talk of a strike and Fred didn't want to give them an excuse to sack him. He was tense and worried all day, anxious to visit the hospital in the evening. It turned out that little Henry Frederick had a bronchial infection, his condition was critical and the family could do nothing but hope and pray. With treatment and rest, Frieda would be fine, they said, but worry about her baby made her recovery slow.

Life for Fred suddenly got very serious. Everton finished the season by winning the title but neither Fred nor Frank was at the final game. The city turned blue for a weekend of celebration but there were bigger things competing for Sadie's attention. She seemed to spend that whole spring waiting. She waited for the baby to recover, she waited for letters from Frank, she waited for news that there would be a war, she waited for news that there wouldn't be a war. And then, just as a soggy spring gave way to a much-anticipated summer, Fred came to Carver Street with the news that his wife and child had, at last, returned home. Sadie, who had been her brother's surrogate mother since he was a boy, cried when she heard the news.

It had taken six long weeks for the baby to show signs of recovery. It was June before Frieda could bring him home and then only because summer had finally arrived bringing sunshine and warmth to give Henry Frederick a fighting chance. It was a quiet homecoming, the atmosphere over the butcher's shop was one of relief rather than joy. Only time would tell how delicate a little boy Henry might be but one thing was sure, he would be nurtured by his mother and cherished by Fred and they were as proud of their son as any parents could be. On a beautiful Sunday in mid-June, Opa, Fred and Frieda proudly walked their child to the German Church where he was baptised.

On the same Sunday, Sadie opened the door to a friend of Frank whom she vaguely recognised. He was in uniform and he thrust a letter into her hand.

"Your Frank asked me to deliver this," he said. "I'm home on a couple of days compassionate leave to go to a funeral, there's stuff we can't write in our letters these days, they read them before they post them."

Jimmy was gone before she could properly thank him, it was obvious that he didn't want to get into conversation. The letter contained news she didn't want to hear. All leave had been cancelled. They were getting ready to move them out, he didn't know exactly when or where, probably Belgium or France. Sadie wasn't to worry, the German army was big but they were mainly volunteers and conscripts, no match for regulars like himself. It would turn out to be a storm in a teacup, it would be over by Christmas. The letter literally took the wind out of Sadie, she slumped into a chair in the parlour. She put the letter in her pocket as if in hiding it she could deny it had ever arrived.

Later that week Sadie was hanging washing on the line in the yard, taking advantage of the glorious weather. William was passing her pegs that she kept in an old enamel pan. Her neighbour was doing the same and though they never tended to chat, they had exchanged pleasantries over the wall. Suddenly Maggie's gate at the bottom of the yard swung open and George, in full uniform, kit bag on his shoulder, walked towards his wife with a grin on his face. Maggie let out a little scream when she saw him.

"What are you doing here?" she said.

"Charming," he replied, "make a man feel wanted why don't you?" George acknowledged Sadie across the wall, said hello to William and asked about Tommy.

"He's with me mam," said Maggie, "she took him to New Brighton with it being such a nice day."

It seemed that the army had recalled most of the soldiers serving in countries in the Empire so George had been shipped home from India and was staying in Liverpool for a couple of days. After that, he had orders to go to Lytham to await possible mobilisation to Europe. Sadie played with Frank's letter in her pocket. She didn't share its contents but now there was no denying the message it contained.

"It's not looking good," said George uneasily, "the Germans are looking for any reason to start a fight, God knows what it will be but they'll find something. Don't worry, we're ready, the army's been expecting this for a long time."

During his visit George was proved right. A young lad from Serbia assassinated the Austrian, Archduke Ferdinand and his pregnant wife giving Germany the perfect excuse to start a war. Sadie had no idea what this Duke had to do with her or Frank or why his death should be the trigger for the British military to go into battle. George tried to explain the politics but the only thing that mattered to Sadie was that now the prospect of war was real.

In July, a heatwave hit and it began as fun, children splashing in fountains in the park, teenagers swimming in rivers, front doors wide open and kitchen chairs brought out onto pavements. But as the weeks dragged on and the temperatures soared, those who had no work to go to stayed indoors and closed their curtains against the searing sun. William and Tommy would start their day outside, usually digging up the tar that was melting between the cobble stones in the street. By noon, though, they were inside, tired and out of sorts, overwhelmed by the heat. Every cloud has a silver lining and for a while, talk about the weather had replaced talk about the war. Occasional thunderstorms brought some light relief but they never lasted long and the rain that bounced on the streets and pavements dried up before it could do any good.

Sadie received two letters from Frank. Bizarrely, they arrived out of sequence, the letter he had written second arrived first. It didn't matter, both letters were full of chat about funny incidences in the barracks and news about his army pals. He told Sadie he missed her and asked for news of William. He wanted to know how they were managing in the heat wave and whether she had had time to go to visit his grandmother. Sadie searched for clues in the letters. Was war coming? Was Frank about to be posted overseas? How soon would he get some leave? But there were no clues, either Frank didn't know any more than she did or he wasn't breathing a word about it. When Sadie wrote to Frank, she talked about the heatwave, she wrote about her last visit to Nan, she told him some of the funny things that William had said and done, she mentioned that George had been home on weekend leave but she didn't mention his new posting. And that's how July and most of August went, unanswered questions and unspoken anxieties hung in the air like the afternoon heat.

Sadie took William and Tommy to the Landing Stage on August Bank Holiday to watch the Isle of Man steam packet loading up and setting sail. It was quite a sight to watch all the holiday makers lining up on the quay side, the women in summer hats, the men in suits despite the temperature, ships' porters relieving them of their weekend luggage. The boys watched as the large ship was led out of the port by the tiny pilot's boat and Tommy and William ran around the dockside pretending to be ships and mimicking the blasts coming from the funnels. Then the three of them sat on a bench looking out to the river and ate egg sandwiches and a pork pie. Maggie had given Tommy a few liquorice sweets that her daughter had brought home from Taveners where she had started work as a sweet packer. The foreman would allow the girls to take a few misshapes so long as they turned a blind eye when he helped himself to a lot more than misshapes. They shared the sweets. The scene on the dockside was idyllic, it was a scene worthy of a painting, full of colour and movement. Sadie tried to memorise the picture so that she could describe it to Frank. Had he been there, it might have been the perfect day.

FIFTEEN
War is Declared.

It rained in the night, the first real rain in nine weeks. It was gentle, summer rain that made no noise. Sadie woke at six, the rain had brought a welcome drop in temperature and she looked in on William who was still sleeping peacefully. Gently, she pulled the quilt over his little body. She thought about the holiday makers in the Isle of Man waking to rain, so unexpected, so disappointing. She wrote a long letter to Frank and tucked it for safe keeping behind the frame of their wedding photo on the wall in the parlour. William made an appearance and at the same time so did Maggie. He came down the stairs into the kitchen, her neighbour made her way through the yard and was knocking on Sadie's back door which was still waiting to be unbolted, she had a newspaper in her hand. Norah Price, from across the street was with her. Norah loved nothing better than to be the bearer of tidings, good news, bad news, it didn't matter to Norah so long as she was the messenger. Luckily for her, her son who was fourteen had got himself an early morning job in the newsagents sorting the papers. The money wasn't great but her husband Hughie had been invalided after a mining accident so every penny counted. One of the perks of the job was a daily newspaper which didn't really interest her son but which Hughie devoured each day and which came in handy for the lavatory.

"We're at war with Germany," declared Norah Price as she brandished the newspaper in front of Sadie as if proof were needed. Poor Sadie tried to take in the headlines. The German army was marching Belgium intent on conquering France. France declared war on Germany and the British Government had announced that Great Britain was now at war with Germany too. British troops had been mobilised overnight. Thousands of service men would be arriving home to be re-deployed. The Royal Navy, Merchant Navy and Coastguard were on high alert.

It was strange but all that Sadie could think about was that the letter she had just written would now be wrongly addressed. "I've just finished writing to Frank," she said pointing to the envelope tucked behind the photo frame, "where will I send the letter, I don't know where he is?"

Maggie sat Sadie down and signalled to Norah to put the kettle on and she said patiently "don't worry about the letter Sadie, keep it safe till they let us know how to contact our men."

They drank sweet tea and Maggie tried to reassure Sadie that the war would probably finish as quickly as it started. Maggie spoke with uncharacteristic sensitivity as if she really understood the impact of the news on Sadie. Sadie was confused, she wasn't used to sympathy from her neighbour, perhaps she felt a kind of solidarity or perhaps she did not want to appear unkind in front of Norah.

Despite the warning signs that had been hanging in the air for weeks, Sadie felt like she was in a dream. Her neighbours left. Maggie had said that since Tommy had heard the news he had been marching up and down the kitchen carrying the broom on his shoulder like a gun saying that he was going to kill all the bloody Germans.

"Isn't Opa a bloody German?" asked William.

"He is, but he's English as well, so it doesn't really count," said Sadie. It was all she could muster. Thankfully it was enough for now.

In the afternoon, Gracie and Jack arrived with Ivy Rose. They had been to see Fred and Frieda and they came with news. William and Tommy had made a tent by throwing a blanket over the clothes maiden and they were sitting in it chatting. Ivy Rose tried to join them but she toddled back to Gracie complaining that she didn't know the password and she had no treasure so the boys wouldn't let her in. Sadie gave her a plate of bread and jam and told her to try Everton. The three children were soon devouring their spoils in the half-light of the tent.

"They've asked Jack to do a special job for the duration of the war," said Gracie. "We have known for a week or so but they made him sign a paper to say that he wouldn't tell anyone until the Government declared war. His boss, Mr. Owen, one of the partners is going to be running everything at the docks. There's a massive amount of stuff that will be coming and going and they have made two huge munitions stores down there. They say the war effort depends on keeping the docks running."

"So, what will you be doing Jack?" asked Sadie

"Mr. Owen has asked me and another bloke to be his assistants Sadie," he said. "For the time being there are just the three of us, it's what they call a protected job."

"That's what we wanted to explain," said Gracie and she bit her bottom lip the way she always did when she was telling her sister something she might not want to hear. Jack took over again. "Anyone in a protected job doesn't need to serve in the military Sadie and what with your Frank on his way to Europe to fight, I wouldn't blame you for being upset that I won't need to go. I promise you the job won't be an easy ride, I'm not sure what it will entail just yet but they have told me it won't be easy."

"Jack," said Sadie, "the last thing I want is for you and our Fred to go joining up, one soldier is enough, I just wish Frank didn't have to go. And anyway, we are going to need you here."

"I'm not sure everyone will see it like that Sadie, the recruitment offices will be open tomorrow, they are expecting queues round the block by eight o'clock. People have a way of seeing things in black and white if you're not a hero you must be coward. When we left Fred and Frieda they were arguing about whether he should sign up for the army. I think we persuaded him to wait for a while. They reckon it could all be over by Christmas." He gently touched Sadie's arm "but I'm glad you understand," he said.

Just then, a minor skirmish broke out in the tent and Sadie had no more time to wrestle with her new reality. She separated the scrapping children, sent Tommy home for his tea and got soup, bread and cheese ready for their own meal.

Jack had been right about the queues at the recruitment offices, thousands of would-be soldiers and sailors presented themselves in those first days, so many that the army and navy had trouble processing them all. The newspapers where full of praise for these brave young men, heroes in the making. Posters appeared everywhere asking for more men to join up. The campaign for recruits was relentless. Still, there was optimism that the whole thing, as Jack had said, would be over and done with by Christmas. Afterall, the British Army had proved time and again that no other country's army was its match, hadn't it?

Sadie posted her letter to Frank and every day she watched and waited for the postman. A week or so later a letter came but it wasn't the letter for which she was waiting. It was a letter from the Council offering William a place in Bray Street School from September. It was an initiative to help the war effort, the letter stated. It was to be a brave experiment. They wanted children who were approaching their fourth birthday to start school so that women could be freed up to take the jobs of the men who had joined the armed forces. What was more, the letter explained, they would be providing free school meals in an attempt to keep the nation's children healthy given the inevitable shortage of food stuff that the war would cause. Sadie was, of course at liberty to refuse the school place given that William would be a full year younger than the required legal age for starting school but it was very much hoped that she would agree to his attendance. The offer of a free meal was an answer to Sadie's prayers. There had been massive panic buying in all the shops, flour was being stock piled to feed the troops and the supply of meat was depleted so that what was left was too expensive for the likes of Sadie. Despite her anxieties, she was glad that her son was going to start at Bray Street.

Sadie travelled to the Admiral to tell the landlord that she would not be able to supply him with pies, it was impossible to buy the ingredients. But before she could say her piece, he was showing her an official letter ordering all pubs to restrict their opening hours.

"I can see us going under if we can only open during the licensed hours that the bloody government has laid down," he said. "Bloody stupid idea if you ask me, anyway Sadie, I'm going to miss our weekly get togethers, but top and bottom of it is I can't use any more pies."

He poured two port and lemons and Jessie and Sadie sat down to drink them together one last time. Despite the warmth of the alcohol, Sadie felt a wave of anxiety about how she would make ends meet. She had already cut back on food and coal prices were rising. She told herself that she would have to make the best of it like everyone else. Frank was God knows where preparing to fight, there were posters everywhere asking people what they could do for their country, now wasn't the time to complain. She left the Admiral for the last time trying hard to be positive. She thought about her son about to start school, she was terrified that someone at the school would ask to see his birth certificate, she had no intention of stating his name as anything but William Jordan, that's how her little boy thought of himself, to all intents and purposes, he was frank's son. Despite the fact that his birth certificate stated "father unknown," William Jordan would be his name for the rest of his life, Sadie would make sure of that.

SIXTEEN
Bray Street School

At Bray Street school, it was enrolment day. Sadie
and William reported to the school hall. It struck Sadie
how tiny the boys were standing beside their mothers in
the queue, especially boys like William who were starting
before they would normally have started school in peace
time. There was an oak table in the centre of the room
which was dwarfed by the vastness of the space. There
was a Proverb from the Bible written on one of the walls
in enormous black, fancy lettering edged in gold.

"The eyes of the Lord are in every place. He sees the
evil and the good."

Sadie shivered. She was glad that Maggie and Tommy
were far enough ahead of her in the queue that she
wouldn't need to speak to them. William waved at
Tommy whilst keeping a tight grip on his mother's skirt.
He was bored by the queuing.

"Name?" asked the headmaster.

William jumped. Sadie hesitated, "William Jordan,"
she replied.

Her breathing quickened when it looked like she was
going to be asked to produce her son's birth certificate
but the moment passed and the rest of the enrolment went
without a hitch. Age, address. Could William tie his
boot laces? Was he healthy? Would Sadie like him to
have his dinners in school? It occurred to Sadie that there
would not have been one mother who would decline the
offer. Finally, the headmaster addressed William.

"See you on Monday morning then William Jordan,
nine o'clock sharp."

And that was it, William was enrolled in school and his new name was established forever. Mother and son made their way home and Sadie was more than relieved at how the morning had gone.

When Sadie and William got near to their house she could see that the door was slightly ajar. She was sure she had closed it behind her but it wouldn't be the first time that the catch had failed. A little gingerly, she pushed the door open and went into the parlour, William ran into the kitchen ahead of her and she heard a squeal of excitement as he shouted "Dad." Instantaneously, an image of William Tierney flashed through Sadie's brain, he was dressed in his sailor's uniform and was sitting at the table, smiling. As quickly as it had come, Sadie shook it out of her head and hurried into the kitchen to hugs and kisses and cries of delight. Frank was home. Naturally, William rehearsed the whole story of the visit to the school. Frank listened patiently.

Sadie stood behind her son and mouthed the words "How long?" to her husband.

"Two days," Frank replied.

Two days seemed so meagre that Sadie had to fight hard not to give in to tears of disappointment.

"William," said Frank, cutting into the story, "there's a present for you and a present for Tommy in my bag, go and have a look."

Overjoyed, the boy searched in the bag and brought back two small, wooden rifles. With the guns in his arms, he raced out of the house to fetch Tommy from next door. "There's a bloke who makes toys out of wood, he's doing a roaring trade, guns for the lads, little rolling pins and wooden spoons for the girls, all the men are buying them.

It kills the time to have something like that to do, I'm spending half my days playing cards! We haven't seen any action yet Sadie, honestly the biggest problem is boredom."

While the two boys played happily at being soldiers, Frank and Sadie spent the next hour talking, laughing and crying. Sadie bathed in the warmth of her husband as they sat together, finally able to touch.

For two days, the three of them were together. They went to see Nan, Frank's Grandmother and they strolled in the park but apart from that they were content to stay at home, shutting out the world and talking about everything but the war. They did their best to make time stand still. When Monday morning arrived, the three of them set off down Carver Street. They held hands until they reached the intersection. They kissed and hugged and Sadie ran her fingers gently around her husband's face as if to carry away an imprint. It was something he had done to her face, many times and she loved it. Frank turned left towards the tram, Sadie and William turned right towards the school. Frank waited on the corner until his wife and son disappeared around the bend, the three of them waving until the very last second.

In the weeks that followed, Sadie missed her husband to the point where her body ached for him. The intensity of her feeling surprised her. She tried to tell herself that she was only one of thousands of women suffering this longing, that feeling sorry for herself was unpatriotic. It didn't help. She felt the aching most when she went to bed and she was lying there waiting for sleep to come to her rescue. Sadie took to planning a future for her little family. It helped to alleviate the loneliness and lull her to sleep. She conjured up future Christmases in her head and outings too. She pictured the three of them at the circus and the theatre, on the front at New Brighton. She saw Frank with William on his shoulders after a game of football in the park. She imagined the children they would have, a girl next and then another boy. She saw herself, clear as daylight, pushing the pram. It was at night that she would compose her next letter to her husband in her head, the words flowed best at night when she was immersed in imagining their future. What Sadie did not imagine was that a few letters later, Frank would be dead.

She had seen the boy on the bicycle through the window as she was making the bed and Sadie's first thought was that he was about to ask for directions to someone else's house. When he knocked on her door, he didn't bother to get off his bike, he simply said "Mrs Jordan, Sadie Jordan?" Sadie nodded and took the telegram from his hand. She didn't speak. She noticed that his jacket was far too big for him as if someone else had owned it and passed it on.

The telegram read, "killed in action at the Battle of the Marne, serving his country, a letter would follow," so few words for such a devastating a message.

Sadie sank to her knees, the telegram still in her hand. Maggie appeared through the back door the moment Sadie shut the front one. She too had seen the boy on the bike and had thought for one moment that he was bringing news of her own husband George.

Maggie despatched a neighbour to fetch Gracie who

deposited Ivy Rose at the dairy with her mother-in-law and could hardly breathe by the time she got to Sadie. Someone had gone to fetch William from school, the kitchen was full of neighbours, making tea, washing dishes, holding Sadie's hand, drawing curtains, putting coal on the fire, collecting eggs from the chickens. They spoke in whispers but it sounded to Sadie like a din, she wished they would go home and leave her to her misery.

Gracie stayed for two long days and nights. Together they tried to explain to William that Frank had died a hero. When eventually the letter came, it said that he was an exemplary soldier, liked and admired by the other men and the officers. His sacrifice would not be in vain. He was buried like so many of his regiment very close to where he fell. His name would live on. Sadie had never been so glad that despite the fact that it wasn't the name on his birth certificate, Frank's name would indeed live on through her son. Shock turned to anger and then to despair. Gracie took William home with her, hoping that Ivy Rose would distract him. The boy was confused, he needed his mother but his mother had nothing to give him.

Sadie took to visiting Nan, Frank's grandmother at every opportunity and the two women cried together and found solace in a sherry bottle. She ate little, neglected the house, got behind with the rent, she ignored letters which came from the school and not even Fred could penetrate the wall of despair. Then something happened which would bring Sadie face to face with herself in a way she could never have imagined.

She was returning from a visit to Nan's house, more than a few sweet sherries inside her. She saw a figure, he appeared to be leaning on the wall of her house. He looked familiar but was muffled inside a duffel coat and scarf. He was smoking. William Tierney had been to Mrs. Carmichael's hoping to find lodgings in his old room for a couple of nights between ships. The boarding house was now occupied by the Brady family consisting of eight red headed children, all girls. They took no time in telling William Tierney that Mrs. Carmichael had gone home to her beloved Scotland at the beginning of the war to live with her sister.

It may have been the alcohol or the anger that raged inside her but Sadie bundled William Tierney through the front door and he stumbled into the parlour. She slammed the door behind them. He was shocked, this wasn't the Sadie he remembered or the reunion he had imagined. On his way into the kitchen from the parlour he saw the wedding photograph hanging on the wall and he noticed the boy standing beside the bride and groom looking bemused. Sadie spat out her story with a venom that she didn't know she had in her. She didn't care if Maggie or the other neighbours could hear, William Tierney would get the full force of her anger and indignation. She blamed him for lying to her, for abandoning her, for leaving her pregnant. She blamed him for the war, for Frank's death, for the fact that she was neglecting her son, for her drinking. She lashed out with her tongue and her fists until finally, Sadie collapsed, exhausted onto a chair. William took the lashing without flinching, he was shocked and hurt. The realisation that he had a son was overwhelming and

William sat next to Sadie, tears streaming down his face.

When William told his story, Sadie was too worn out to do anything but sit quietly and listen. He had no idea that she had been pregnant. He had lied about sailing to America to impress her. He intended to travel to Portsmouth to get on a cargo ship to Antigua. But the night of the fireworks he had returned to Mrs. Carmichael's boarding house where his brother told him that a girl he had been courting was having his child. He had known her all his life. He married her and weeks later she lost the baby. They lost another child soon after and then six weeks ago his wife had passed away giving birth to one more dead child. William told his story as if he was a stranger to it. Silent tears fell onto his hands. Sadie remembered how she had loved his hands, how she had loved him. There was no life in his eyes. She felt for William in his grief, strangely she felt human again, it was the first time she had felt anything for anyone but herself since the day the telegram arrived. Something in Sadie broke, like a great river bursting its banks. She fell onto her knees with her head in William's lap, he cupped her face in his hands and drew her into his body. He was warm, strong, she remembered his smell. His touch was overwhelming. In that moment, Sadie had no thought for the future, life had dealt her the cruelest of blows and now she yearned for the human contact that William Tierney was offering. She was like a drowning woman clinging to driftwood.

Sadie woke just after dawn but William Tierney was already up and dressed. Sadie shuddered, there had been none of the warmth and companionship which Sadie experienced with Frank.

"Too many ghosts," she said and he nodded in agreement.

They parted for a second time; they both knew that this time it was forever. Minutes later, Sadie rose, dressed and was working her way through the whole house, scrubbing, cleaning, reinstating some version of normality. Next, she lifted down the tin bath from the yard wall, half filled it with hot water from kettles and pans, closed the kitchen curtains and washed herself clean. After that, she left for Gracie's to fetch back her son. She thought she saw Maggie's curtains twitch, for a second, she considered a defiant wave but she focused on her new start, on repairing her relationship with William and she pressed on towards the tram.

The scene that met her at her sister's house made her realise that she was not the only one with troubles. She pushed open the door which was ajar. The children were playing in the yard, they had jam jars in their hands. Jack was burning something on the fire which was filling the kitchen with an acrid smell and Gracie had been crying. Jack had finished an early shift and had arrived home to find a parcel addressed to him on the doorstep. It was a box of white feathers, mostly chicken feathers but some were the tail feathers of a pigeon. There was a note which simply said "coward."

"So much for the badges they gave us to wear and all those bloody certificates of exemption they've issued," said Jack. "Don't people realise that if we can't keep the bloody docks moving we'll lose the war?"

Sadie wanted to sympathise but momentarily, she hesitated. Some dead soldier's mother or sister or wife had probably delivered the feathers and she knew first - hand how grief and anger could make you lash out. Luckily for Sadie, her sister didn't notice the second's hesitation because the back door crashed open and in ran William followed closely by his cousin, each proffering jam jars stuffed with twigs and soil housing collections of worms and insects. William stopped in his tracks when he saw his mother and though it wasn't entirely unexpected, Sadie was devastated when he ignored her and proudly showed the fruits of his afternoon's labour to Gracie.

The tram ride home was silent and William insisted on running ahead of his mother on the walk up to Carver Street. As they were passing the school, Sadie noticed that the gate was open despite it being a little after four thirty. She wanted to reinstate William in school as soon as possible, for one thing, she needed to find a job and her son needed some normality in his days. She was hoping that the headmaster was still on the school premises. It was eerie walking around the deserted classrooms. The only light she could see was coming from a room in the corner which she presumed was the headmaster's office. She and William were making their way towards the light when they heard a voice behind them.

"Can I help you?"

It was the school caretaker, Cyril Harmer. Sadie had known him for years, everybody knew him. He lived on the other side of the main road from Sadie with his mother. It was strange how the two communities never really mixed. But everybody knew Cyril. He was about ten years older than Sadie. He was a tall man, lean rather than thin with jet black hair that was greying at the temples. He wore a black eye patch and that's the reason everybody knew him. He had been an only child, his father used to take him shooting on Sunday mornings while his mother went to the service at the Methodist church. In the afternoons she would deposit him in Sunday school while she and her husband took advantage of an empty house. His father gave Cyril an air rifle and the boy would sit on the wooden plank of a toilet seat in the outside lavatory, open the door and fire at a makeshift target he had drawn on the yard wall. One morning, just before his thirteenth birthday, the gun misfired and the tiny bullet went straight through his left eye. It took months and months of care and several operations and still they did not manage to save his eye.

"Mrs. Jordan, isn't it?" Cyril said looking at William, "Sadie?"

"I wondered if the headmaster was still here," she replied. William reached up and held her hand for the first time since their reunion.

"You're lucky," Cyril said, "that's his room over there." He pointed towards the light. "I was very sorry to hear about your husband." Sadie nodded and turned to walk away.

"You won't have got the letter from the headmaster," he said, "they sent letters home with all the boys yesterday."

"No," said Sadie picturing the pile of letters which she had thrown onto a chair in the parlour unopened, "no, I don't think I did."

"I hope I'm not speaking out of turn but there's a job going, here in the school. Assistant to the cook. The applications need to be in by tomorrow, only I know you used to work in the bakers, I used to come in every Saturday with my mother."

"I know, I remember," replied Sadie, she thought he seemed flattered that she had remembered.

William and Sadie made their way over to the headmaster's office and after her apologies for unanswered letters and his condolences for their loss, William was told to return to school the following morning.

"And don't be late young Jordan," said the headmaster. Before he could usher them out of his office Sadie plucked up courage and asked about the job vacancy and he gave her a form to complete.

"Bring it back in the morning when you come with William," he said anxious to get home for the evening.

For the first time in a long time, Sadie felt the tiniest glimmer of hope and she and William made their way home.

That evening, Sadie gave Emma Moran's name as a referee when she completed the application form for the job. She hoped her former employer would be as good as her word and supply a favourable reference. She wasn't sure whether it was this or whether Cyril, the caretaker had put in a good word for her but in any case, she was called for a short interview and was told the job was hers. The cook turned out to be a woman in her late sixties called Ada. She had retired from a job in the kitchens at the Adelphi Hotel, but then war broke out and she didn't want to sit at home all day on her own. Ada's retirement was short lived, everyone said the job in the school was made for her. The third member of the team was a slip of a girl, a shy fifteen-year-old called Cora. She was hired to wash up, scrub pans and clean tables. Sadie's role was largely preparation of vegetables. Ada turned out to be a genius at making tasty meals on a shoestring and she had useful contacts with suppliers from her hotel days. Happily, she wasn't averse to suggestions from Sadie and soon recognised her talents with pastry.

When Sadie was working she managed to block out the waves of grief and sadness which threatened to overwhelm her at other times. By and large, the school was a happy enough place and provided that the cook kept within her meagre budget, she, Cora and Sadie were left alone by the headmaster to get on with the job, mainly because he saw the kitchen as the domain of women and had no idea how to wash a dish let alone cook a meal. They worked well together and soon, a bond was formed between the three women, surrounded as they were by two hundred and fifty boys, four male teachers, two of whom had come out of retirement to replace younger teachers who had joined the military, one female teacher, a headmaster and a male caretaker.

Every day the male staff came along to the hall which the women transformed into a canteen each lunch time and were fed alongside the older boys. The younger boys ate in their classroom, supervised by the only female teacher. Ada noticed that the caretaker always made sure he was served by Sadie, she commented on it but Sadie batted away the suggestion like a nuisance wasp.

William continued to be withdrawn, he struggled to understand Frank's death and kept waiting for him to come home. Sadie had no idea how to help him, she could barely understand her own feelings, she struggled with guilt, remorse, anger and her way of dealing with the chaos inside her was to push it down to stop it from choking her. Then one Saturday morning she woke with a headache and a feeling of nausea. There was an illness spreading through the school which was causing the boys to vomit. Lots of them had been sent home and Sadie had been concerned in case William caught it since she would have found it difficult to take time off to care for him. She drank tea and ate dry bread and began to feel better and it wasn't until she was dressing that she looked in the mirror and noticed the changes in her breasts. She had lost a lot of weight during the last few months, but it wasn't that which caught her eye, it was the slight change in her body shape. She knew, of course that her last period hadn't come but she had put it down to the trauma of Frank's death. Staring at her image in the glass, she had no doubt that she was carrying William Tierney's baby, it could only have been his. She stared in utter disbelief. She was surprised at how calm she felt. She thought about her son, his son, sleeping, oblivious in the next room. The only thoughts in her head were about how they might survive. This time, she could not claim the innocence of youth and she could not burden her family. There was a war raging, brave men were being slaughtered and others were returning home maimed, there would be no surfeit of sympathy for mature women who got themselves into trouble. She could hear it now, "she didn't waste much time, her poor husband's only been dead five minutes…" But it wasn't the sneering criticism of the neighbours that terrified Sadie, it was the idea of the workhouse. Even if she could pass off the baby as Frank's which would be implausible given the time lapse, how would she survive with two children? In the time it took to dress herself, Sadie had hatched a plan. Even as she concocted her scheme, Sadie loathed herself. She could hardly recognise who she was but she was trapped. She had two children to protect, she would do what she needed to do and wrestle with her conscience the best way she could.

On Monday morning she dressed in her best blouse, paid attention to her hair and smoothed rouge onto her lips and cheek bones trying not to look so pale. She took a clean white apron from the drawer. At lunchtime she saw Cyril coming into the school hall, he was walking towards her, by-passing the queue of boys waiting to be served. She piled rabbit stew onto his plate making sure to give him the best of the meat. She smiled and struck up a cheerful conversation. How was his weekend? How was his mother? He was delighted by the attention. His mother was ill as it happened and confined to the house. Sadie's fingers brushed against the inside of his wrist as she handed him his plate.

"Actually Sadie," he began, emboldened by the touch, "I was going to ask you if you fancied coming with me to the theatre on Saturday night. The thing is, I have two tickets, I was planning to take my mother but she won't be well enough. It's the Hippodrome, there are some great acts on the bill, pity to waste the tickets."

"That's very kind, Cyril," said Sadie "I'd love to go to the Hippodrome, I've heard about it but I've never been."

Cyril was both surprised and delighted. Sadie saw Ada's face out of the corner of her eye. Her eyebrows gave away her disbelief but Ada knew better than to say anything. Sadie took a moment to steady her breathing and then, head down, busied herself with serving the stew.

Sadie made arrangements for the theatre visit. She had never been able to lie to Gracie but she wasn't ready to be judged, she had enough self-loathing to be going on with. So, she arranged to take William to Frieda on the Saturday. She told her that Ada had planned a trip to the Hippodrome but that her friend had taken ill and that she had offered the spare ticket to Sadie.

"I don't need to pay for the ticket," lied Sadie, Ada was given them by the night porter at the Adelphi, he's a cousin of hers…"

"That's good Sadie, it's about time you started living a bit after what you've been through. I'd love to go to the Hippodrome; people say it's a great night out. William will be fine with us, he can help me with the baby, we'll bring him back on Sunday afternoon if you like, give you chance to have a lie-in for a change."

Sadie ached with the weight of the lies that seemed to be coming so easily to her but she pressed on with her plan with a determination that came from her need to survive. She was like a spider weaving a web, waiting for its prey.

SEVENTEEN
Sadie and Cyril

When Sadie got into the theatre with Cyril she wasn't prepared for the vastness of the space or for the magnificent painted panels and mosaic floor, the three thousand red and gold plush velvet seats or the massive stage. Her mouth fell open and Cyril smiled, delighted with her response.

"It used to be a circus," he said, "that's why the stage is so big, it was the old circus ring. There's a massive water tank under the stage," and he went into detail about the variety acts he had seen. He made sure to mention Charlie Chaplin and Houdini.

"My mother loves it but it's getting too much for her now her health is not so good."

Cyril's love of the theatre was genuinely infectious and it occurred to Sadie that she had never heard him sounding enthusiastic like this about anything before.

Sadie didn't know what to expect. When the curtain rose, she clapped enthusiastically after every act, the violinist, the soprano, the comedian, each was better than the last and at the end of the first half, she couldn't believe her eyes when a real live camel was led onto the stage carrying two exotic dancers who were soon joined by a troupe of beautiful girls dressed in gold and turquoise costumes. Sadie was mesmerised. Cyril loved her eagerness, it gave him confidence, it boosted his ego. Sadie got up to go, thinking that the show was at an end and Cyril laughed and told her that they were going to get drinks that he had ordered in the bar. It was almost impossible to believe that there was a war raging in

Europe and the only thing which marred Sadie's enjoyment of the spectacle was that she would have loved to be in the Hippodrome with Frank.

"You haven't seen anything yet Sadie," Cyril said, "the second half is always really good and wait till you see the finale, it's going to be amazing."

He was right. When the curtain rose for the finale, they had laid flags in an enormous circle on the stage. The Union Jack was there of course as well as flags from France and Belgium and other Allies. And then there was the German flag with its menacing black eagle staring out into the audience. The atmosphere in the auditorium was tense, quiet, the orchestra struck up and onto the stage trotted a magnificent white stallion led by his trainer dressed in red livery. The horse did some amazingly clever tricks, entertaining the crowd with his brilliance. Then the trainer led him into the middle of the ring of flags. He got the horse to rise up onto his hind legs in front of each of the allied flags and bellow in triumph, his head in the air. When he got to the German flag, he came crashing down on top of it with his enormous front legs, crushing the eagle with his hooves and snorting and shaking his huge head. The audience went wild. They clapped and cheered and got to their feet, Sadie thought her ears would burst. Cyril could not have been more delighted at the success of the evening.

They left the Hippodrome in high spirits, conversation about the entertainment flowed effortlessly as they walked the mile and a half home. Once or twice Cyril took the opportunity to rest his arm on Sadie's shoulder, he took her hand when they crossed the roads. Sadie worried that Cyril might suggest leaving her at the bottom of Carver Street and continue on alone to his own house. But at the intersection, they turned together into her street, still chatting amiably about their evening. Sadie was glad to be able to turn her back on Cyril in order to put her key in the lock, she threw a glance at her neighbour's house and was relieved that it was in darkness. She took courage in her hands and asked him if he would like to come in for a drink. She held her breath and her grip tightened on the key. Seconds later they walked through the parlour and into the kitchen. Sadie fiddled with the gas light and asked Cyril to stir the embers in the fire and throw on some kindling and a couple of pieces of coal. The gas light fizzed into life and the kitchen took on a yellow glow. Sadie took down a half bottle of sherry and two small glasses from the shelf. She and Cyril sat at the table and drank a toast to the end of the war. She poured a second glass from the bottle and laid her hand on his, hoping against hope that he would respond. He did. As they climbed the stairs Sadie knew that she could not afford to give way to her misgivings. She quelled her feelings of guilt and shame even as she welcomed Cyril into her bed.

It was still dark when Sadie woke. Her cheeks were wet with tears. She had dreamt of Frank, they were sitting by the fire in the kitchen together, she was at his feet with her head on his lap. The moon threw shadows round the bedroom and for a moment she thought she caught sight of Frank in front of the tall chest of drawers. She stopped herself from calling to him. It was Cyril, up and dressed and ready to leave. Sadie thought about pretending to be asleep but she needed to know whether he intended to continue their relationship and she knew she would have to face him at school. Better here than in the dinner queue.

"Sadie, I didn't mean to wake you," he said. "I had a wonderful evening, can I assume we will be doing it again? It's just that I need to get back to mother before she wakes up. She'll worry if she thinks I have been out all night and she depends on me to take her to the early service at the Methodist Church on Sunday mornings, she never misses unless she's really ill."

The sense of relief in Sadie was so consuming she felt sure it must have been obvious to Cyril, but he took her acceptance as an endorsement of his suitability. He had won her affections.

"I'll leave quietly," he added, "don't want any curtains twitching."

Sadie heard the front door close, she lay motionless, drained of energy. She hardly recognised herself, hardly believed the ease with which the lies had come from her lips. Self-recriminations flooded through her, she buried them along with the guilt she had already hidden away. She was a widow, about to be alone with two children, she was grieving the only man she would ever love, she could hardly afford to pay her rent. There was no room to indulge in recriminations, she must make the best of things, she must survive. In the bedroom, Sadie waited for the gloom to give way to the first of the sun's light and with it came a fresh determination, she would do what she had to do. The fly was in the web and now she must continue with her plan.

Sadie waited for a month and then broke the news that

she was pregnant to Cyril. She couldn't tell whether he was pleased or displeased. She had been careful to do everything possible to make him happy and he had shown no signs of running for the hills when he heard the news.

"No need to mention the baby to mother when I take you to meet her, Sadie," said Cyril, "she means well but she can be a bit critical, best if we keep it to ourselves until after wedding."

Sadie had no intentions of disclosing to the old lady that she was pregnant. She had memories of Cyril's mother from her time in the bakery when she would come in to gossip with Mrs. Morris, all of it to the detriment of other people. She was relieved to find Cyril's cousin, Mary was at the house when she and Cyril arrived. Mary was one of those dutiful women who had sacrificed her best years caring for her own mother and her mother's sister, her aunt. She lived next door to Cyril and would fetch in meals and medicines, clean and cook and dole out sympathy when her aunt complained. Mary was the sort of woman whom people described in one of two ways, a saint or a fool. Mary's presence meant that his mother could not pursue some of the more delicate lines of enquiry she would like to have asked. It was obvious she thought that her son was rushing into this marriage, that he had been snared as a meal ticket and substitute father for Sadie's son. Sadie was glad that William wasn't with them. She understood only too well that Cyril's mother might be the stumbling block to her intentions.

A short time later, to her relief, the tiny wedding party gathered at the Methodist Church. Sadie was dressed in the same suit and hat she had worn when she married

Frank. Gracie was there by her sister's side. Cyril wore a suit that Sadie had never seen before, though from the style of it, Gracie had said, it wasn't a new one. His mother dressed in a sensible, brown coat and hat was accompanied by Mary. The Minister gave the appropriate amount of attention to Cyril's mother, which pleased her and made Mary's life a little easier. The service lasted twenty minutes, the registers were signed and they returned to Cyril's mother's house for a salad that Mary had prepared and left under clean tea towels in the kitchen. Sadie was glad that none of it was even vaguely reminiscent of the day she married Frank.

The wedding arrangements were not the only compromise that Sadie had been glad to make. The old lady had wanted them to move in with her.

"It'll save Mary from having to come in and see to me so often," she had said.

Instead, Sadie suggested that Cyril should spend every Saturday afternoon with his mother, stay the night and take her to church on Sunday mornings, returning home to Carver Street on Sunday afternoons. Sadie felt a pinch of shame at the gratitude with which Cyril seemed to jump at the suggestion. It suited everyone, especially William who would never bring himself to forgive his mother for inviting the school caretaker into their home.

It turned out that Cyril was something of a handyman, he could make things out of nothing, he grew vegetables in boxes at school and brought home the spoils, he made a cradle for Daisy when she was born, he fixed taps that had dripped since Sadie's family had moved there from the Courts. He mended window frames which had rattled for years. What he lacked in willingness to communicate and in emotion, Cyril attempted to make up for in practical ways. Sadie often thought that she and the children got in the way of the solitary life which Cyril found comfortable, that had he really had a choice, he would have remained a single man. She thought he would have loved to have been able to take Sadie on his arm to the theatre at the end of every month, a replacement companion for his mother, but that to have a wife and children was too demanding on his emotions and his stamina. Their marriage was what you might call mutually functional. She provided regular meals, she listened to him on the odd occasions when something sparked his interest or was weighing on his mind, she was genuinely vociferous in her praise of her husband's skills. They had sex once a week and that was satisfactory, she kept a clean and comfortable house and though she never interfered with the care that Mary provided, Sadie sent round scones and treats and kept up an all be it distant relationship with Cyril's mother for the rest of the old lady's life.

When Daisy was born, Cyril's mother remarked that she had arrived very early. She tried to point out to Cyril just how early. Sadie was never sure whether Cyril believed her story that the baby was premature, he was an intelligent man and it would not have surprised her if he had guessed at her plan even before their marriage but that he did not have the emotional resilience to challenge her with it. To his credit, he was not unkind or cruel to Daisy or to William even when his mother, on a rare family visit, took pains to point out that Daisy was the image of William and nothing like Cyril. He was distant with the children, they found no comfort or warmth in him but plenty of criticism. William longed for the companionship he had found in Frank and in his uncle Fred, the football banter, the shared love of his team, the ruffle of the hair, the kick about in the yard. Cyril might have taught him to knock in nails or paint the back gate but these pursuits were his step-father's domain, solitary activities not to be shared, especially with a child. He did offer to take William shooting, which Sadie found strange considering that her husband had lost his eye in an accident with a gun and she made it clear she wasn't keen on the idea and neither was her son.

William became a lonely child. He saw that his mother's time was taken up by his sister, he never really got over Frank's death and when Uncle Fred announced that he had been conscripted into the army, poor William was afraid of losing his uncle in the same way that he had lost Frank. Several times, Sadie caught sight of her son staring at the wedding photo that still hung on the parlour wall. She had waited for Cyril to ask her to take down the photograph but he never had. She wasn't sure whether it bothered him to see it hanging there or whether he had simply consigned it to a different part of Sadie's life and put it out of his mind. He never asked her about William's father. Young William had occasional nightmares which disturbed the whole household and Sadie found it difficult to get him to talk to her. Deep down she knew that he deserved the truth about who he was but she had buried those secrets so deeply that she could not take the risk of telling the truth to herself let alone to William. When Sadie was busy weaving her web, she did not realise that she, too would be caught in its gossamer threads. The only thing to do was to carry on pretending.

Sadie's third child, Charles was born just before Cyril's mother died. They named him Charles after Cyril's father and the old lady complained when Sadie and the children called him Charlie, this, of course meant he would be called Charlie forever. Cyril seemed pleased to have a son of his own, he was a little more animated, especially when his mother was vocal in her approval. "Lovely dark eyes," she said, "just like your father Cyril." Cyril was obviously pleased and there was no denying that Charlie was very like him.

Cyril's mother died on a Sunday. The timing was fortunate because Cyril was with her. She had a massive stroke and breathed her last early on the Sunday morning. Cyril had held her hand sitting in silence for the whole night, never moving until Mary arrived with the minister at eleven thirty. He prayed with them and encouraged Cyril to send for the doctor to verify the death. Back in Carver Street, Sadie suspected the old lady might be ill. Her health had always been up and down and lately, it had taken a turn for the worse. She wasn't too shocked when her husband returned home at seven o'clock looking pale and tired. He was carrying an old leather bag.

"I'm really sorry Cyril, was the end peaceful for her?" she asked.

Cyril nodded, "a massive stroke, the doctor said, the minister's coming here tomorrow night to organise the funeral. I asked the undertaker to take her to the funeral parlour tomorrow, we can go and see her on Tuesday, I thought you wouldn't want her here," he said, but there were no tears, he didn't reach out to be held. He simply took himself up the stairs, placed the leather bag on the wardrobe, undressed and got into bed. Sadie took up a cup of tea when she heard him moving a few hours later but, though she tried, communication was limited to a few sentences. Sadie thought about the comfort she had received from her sister and brother when their mother had died so she asked how Mary might be coping and whether she should call on her.

"Leave it for now, Sadie," he said and she knew this was not the time to argue.

It was a quiet funeral, a handful of mourners including a couple from the Methodist Church and the minister. Everyone said when people live to a good age like Cyril's mother all their friends have gone before and you couldn't expect a good turnout but they all knew that had she been more gregarious, more generous, less judgemental, there would have been more people at the graveside. It turned out that the minister was also the executor of the will. Cyril was unaware there was a will. He and Mary had cleared his mother's house in the first few days, he had brought a couple of bits and pieces to Carver Street, a china tea set, a couple of books and a brass eagle which had stood on the fireplace. Mary had suggested several times that her aunt should take down the eagle and store it in a cupboard because it resembled the hated German emblem but she never would and Cyril had said that he didn't know what all the fuss was about. When the house was empty, Cyril gave the keys back to the landlord. When Sadie asked Cyril how he was feeling about letting go of his childhood home, he shrugged and said, "it's just a house." When the funeral was over, the little party walked to Carver Street where Sadie had prepared a few refreshments out of the bits and pieces she was able to get her hands on in the grocers. She made tea for everyone and they sat chatting. It was a relief to open the curtains and let in the daylight. She had noticed Maggie watching them as they got back from the burial. She got the feeling that Maggie disapproved of her marriage to Cyril, the two of them had become even more distanced over the last couple of years. Maggie had been helpful when Frank had died and Sadie took it as a sign that her neighbour was warming to her but it hadn't lasted and if anything she gave the impression that she was judging Sadie's every move. It was obvious to Sadie that Maggie didn't like Cyril. He could be curt with the neighbours, preferring to keep himself to himself but she wondered if it was more than that, she felt a disapproval from Maggie on which she was reluctant to dwell. She suspected that Maggie knew that William Tierney had returned that night and if she did it would not have been difficult for her to figure out that Daisy was his child.

As the mourners were leaving, the minister took Cyril aside and suggested a time for Cyril to come to the church to talk about the will. Mary would need to come too. They fixed on the following evening.

"It's not a fortune, Cyril, but it's a healthy sum," began the minister, "she's left a small sum to the church, thirty pounds to you Mary and the rest, one hundred and seventy odd pounds goes to you Cyril, along with whatever was in the house of course."

When Cyril returned home, Sadie was surprised that he opened a conversation about the will. She wanted to know, of course, but Cyril was such a private person, she had made up her mind that it would be fruitless to pursue him for details and she imagined there had been enough to pay for the funeral and her mother-in-law had left little else. As it was, Cyril told her that the old lady had left a substantial amount of money in a trust fund for their youngest child, Charles, to be accessed when he reached twenty-one.

"There's no rush, I'll get the bank to open the trust fund next week," he said.

"All of it for Charlie?" asked Sadie, incredulous.

"Yes, I'm a bit surprised she didn't leave it to me but there you are," replied Cyril.

"But nothing for the other children, for Daisy or William?" came the response.

"No doubt she had her reasons," said Cyril sarcastically and Sadie was sure she had. Cyril's mother could not have spoken more clearly. As far as the old woman was concerned, Charles was her only grandchild. She had never swallowed Sadie's story about Daisy's origins and as for William he was simply an imposition on her son, a burden in Cyril's life.

Cyril Harmer retreated into his own world and life in Carver Street continued as before. It was as if William, Cyril and Sadie were living in their own separate bubbles, a polite veneer coupled with a need to function or at least to avoid disaster kept them on a course that was just about tolerable. When Sadie felt despondency threatening, she thought about the men who were returning from the front with missing limbs and shattered brains, she thought about the women who had taken the jobs of men and who would be forced back into their old unwanted lives whenever the fighting ended. Everybody knew it, nobody wanted to say it. She thought about Frieda, waiting constantly for news of Fred, struggling with their little boy who was seldom in good health. She settled for what she had, told herself to be grateful for a man who didn't get drunk, tipped up just about enough money each week, never hit her or the children and largely kept out of her way. Lots of people were anticipating a new world that would come with the end of the war, they clung to the hope that the end of the conflict would bring the changes they longed for, but not Sadie, she had never been so lonely.

Early one morning, Sadie got Daisy and Charlie into the pram and was leaving the house to go shopping. The queues were endless in all the shops, especially the grocers, she would be in for a long wait. She didn't mind for herself, there was always a bit of gossip and banter to interest the women, but she felt for the children when they got restless. Sometimes in the rations queue one of the women would come up with a scheme to amuse the children, to lighten things up as they put it. Gertie Jenning's husband who was a rope maker had brought home a very long, thin rope from work. As she waited for her share of the new batch of flour that had arrived at the grocers, Gertie suggested they should get together after tea and use the rope for a skipping competition.

"It'll stretch halfway down the street," she said, "let's get the children together and we can turn the rope for them, see how many we can get skipping at one time, only the weather's set to be fine and there's only so much moping around the house you can do isn't there?"

So, the women and children turned out in force for an evening of skipping. A few men stood smoking watching the fun.   Chairs and stools were brought out and the women cobbled together a few treats and cups of water and tea were distributed.   The children loved it all; the singing of rhymes, the attempts to get dozens of them skipping together, a game of " under the stars and over the moon,"   the banter when one of them broke the rhythm. It was a happy evening, a lightening of the mood with no time to dwell on the horrors that were blighting all of their lives.   For Sadie, the optimistic mood would be short lived.

EIGHTEEN
The Lusitania

Norah Price called from across the street, bursting with news. Had Sadie heard what had been going on, she asked. Norah was delighted to find that she hadn't. "The Lusitania has been sunk by a U boat just off the Irish coast. She was torpedoed last night. The Germans said she had guns and ammunition on board, that she wasn't just a passenger ship, but the papers are saying that's just an excuse. We all know they're animals. The ship was coming from New York to Liverpool. There's twelve hundred people dead. Loads of children too. Most of the crew were from round here, nearly all from Irish families, like your poor mam Sadie, they're all dead. There's murder going on, gangs have been on the rampage and smashed up loads of German shops. They've arrested the lot of them, they are all up in front of the magistrates for rioting and looting but there's too many to keep them all locked up for long. I don't blame them for rioting, I've said all along, if they're German you can't trust them, I don't care how long they've been living here."

Sadie tried her best to quell the rising panic and, pushing the children in the pram, headed towards the pork butchers where she hoped that Opa and Frieda and little George were safe. When Fred had volunteered for the army, Frieda's mother had begged her daughter to move back to the family home but Opa would not go with her so Frieda opted to stay with her grandfather, she could see that he was frail and could not bring herself to leave him even though he encouraged her to go.

"It's so obvious that Opa is German", her mother had said, he has never changed his name for a start and he's living over a German shop. If you and George come here to live with me, no-one will know that you are German, we have your dad's name and we speak as scouse as everyone else round here." But Freida had made up her mind and Opa was so well liked by his neighbours and for that matter so was the butcher that she could not envisage the desperate hatred that would be unleashed by the sinking of the liner. Besides, the English surname and the scouse accent had not been enough to prevent her brother Michael from being bullied out of his job and into the navy.

Sadie arrived at the butcher's shop, breathless and sweating. Daisy was fractious and Charlie would need feeding soon too. What she saw struck fear into her. Every window in the front of the shop and the little flat above was smashed. Freida and her mother were upstairs in the bedroom collecting together some belongings and crying as they stuffed clothes and blankets and personal items into three suitcases. There was little of any value to pack into Opa's case but he would need his shaving kit and his mirror and there was a packet of old letters tied with string that were important enough for him to have saved over the years. Freida found his pipe and tobacco, his pyjamas were under the pillow on his bed. She looked for his overcoat, thinking that he might feel the cold when they released him from the police station but he must have put it on when they came to arrest him. She folded what meagre clothing she could find and everything went into one of the suitcases. Two of Fred's pals from the docks arrived with a handcart to take bits of furniture to Freida's mother's house. She gave them the address of her three rooms in one of the tenement blocks in Netherfield Road. They loaded the suitcases onto the cart.

Opa wasn't on his own at the police station, they had rounded up all the German tenants and property owners in North Liverpool and locked them up for what they said was their own safety. Freida's mother appealed on the grounds that Opa was frail and old but the police said that his great age only made him more vulnerable and that was a good reason to keep him incarcerated.

It was the injustice and unfairness with which Sadie couldn't deal. Freida's brother had been one of the first to go to war with the Royal Navy, gentle Fred was fighting on the front, Frank had given his life. All Opa had ever done was to move to another country and make it his own. Days later, Opa was taken away on the Isle of Man Steam Ferry to a camp set up on the island for Germans who might be a threat to homeland security. Here, he would see out the rest of the war. The rioters were fined and the able bodied among them encouraged to join up as soon as possible so that they could benefit the war effort with all that aggression.

In the days and weeks that followed, people were so incensed at the fatalities from the sinking of the Lusitania, especially the dead children, that no-one saw things from Sadie's point of view, certainly not Cyril. The anger she felt became one more thing to keep hidden one more thing to bury with the rest of the sadness she dragged around. Then one awful Saturday morning, Frieda got a telegram to say that Fred was missing and her whole world collapsed. Her mother and Sadie tried to persuade her that there was still hope, that Fred was probably in some German factory making armaments or in one of those camps where they sent the Red Cross parcels. Frieda took to her bed and kept little George so close to her that it became unhealthy. Sadie would go to the tenement with Daisy and Charlie while William and Cyril were at school and persuade her to let her little boy go with them to the park. Sadie was close to despairing about Fred too, he was her baby brother but she couldn't let down her guard in front of Freida or William who was clinging to the hope that he would be re-united with Uncle Fred when the war came to an end.

"You see, William," said his mother hoping that her words did not sound too hollow, "you and Uncle Fred will be over at Goodison Park watching the Blues win that cup just as soon as this fighting stops. I bet he thinks about that every day. And just wait till he sees how good you are now with that football, far better than he ever was, he'll be taking you for a trial at Tranmere one day you'll see. You know what they are all saying, when we win this war there will never be another war ever again."

These rare moments of intimacy with his mother gave William solace. He yearned for the closeness he used to enjoy with her but life was too full of difficulties for Sadie. She was unable to summon up the energy to give any more than she was already giving and as for William, he didn't know how to find the courage to ask for her help. The last thing he wanted his mother to do was to confirm his suspicion that all this sadness was his fault. The little boy was haunted by the memory of his last goodbye with Frank. All he knew was that Frank was dead and Fred was missing, there was sadness everywhere and he would never regard Cyril as a friend let alone a father as long as he lived.

NINETEEN
Living With Shame

As the war rolled on, there were moments of elation when the allies made gains and moments of despair when the Germans sank yet another ship. The threat of air raids from German Zeppelins became a real possibility. The papers were full of stories about bombs falling from the sky on ordinary peoples' homes in London and the coast. Fear spread like wildfire from family to family. The authorities talked about a blackout and everyone went into a panic looking for sacks and old blankets to cover their windows. A story circulated that a German Zeppelin had been on its way to bomb Liverpool but the pilot had miscalculated and the bombs ended up falling on some poor village in the Midlands. In the end, they decided against the blackout because they didn't believe those strange looking balloons could ever get as far as Liverpool. Telegrams arrived, letters followed, men were dead or wounded in action or lost somewhere like Fred. Recruitment was relentless. Women would bravely wave their men off at the railway station with smiles on their lips and pride in their eyes only to meet them months later when they returned on the hospital trains to the same station. Now it was pity on their faces and anxiety about how they would manage in their heads. Soldiers returned home unable and unwilling to even talk about the horrors they had seen and all the time the women got on with life, clinging to hope, being cheerful, queuing at the grocers to pay ridiculous prices for basic stuff, cobbling together meals from whatever they could buy or grow, bringing up their children and waiting, endlessly waiting for the end of the war which was going to end all wars. Sadie was one of them. It wasn't the deprivation or the hard work or even the fear of the sky bombs that got her down, it was the loneliness of a marriage devoid of emotion and the secret shame she carried.

Occasionally, Sadie thought she might confide in Gracie. Her sister had never been judgemental, she knew that. But it wasn't Gracie's judgement that Sadie was afraid of, it was her own. She was so ashamed of things she had done, decisions she had made, lies she had told and secrets she had kept that she couldn't risk exposing any of it to the light of day. Much of the time, she pretended. She pretended to be happy with Cyril, she couldn't criticise him or share her concern about his coldness, she was too ashamed of the way she had deceived him. She couldn't talk to Gracie about William Tierney, though she suspected that her sister had guessed that Daisy was not Cyril's daughter. She could not confess that she was so distant from her son because Gracie seemed so much better at being a wife and a mother than she did.

Gracie seemed to be successful at most things, she even had a wonderful relationship with her mother-in-law and the sisters would often meet at the dairy so that the children could run around with space to play. Sadie tried hard not to begrudge the fact that Gracie managed to keep her husband by her side while Frank had sacrificed his life and left hers in ruin but now and again, the resentment surfaced and when it did, she wondered if Gracie knew how she felt and she asked herself if this was the real reason she could not take her sister into her confidence. When and how had Gracie turned into the sensible, reliable sister, she wondered. Sadie had always been the one who could be relied upon, the dependable sibling, the surrogate parent in the family. Gracie had been the frivolous one. How different the future had turned out from how she had pictured it. She wondered if their mother had been alive whether she would even recognise her two daughters.

TWENTY
The Fire.

The sisters were reunited in a way that neither of them could have predicted. It was Sunday evening, Cyril and Sadie were sitting in the kitchen, the children were asleep in their beds. Cyril was putting the finishing touches to a model ship he was making. Sadie wished with all her heart that he would teach William how to make models but the offer never came, her husband would wait until the children were out of sight before he sat down to immerse himself in his hobby, always on his own. Sadie was darning William's school jumper when suddenly they heard a massive bang followed by the sound of multiple explosions at the rear of the house. They ran into the yard, there was a distinct tremor all around them and at first they thought what everybody thought, that a German zeppelin had dropped a bomb. Maggie and the rest of the neighbours ran into the entry behind the houses, the noise was deafening. A few of the neighbours ran to the end of the entry as far as the intersection at the bottom of the street. A small crowd had already gathered. They were looking towards the river where blue and orange flames lit up the night sky.

"It's the docks," they were shouting, "it's on our side of the river."

William had woken and had run down the yard dressed in his pyjamas and shoes, alarm written all over his little face. He joined a group of children further down the entry and Sadie kept her eyes on them as they shouted and pointed and craned their necks towards the blaze. Even in the midst of the pandemonium Sadie found herself thinking that despite his tender years, her son was rapidly becoming one of the big boys. How had she not seen him growing up? The men who were there made their way down to the docks to see if they could help in any way. Cyril would have gone with them but Sadie begged him to stay and look after the children while she went to see Gracie.

"Jack had a shift tonight, he's bound to be down there," she cried, "please Cyril, I need to go and see if he and Gracie are ok."

Cyril nodded, he looked a bit bemused, as though he couldn't really understand what use a visit from his wife would be even if Jack had been involved in the incident. However, he agreed without too much grumbling and Sadie put out milk and the remains of a loaf and some jam on the table for the children's breakfast.

"I'll be back on an early tram in the morning, you feed the children and get ready for work, I'll be home before you need to leave," she said. Cyril surprised her when he replied, "it might be better to go to the dairy before you go to Gracie's house. The dairy's in town, they'll get to know what's happening before the rest of us and anyway, your Gracie spends so much time with her in-laws she might even be there with them, it might save you a journey down to the Dingle."

Cyril had a habit of turning an observation into a criticism and Sadie couldn't tell if he was suggesting that her sister and by implication Sadie, spent too much time visiting Dilys at the dairy. She was grateful, however, for his offer to help with the children and for his suggestion. Suddenly, William appeared at the bottom of the stairs, dressed and wearing his coat.

"I'm coming with you Mam," he insisted, "I can look

after Ivy Rose, please Mam, I want to find out if Uncle Jack is ok." Sadie agreed and Cyril looked relieved that he had one less child to consider.

The journey into town was stressful. Sadie was glad of her son's company, on the tram he put his head on her lap and she stroked his hair. Everywhere there was a smell of smoke and though the explosions had ceased, the flames were leaping high and wide lighting up a large portion of the docks. Crowds of people were making their way down the hill to the river. Sadie fought hard to dispel an image of Jack running out of the inferno, his clothes on fire. It was like living in a nightmare. When they arrived at the dairy, Alun was fastening Dragon, the horse into the cart.

"Sadie, William, thank God you're here. Our Jack is at work, we are worried sick about him. Dilys is in the kitchen, I'm just going to take her to Gracie's and then I'll get down to the docks to find him. Gracie was here today but she went home with Ivy Rose to get the tea on about four o'clock."

William reached out to pat the horse on his nose and Alun said a little gruffly, "watch you don't spook him William, he's a bit nervous with all this noise going on."

"Do you know what's happened down there?" asked Sadie.

"There was an accident in one of the munition stores and tons of explosives went up," Alun answered, "I don't know much more except people have died."

Sadie was shaking when Dilys joined them and they set off in the cart to go to Gracie's house. Dilys was glad to see her.

"I'm just praying Jack is ok Sadie, Gracie is going to need you, especially after losing the baby, she hasn't been well for a couple of weeks."

Sadie was confused. "The baby?" she said and Dilys realised that Gracie had not told her sister that she had miscarried for a second time in a year only two weeks ago. Sadie had no idea and she felt the shock like a hammer blow. How could they have drifted so far apart?

As the cart approached the house, a lad on a bicycle was just closing the gate, Gracie was silhouetted in the doorway.

"He's ok," she yelled.

"They sent me with a message," explained the lad, "Mr. Evans said to say he is ok but he won't be home until tomorrow, no-one is to worry."

As he cycled away, he called "everyone is saying Mr. Evans should get a medal for what he's done tonight."

With that, he disappeared into the darkness, Sadie, Dilys and William went into the house and Alun turned around his horse and cart, determined to see with his own eyes that his son was not a casualty.

"Are you sure Gracie?" asked Dilys, "are you sure Jack's ok, what did the message say?" Sadie watched as Gracie took her mother-in-law in her arms and held her.

"He wrote the note himself Dilys, look," she said. She picked up a piece of paper from the table and showed it to Dilys.

"Don't worry. I'm fine, it's madness down here, I won't be home until some time tomorrow. I love you. Jack."

"Alun has gone to see if he can find him, I don't know

if they will let him get near but he won't be satisfied until he's tried," explained Dilys.

"According to the young lad who came with the message, one of the munitions stores has gone up, it was Jack's biggest nightmare even when they built them. There are five dead but there could be more," explained Gracie running her hands through her hair. Sadie poured hot tea from the teapot and encouraged the women to sit down at the table. She glanced at William and drew him towards her.

"Let's go upstairs and check on that cousin of yours," suggested Sadie, "she may have woken up with all this commotion."

Ivy Rose was fast asleep, oblivious to the chaos that was rocking her family.

"She's still asleep, Mam," said William, "that's good isn't it?"

Sadie pulled up the blanket that the little girl had kicked off, it was a warm night it wasn't necessary but it made Sadie feel better. She and William went back into the kitchen, William hugged his favourite aunt and she stroked his head. Sadie noticed how thin her sister appeared. She had dark circles under her eyes. For the first time, Sadie thought Gracie looked every year of her age.

Alun returned with the news that he had spoken to Jack.

"He's got cuts and bruises, but he'll be fine when they get everything under control. They've got a load of fire boats concentrated on the blaze, it'll be out before morning if there are no more explosions. There are five dead, all women on the evening shift but Jack and his boss managed to get six others out before the whole thing went up. They sent doctors up from the Northern and nurses from one of the hospital trains that happened to be in Lime Street Station waiting to leave. Jack didn't know how many casualties there are, a lot, he said, but it looks like they are all being treated now."

They listened in silence as Alun described the horror.

"How did he seem?" asked Dilys.

"I thought he would be drained," said Alun "but he's not, he's giving orders and making decisions, everyone seems to need him. He seems to have got a load of energy from somewhere. He told me to tell you and Gracie that he is fine so you don't need to worry."

Satisfied for the moment, Dilys and Alun left for the dairy, Dilys promising to return the next day and Sadie helped her son to bed.

The sisters sat in silence for a while, each caught up in their own thoughts.

"Why didn't you tell me Gracie?" asked Sadie.

"Tell you what?" replied her sister.

"Tell me about the babies you've lost," said Sadie.

"What, like you told me that William Tierney had paid you a visit," retorted Gracie and then was immediately sorry.

Sadie was shocked into silence for a moment. She saw the hurt in Gracie's eyes, she felt shame rising like bile in her throat.

"How do you know?" she asked.

"Your lovely neighbour Maggie took great delight in telling me. She tried to make it sound like she was concerned for you because you were drinking a bit too much and you were so down after Frank died. I know she is your neighbour Sadie and Tommy's a great friend to William but Maggie has always had a problem with you, she couldn't wait to tell me that she saw William Tierney at your door and she loved it when she realised I didn't know."

"Why didn't you tell me what Maggie had said?" asked Sadie.

"Because you were hell bent on marrying Cyril and I couldn't understand why. Then when Daisy was born, I put two and two together and it was too late. I didn't think you would want to know that I had guessed your secret what good would it have done to tell you? I don't know why we got so distant Sadie, there have been times when I've longed to talk to you but secrets have a habit of getting in the way even between us."

With that, Sadie took hold of her sister and cradled her. Gracie was exhausted, too exhausted to cry but Sadie cried for both of them.

"I'm sorry Gracie, I'm so sorry," she sobbed "I was too ashamed to tell you the truth, I can hardly believe what I have turned into…."

Sleep came easily to them both that night. They slept in the same bed as if they were girls again and when morning broke, Sadie got William up and ready, kissed her sister and Ivy Rose goodbye and headed for an early tram back to Carver Street. The trams were running late, the whole city seemed out of sorts. The morning brought news that two more women had died overnight in the hospital. The death toll was now at seven and there were sixteen serious casualties, dozens more people had been treated and sent home.

When Sadie and William got home, it was obvious

that Cyril was spoiling for a confrontation.

"I thought you would be on an earlier tram," he complained.

"Sorry," she replied, "the trams are running late, we waited for half an hour, thanks for seeing to their breakfast."

She nodded towards the younger children who were happily dipping bread into warm milk, Daisy sitting at the table and Charlie in his chair. Sadie was genuinely grateful to see that Cyril was caring for them.

"I wanted to be at school early this morning, one of the boilers needs attention. I should be there by now," said Cyril.

Anxious to stop this from escalating, Sadie bit her bottom lip and managed to sound conciliatory. It was the last thing she was feeling.

"You'd best be off then Cyril, I can take over now," and she passed him his overcoat from the back of the door.

This was not going to be the end of it for Cyril.

"Come on then lad," he turned to William. " You may as well walk with me this morning, don't want you turning up late as well."

"He's had no breakfast yet Cyril, he's hungry, he can run to school as soon as I've given him some porridge, I'm sure they won't be bothered this morning, not after seven people have been killed. It's been a hell of a night, Jack's not even home yet."

But if Sadie was hoping for empathy from her husband, she was disappointed.

"It doesn't mean he should be encouraged to get into bad habits, he needs to grow up and take responsibility, he insisted on going with you last night, nobody forced him, now it's time for school."

Sadie could feel the anger rising but before she could retaliate William, who had watched the drama unfolding and was feeling his mother's discomfort, said "it's ok Mam, I'm not that hungry, I can wait till dinner time. If I run fast, I'll catch up with Tommy at the corner." In seconds, he had brushed past them both and was out of the door chasing his friend like a whippet.

Cyril left without another word and Sadie, exhausted, slumped into a chair beside her children but she was delighted to have re-opened her relationship with Gracie and was not about to let her husband ruin the day. Despite her exhaustion she would get out into the fresh air with the children and use the walk to keep her anxiety at bay.

TWENTY-ONE
Jack Comes Home

At Gracie's house there were anxieties of a different kind. This would be a day of waiting and watching. Gracie had no idea when her husband would return and it took all her resolve to remain calm for her daughter's sake. Gracie found herself mulling over her conversation with her sister. She had never liked Cyril, she found him cold and unresponsive but Sadie had said so little about their relationship and she didn't see them often enough as a couple to make a judgement about the state of their marriage. It was a relief that they had cleared the air and it would have to be enough for now that they could be sisters again.

Dilys arrived just before two, she brought a golden rice pudding for them to eat when Jack got home. Ivy Rose was insisting on eating her share there and then but Gracie won the battle and the pudding was placed on the top of a high cupboard. When it got to five o'clock and Dilys had left to do the evening milking, leek and potato soup was bubbling and a fresh loaf had been bought. Gracie was standing at the window looking for signs of Jack in the street. Ivy Rose played at her feet with her two peg dolls that Dilys had dressed for her from an old pair of kitchen curtains and a ball of wool that she used to make their hair. Ivy called them her twins. It was two hours before Gracie watched her husband wearily making his way up the pavement and through the gate. She thought about rushing out to greet him but something in the way he held himself told her that the last thing he wanted was more drama. She opened the door and when she looked closely at Jack, all of Gracie's resolve to be strong and calm evaporated. The two of them stood motionless, both in floods of silent tears.

"Please Gracie, don't ask me about it, I don't know how those lads at the front are doing it, no wonder they are coming home half mad," he said.

Gracie led Jack into the kitchen where his meal was waiting. His left forearm was bandaged, his eyebrows were blackened and his left ear was clogged with dried blood. The hair on the left side of his head was singed and he had a nasty gash along his cheekbone. Gracie found it hard to look at him without crying. Jack refused the soup but Gracie insisted and when Ivy told him that he wouldn't get any rice pudding unless he ate it, he laughed and said "Oh well I'd better get on and eat it then."

Gracie put their daughter to bed and filled the tin bath with hot water that she had heated in large pans. She helped her husband into the water and gently removed the grimy bandage from his arm. She poured tepid water over his wounded head from a jug and washed away debris from his body. She dressed the burn on his arm with fresh bandages and while Jack took himself upstairs to their bed, Gracie took a bucket and emptied the contents of the tin bath down the sink. She doubted that she would ever get to know what had happened in the fire, if she did it would be in her husband's time. It struck her that loving someone like she loved Jack was painful. The sadness of the lost pregnancies had been hard but at least it was a pain they had shared. She felt shut out of the tragedy of the previous night and all she could do was respect Jack's wishes not to press him to share it. It struck her, too that her sister felt like this most of the time, trapped, as she was in a loveless marriage.

TWENTY-TWO
A Meeting In The Park.

In Carver Street, Sadie fed and dressed Charlie and Daisy and placed them at the top and bottom of the pram, much to Daisy's disgust as she wanted to run along the pavement on her own on the way to the park. They took a longer route in order to walk past the school where Sadie thought she might get a glimpse of William in the playground. Her heart was heavy as she thought about her eldest son. Every time there was one of these spats with Cyril, her biggest concern was that William would start to resent her for not supporting him. She never challenged Cyril even though she felt that Cyril's criticisms of William were unjust. Sadie was afraid that if she challenged him, Cyril's resentment would boil over and he would accuse her of deceiving him into marrying her. She couldn't take the risk.

The park was quiet, Sadie headed for the bandstand where she could sit on a bench and watch the children playing on the wooden steps. Charlie and Daisy were glad to be freed from the pram and were happily collecting tiny stones and placing them in small piles on each step. Now and again Daisy would squeal and stamp her feet when a pigeon threatened to make off with her treasure. Charlie tried to copy but wasn't yet steady enough to walk, let alone stamp his feet. Sadie couldn't help smiling as she watched their antics. An older woman with a dog on a lead approached from the other side of the bandstand. Sadie recognised her at once.

"Mrs. Murdock, how are you doing, it's been a long

time?" she said.

"Sadie, how are you, I haven't seen you since your poor mother's funeral?" Mavis Murdock replied. She joined Sadie on the bench, her little dog straining at the leash to get near to the children.

Mrs. Murdock had been one of the friends who had called to see Sadie's mother on a regular basis during the years she had been too ill to leave the house. When she was widowed early in her marriage Mavis Murdock had bought a black highland terrier and never went anywhere without him. Sadie wasn't sure if this was the same dog. Over the years, Mrs. Murdock had had several highland terriers, all the same colour and for some reason she chose to call all of them Angus. At least it made it easy for Sadie to ask how Angus was.

"I was so sorry to hear about your husband, Sadie," said Mavis Murdock. " I heard you got married again and these must be your children." She smiled at Charlie and Daisy as she gathered Angus up so that he could sit on her knee.

"How's your eldest boy, such a shame that your poor mother never got to see him grow up, she couldn't wait to be a grandma?"

The two women chatted amiably while the children played and Mrs. Murdock asked about Fred.

"Have you had any news about your brother?" she asked, "I know he was declared missing in action. Fred was always such a gentle boy, sometimes I am glad I didn't have any children, no-one to worry about but my Angus, and I can keep him on a lead."

Sadie explained that Fred had married Frieda and they had had a son called Henry, named after his great grandad.

"Frieda and Henry live with Frieda's mother," explained Sadie. "Frieda took a job in the Shell Company in Bootle, she's working on munitions. It's good money and her mam looks after Henry."

There had been no news about where Fred might be, presumably in a prisoner of war camp somewhere but they were all keeping hopeful that he would be back with them when the war came to an end. She didn't mention the fact that Frieda's family were German or that her grandfather was currently incarcerated in a camp in the Isle of Man. Even when she was talking to people as sympathetic as Mavis Murdock, Sadie was never confident of a positive response.

"Have you heard about the Red Cross Sadie?" asked Mrs. Murdock. "They operate out of one of those lovely big houses in Gambia Terrace, right opposite the site where they are building the new Cathedral. They search for missing soldiers, I'm not sure how much luck they have but they managed to find my neighbour's son. I know that much. It might be worth going to see them, you never know."

Sadie was more than grateful for the information and started planning a trip to Gambier Terrace in her head. "Thank you so much Mrs. Murdock," she said, "I'll go along tomorrow and see if they can help. You have given me a bit more hope."

"I hope I haven't got your hopes up for no reason," replied the older woman. "I wouldn't like to be responsible for worrying you even more. If you do go, take along Fred's army number and anything else you have got to help them to search. I remember that's what my neighbour had to do."

Sadie took Mrs. Murdock's hands in hers, thanked her

for her friendship and while Mavis started for the other side of the park, with Angus sniffing at every tree, Sadie got Charlie back into the pram and relented when Daisy decided she was walking home. It was a slow journey but by the time they reached Carver Street, Sadie had resolved to go to Gambia Terrace the next day to see if any information about her brother could be found. William arrived home ten minutes after Sadie and she looked at his face, searching for signs that he was harbouring resentment from the fight with Cyril that morning. She assumed he did not because in seconds, he was playing with the hoop in the street with Tommy.

Despite her best intentions, Sadie did not visit the Red Cross headquarters the following morning. Daisy woke during the night with a fever and Sadie got into bed beside the little girl, Charlie, inches away in his cot, slept happily. Her mother's presence soothed Daisy enough for them all to get a few hours sleep but, in the morning, she woke with a cough and a streaming cold scuppering any chances of leaving the house that day. Instead, Sadie wrote a letter to Frieda and repeated what Mrs. Murdock had told her.

"It's a long shot, Frieda, I wouldn't want to raise your hopes but if you post any useful information about Fred to me I'll go to Gambier Terrace as soon as Daisy is better."

Two days later Frieda arrived at Carver Street after she finished an early shift at the factory. Sadie thought her sister-in-law looked tired, her skin had taken on a yellowish tint from the chemicals that she was using at work. They sat and drank tea, chatting about the children and about Opa.

"He's not well, Sadie, he's having trouble breathing, it's a chest infection," said Frieda. "We have had a letter from the pastor, he says we shouldn't worry, he's not confined to bed, but Opa has stopped smoking his pipe so we shouldn't send any more tobacco in his parcels. I don't think he would have given up his pipe unless it was serious."

The pastor at the German church had volunteered to be incarcerated in the Isle of Man camp so that he could minister to the men over there. Frieda's mother called him a saint. He was in touch by letter with the German families back in Liverpool while his wife and a couple of the Elders had taken over his duties at the church.

"We keep a candle burning for them all at the church," said Frieda "and Mam has a lot of friends there, they support each other. We pray for Fred every Sunday too. The pastor said he'd keep us posted if there was any change in Opa."

Frieda reached in her handbag for a piece of paper on which she had written details about Fred that she thought might be helpful if the Red Cross agreed to search for him. She had written them down in a neat list and carefully numbered each bit of information.

"This is everything I can think of," she said, "and I have brought the letter that the army sent to let us know that he was missing."

Frieda got up to leave and kissed the children goodbye. "I think I'd know if he was dead Sadie, I'm sure I would have a feeling," she said.

"I feel the same, Frieda," replied Sadie, "this bloody war can't go on forever, he'll be back. I'll let you know how I get on with the Red Cross."

"I'd better get home to Henry, I see so little of him with these extra shifts, he'll be forgetting who his mam is," Frieda said with the hint of a smile.

With that, the two women hugged and parted.

TWENTY-THREE
The Search For Fred.

It was another five days before Daisy recovered from her cold but on day six, Sadie closed the door at Carver Street and headed for the tram to Gambier Terrace. She carried Charlie and Daisy trotted contentedly at her side. She noticed new posters had appeared in shop windows and on church notice boards and lamp posts, they seemed to be everywhere, even on a few windowpanes in peoples' homes. There was to be a fresh recruitment drive, more soldiers were needed. They were calling it "The Big Push", it was going to be the final blow which would force the German army into capitulating. Cyril had told Sadie that German morale was at its lowest since the war started, people in Germany were starving, he had said, malnutrition was rife and the German army was weary because supplies of food and ammunition weren't reaching them. Now was the time for the allies to step up but thousands more men would need to be recruited, volunteers and conscripts. "They are raising the upper age for recruitment to fifty-two," Cyril said "and they are calling up lads who are working in essential jobs now too, miners and dockers are going to the front, I wouldn't be surprised if they conscripted Jack."

The tram stopped just a few yards from Gambier Terrace and Sadie walked slowly up to the black wrought iron gates that led her into a garden, neatly laid out with several varieties of vegetables in raised beds. The only concession to flowers was a small circular patch given over to a rose bed in the centre. Sadie stood looking at the terrace of houses in front of her, she was daunted by the size of them and wasn't sure which house she needed to find. It only took seconds to see the flag of the Red Cross in the huge bay window of a house at the far end of the terrace. Charlie struggled to get down from his mother's arms so that he could toddle up the steps after his sister but Sadie kept a firm grip. The door was ajar and she saw a notice that someone had made hanging on the knocker.

"Welcome, please enter," it read.

Sadie and the children found themselves in a large, square hall which was littered with boxes of all sizes. Sadie was drawn to a door on her right through which she could see movement and hear women chatting and someone softly singing. She pushed the door and stepped into a huge room which looked out into the garden through which she had just walked. The room was cluttered with piles of clothes, shoes, tins of food, tobacco and cigarettes, pencils, paper, envelopes, blankets, utensils, tea and coffee, all manner of items as well as more boxes. There were half a dozen women sorting and packing and labelling, one of them approached Sadie. She was no more than eighteen, tall and angular, she spoke with her eyes. Sadie's first thought was that confidence oozed out of her every pore.

"Hello," she said, "I'm Sophie, is there something I can help you with?"

Sophie held her hand out expecting Sadie to shake it but Sadie hesitated, never having shaken hands with anyone before. It didn't deter Sophie.

"What lovely children," she continued, "why don't you all sit here and tell me why you have come to see us today?"

She ushered Sadie and the children towards some wooden chairs placed on the edge of the room and Sadie introduced herself and explained the purpose of her mission.

"Well," responded Sophie, "you are in luck today because the person who can help you works in that office there, behind the dark green door. But before you see her, I'll fetch Isabelle, she'll take a few details and then take you in to see Emma."

With that, Sophie disappeared into what looked like a cupboard and a minute later, a short, stocky woman in her mid-forties appeared. She looked like she was glad to have escaped from the cupboard, she was wearing an overall which had seen better days and a thick strand of dark hair had escaped from the bun on the top of her head. She kept pushing it back with the palm of her hand but the strand of hair was too heavy to stay in place unaided. Sadie had a strong urge to pin it into the bun for her. She resisted.

"I won't shake hands," said the woman, "I'm filthy, trying to make a bit more space in that old cupboard, I've found two dead mice already," she laughed. "I'm Issy, we all work for the Red Cross here, we've got a few consignments of parcels going off to the front and to P.O.W camps in Germany. We are not usually quite so disorganised but they need to be on their way to the docks by five o'clock. Sophie tells me you are looking for a missing soldier. You've come to the right place, we have a woman called Emma whose job it is to organise searches. Now, just give me a few details and I'll take you in to see Emma. She knows you're here, Sophie has told her."

Sadie gave Issy the paper which Frieda had written and the letter from the army which had informed them that Fred was missing.

"That's wonderful," said Issy, "you've no idea how much time that saves, someone is very organised!"

As Issy led the three of them towards the office door, Sophie reappeared and suggested that she should take the children into the garden to see the rabbits. The women were breeding rabbits to help with the food supply for the soldiers but she didn't mention that to the children. Sadie looked at Daisy and was unsure if she would want to go with Sophie, she had been more clingy than usual since she had been ill but Daisy couldn't resist the idea of a hutch full of rabbits and Sophie assured Sadie that the children would be fine with her, she had four siblings at home, none of them anywhere near as well behaved as these two.

When Sadie finally met Emma, she couldn't believe her eyes or her luck.

"Sadie," said Emma Moran, "how wonderful to see you again."

Emma turned to Issy, "Issy, this woman was my right hand for a few years, back before the war when we all lived in a different world, I didn't want to lose her but she started her own little business. I never found anyone as good to replace her."

Sadie was a little embarrassed but she was touched that her former employer had realised how awkward she was feeling and was trying to make her feel comfortable. It never occurred to Sadie that Emma Moran meant what she was saying. Emma pulled up a chair for Sadie and went over to a little side table where she kept a camping stove to make tea for them both. Sadie considered offering to help but thought better of it.

"Mrs. Johnson told me about your husband, Sadie, I was really sorry to hear he had been killed. She said that you had married again, I'm glad. How's your son, William isn't it, have I remembered that right?"

Sadie explained that William was growing up fast and that he was doing well at school. "I have two other children, they are outside with Sophie looking at the rabbits," said Sadie.

"Sophie's a natural with little ones," said Emma, "they all seem to warm to her."

The two women chatted amiably and then Emma Moran looked closely at the information which had been supplied by Freida.

"She would have come with me to see you, but she works in the shell factory and she can't take time off," explained Sadie.

"All the factories have stepped up production of munitions for the Big Push," replied Emma, the response to the latest recruitment drive was so good that now they're complaining about a shortage of munitions and food for the number of soldiers. That's why the girls are so busy out there in the parcels room. Our work has doubled since they announced the Big Push. Strikes me the army would do well to have a few women in the ranks, they wouldn't be running out of food."

"I believe the upper age for soldiers is fifty something now," said Sadie. "It seems impossible."

"They're not sending them to the front," replied Emma, they are using the older recruits to release the young men to fight, but you're right, no-one expected the war to go on for so long. They've called up men in protected occupations too, a lot of women are joining the land army to fill in for the farm labourers."

"My brother-in-law, Jack Evans works at the docks, my husband thinks he will be called up, I don't think so though, he has an important job down there. I hope not anyway for my sister's sake."

"You've got no worries there Sadie, you're right and your husband is wrong. I know Jack, everybody knows him especially since the fire and my husband is on the board at the docks. He says they couldn't do without him."

Emma Moran didn't want to mislead Sadie into believing that searches for missing soldiers were highly successful or that finding missing men was quick. She also said that she felt it was her duty to warn families that often the news wasn't good and if they started a search they must be prepared for that. Sadie explained that Fred had married into a German family and that Opa was one of the alien community incarcerated in the Isle of Man. Frieda hadn't mentioned it when she wrote her information sheet, she feared it might lessen their chances of getting help but Sadie knew Emma Moran and she knew that she would not let that colour her judgement.

Emma escorted Sadie from her office back into the parcel room where Charlie and Daisy were sat at a table, Charlie on Sophie's knee and Daisy drawing a picture of a rabbit, both of them eating slices of apple from Sophie's lunch box.

"Thank you so much Sophie," said Sadie, "they look

as if they've had a lovely time, I hope they've been well behaved."

"Perfectly well behaved," answered the young woman. "I hope you bring them next time you come."

"Say thankyou to Sophie," said Sadie to her daughter.

Daisy said nothing, instead she lifted her little arms up towards Sophie who picked her up and the child planted a kiss on her cheek.

"That's a wonderful thankyou," said Sophie.

"I'll be in touch when I hear anything of interest," said Emma Moran, "we don't tend to write details in letters, we need to be discreet but I'll write to you and perhaps you can come in again and bring Frieda with you. It's been a real treat to meet up again, Sadie, let's hope it won't be too long."

With that, Emma returned to her office and the flurry of urgent work that the women were doing resumed at a pace in the parcel room. Sadie thanked the women again, walked down the steps at the front of the house, strolled the length of the garden and pulled open the wrought iron gate. As she left, she looked back at the terrace of houses. She felt like she had been in another world, a world which seemed to have more colour than the one she inhabited. Strangely, she felt uplifted. For the first time since Frank had died, she felt like there may be possibilities in life.

That evening, Sadie wrote to Frieda with an account of what had happened at Gambia Terrace. She didn't want to mention her excursion to Cyril because she didn't want to hear that she was wasting her time but he asked her directly what she was writing so she gave a brief explanation of events, giving the deliberate impression that she knew it was a long shot.

"Bunch of female do-gooders, I expect, I wouldn't get your hopes up. Anyway, shouldn't Frieda be doing the running round, she's his wife."

Sadie continued with her letter, trying to block out his words. Cyril went back to his model making.

Over the next days, Sadie pushed hopes of finding Fred to the back of her mind, she was aware that she could easily get obsessed by the idea of the search so she got on with the ordinary stuff of life. Cyril seemed to be in a more conciliatory mood and Sadie was surprised to hear him say that he had been to visit his cousin, Mary. As far as Sadie was aware, he had hardly bothered with her since his mother had passed away. Sadie had tried to encourage him to visit but Cyril said that there was simply no need. Sadie thought there was every need, given that Mary had devoted her life to his mother for years and for that matter to Cyril and that her home was next door to theirs. Apparently, Cyril had heard that Mary had been under the weather and had called on his cousin after work.

"I said I would go and see her on Saturday afternoon," Cyril said, "I might even see what's on at the theatre and take her out for the evening."

He glanced at Sadie while he hung up his coat on the back of the door. She realized he was waiting for a response. She was so unused to conversation that it took Sadie a few seconds to respond. She was surprised but glad that her husband was proposing this act of kindness. She had never had a problem with Mary and was actually grateful that because Cyril's cousin had been prepared to care for his mother, she had been spared that responsibility. Truthfully, Sadie was also relieved that Cyril would be going out for a few hours, there was always less tension when she and the children had the house to themselves.

"That's a lovely idea Cyril," she said, "you'll enjoy the show as well as Mary, did she say what has been wrong with her?"

"Oh no, I got the feeling it was women's problems so I didn't ask. I might go round and visit her a bit more often, maybe Saturday afternoons," he responded.

Cyril was as good as his word and so began several visits to Mary on Saturday afternoons.

"Don't bother yourself with my tea Sadie," said Cyril as he got ready to leave for his cousin's house, "our Mary likes to cook, you just see to yourself and the children, I'll see you later."

With that Cyril was gone and everyone felt a little relieved, especially William.

"Can Tommy come round and play, Mam?" William asked, "his mam's out and he doesn't like their Cate looking after him, she sends him upstairs when her boyfriend's there."

Sadie smiled. Tommy's sister, Cate was seventeen. Maggie had started a cleaning job in the Feathers hotel in town at weekends and Cate was left to look after Tommy. She was obviously less than pleased with the arrangement. Sadie tried not to be judgemental. Whatever else Maggie was, she was certainly a worker, taking on two, demanding jobs. The relationship between Sadie and Maggie could never have been called a friendship. Out of sheer necessity, they had helped one another in various crises but Maggie always made it clear that she wasn't looking for a friend. Sadie had considered challenging Maggie after Gracie told her what Maggie had said about witnessing William Tierney's visit but she couldn't risk raising speculation about Daisy's parentage. Instead, Sadie kept the neighbourliness to a minimum and the relationship was less than warm.

No sooner had Sadie agreed that Tommy could come to play than the two boys were sitting cross legged on a rag rug under the stairs playing with a box of soldiers that Tommy had brought with him. Sadie sat looking at them and her thoughts turned to Fred. Her brother used to sit and play in that space too, she had memories of her mother making the rug so that Fred wouldn't have to sit on the cold quarry tiles.

It was just over a fortnight since Emma Moran had begun the search for Fred. She had warned that it would not be a quick process but now that Sadie had set things in motion, she longed for news and she was finding it hard to be patient. In the two weeks since her visit to Gambier Terrace, rationing had become even more strict. They needed to send extra food to the troops whose numbers had increased since the recruitment drive. Sometimes it looked as if the Big Push was succeeding, there were rumours that the German army was losing ground but the end was never quite in sight despite news of near rebellion in German Cities because people were literally starving. In Liverpool, Sadie noticed that more and more canteens were opening where people could buy cheap, healthy meals. When she saw the queues, she was grateful for the school dinners that Cyril and William were enjoying.   There was no flour to be bought anywhere, it was being diverted to the troops to make into loaves. Leaflets arrived with what they said was an ingenious recipe from the Government for making bread out of potatoes. Sadie made a loaf which she served up with soup but the faces of the children and her husband told her exactly what they thought of the potato bread. Despite the hardships and the tragic losses, people rallied and managed to contribute to funds for parcels to send to the soldiers. Sadie, Gracie and Frieda gave what they could to the cigarette fund. None of them said it but they were all thinking of how much Fred enjoyed his Woodbines.

The following morning, the letter arrived. From the bedroom window, Sadie spotted the postwoman weaving her way down Carver Street. She watched the small, brown envelope as it fell silently onto the floor. She stood motionless in the doorway between the kitchen and the parlour. Sadie felt her heart racing, she was stopped in her tracks by the sudden anticipation of bad news. It seemed like minutes standing there, eyes fixed on the envelope. Finally, she turned and headed for the sink in the kitchen. She splashed her face with cold water from the tap and soaked a cloth which she placed on the back of her neck. Charlie started to whimper and Daisy clambered down from her chair to comfort him.

"Mammy you're all wet," said the little girl approaching her mother. Sadie heard her daughter and drew her towards her then gathering up Charlie she walked into the parlour and picked up the letter. She sat down in the armchair, her two children at her feet and with trembling hands, she opened the envelope. Emma Moran hoped she was well and would be calling at Carver Street on Friday next at two o'clock with news of her brother Fred who had been located. She had written to his wife, Frieda, asking her to be at the meeting and was looking forward to making her acquaintance for the first time and to seeing Sadie again. Sadie felt a surge of energy shoot through her body like lightening in a storm. Tears rolled down her face as she lifted her children onto her lap and told them she was very, very happy.

Sadie knew that she couldn't wash dishes and sweep floors as if this was a normal day. She put both children in the pram and pushed it out into the street. She needed to be outside, she needed air and she needed to walk. She found herself on the pavement in front of St. Saviors, though how and why she had gone there, she didn't know. She left the pram at the bottom of the steps and carrying a struggling Charlie who wanted to join his sister as she ran ahead, Sadie pushed open the heavy door and entered the church. It took a minute or so for her eyes to adjust to the gloom inside the building. She was glad there was no-one else in the place. Sadie walked towards the half dozen lighted candles arranged on a wrought iron stand in front of the altar. The children were mesmerised by the flickering flames. She sat Charlie on a pew a few feet away. She took a taper and holding Daisy's little hand, they lit a new candle. She had prayed so many prayers since Fred had gone missing but none of them came to her now.

"The candle will have to be enough," she murmured as she and Daisy stood watching it dance in the darkness.

"Mammy, look at Charlie…" cried Daisy.

Jolted into the present, Sadie saw her son about to launch himself from the end of the pew onto the hard floor. She grabbed his little body in the nick of time and to avert a disastrous screaming match, she gave him a coin to push into the collection box to pay for the candle then headed for the greengrocers to buy potatoes. The hens had laid and she had six brown eggs in the cupboard, she would fry slices of potato and eggs as a treat and tell Cyril about the letter over tea. It was slow progress because Daisy was walking beside the pram which gave Sadie time to think. She resolved to write to Gracie when she got home, to share the good news and ask her to come to the Friday meeting so that her sister could hear firsthand what Emma Moran had discovered.

There was the usual queue for rations outside the shop and plenty of banter between the women. Mrs. Finch, the greengrocer's wife was in no hurry to serve since she was enjoying the gossip while she weighed the potatoes and the carrots. There was a group of small children playing on the pavement, they were drawn to Charlie like moths to a flame and he was enjoying the fuss.

"Have you heard anything about your Fred Sadie?" said an old neighbour.

It was a question Sadie had answered many times over the last months. She didn't intend to tell anyone about the letter but the words that came from her mouth seemed to have an energy of their own and wouldn't be stopped.

"I had a letter from the Red Cross this morning, they have located him, that's all I know for now but I may know more on Friday."

Sadie saw a flicker of hope in the woman's eyes and she was glad she had shared the good news, it was as if it belonged to everyone.

TWENTY-FOUR
The Rabbit Cull

Sadie always knew what kind of mood her husband was bringing home as he entered the house. When Sadie was home, she left the front door open all day but Cyril disapproved and made a point of closing it as he entered each evening. There was something in the way he shut the door which gave away his mood. Tonight was a gentle click. Sadie was grateful, she didn't want anything to spoil the optimism she was feeling. Sadie had propped the letter against the sugar bowl in the middle of the table. The three children were tucking into fried potato and eggs, enjoying every mouthful.

"That smells good," said Cyril as he took off his coat.

"A bit of a treat," replied Sadie and she placed his dinner on the table and put her own food onto a plate.

"I had some good news today," continued Cyril, "the headmaster popped in to see me. The Ministry of Food has called for a national cull of wild rabbits. They need the meat to send out to the front, they want every man who can shoot to go on a hunt this Saturday. The headmaster asked me to join his group."

It was clear that Cyril thought of the invitation as an honour and Sadie nodded encouragement as she sat down.

Cyril looked at William. "I thought the lad could come with me, I asked the headmaster and he said the boy scouts are volunteering."

Sadie saw the panic in her son's eyes and more forcibly than she intended, she said, "no, Cyril, he's too young to go shooting."

"Nonsense," said Cyril, "I was out hunting before I went to school, it'll do him good. You've got the lad tied to your apron strings Sadie, it's time he grew up, he's not eighteen months anymore."

"He's seven, Cyril, I don't want him to go, that's the end of it. You go and enjoy the day."

But Cyril wasn't about to give up. "Look at him, he never stops crying, our Daisy's got more about her than he has. He's a big girl's blouse."

"He's my son," replied Sadie, "and I don't want him to be handling guns. Hasn't he had enough of death already in his life?"

"Now we're getting there," spat Cyril, "you mean he's your son, he's not mine. Well just look at the bloody photo you're so proud of in the parlour maybe it's time you told him he's not Frank's son either. There's plenty of boys lost their real dads in the war, I bet they'll be out on the shoot."

Sadie looked at William, he was white and silent tears rolled down his face. She had no idea where this argument was going to lead and her son was scared. "Why don't you go and get ready for bed William," she said.

Silently the little lad climbed the stairs and when he reached the top he sat on the landing with his head in his hands, listening to the row that raged below. Charlie had begun to whimper, Sadie scooped him up and Daisy came and stood as close to her mother as she could, gripping her skirt.

"That's right, let him run away, when is he going to learn to stand up for himself? No wonder the boys in school call him names. By God if you think you are going to treat Charlie like this when he gets a bit older you've got another thing coming." Cyril was relentless. "You're not doing the lad any favours," his rant continued, "all that stuff about him being a good footballer. He's got more chance of flying to the moon than playing for Everton, all the boys think they are going to be footballers, he's no better than anyone else. He needs a dose of reality and so do you Sadie."

Of all the spiteful comments flung at her by her husband, it was his throw away remark about the name calling in school which stung Sadie the most. Was there any truth in it, she wondered? She had never understood her husband's passion for shooting given that he had lost his eye to an accident with a gun. She struggled to understand why he would want to go shooting himself let alone take William with him.

"It's just not safe," she said, trying to placate Cyril.

"It's perfectly safe," retorted Cyril, "he's just a spoiled brat, I bet if I asked Tommy he'd jump at the chance."

The anger that Sadie felt at this injustice would not now be contained.

"How can you say it's not dangerous when your half blind because of a gun?" she shouted, "and if you think Tommy would jump at the chance go and ask his bloody mother, that's if you can find her, she's never there to look after Tommy, she wouldn't know if he went or not."

"Don't be so bloody stupid, no wonder the boy's like he is, that gun was faulty, this is totally different, anyway, you fall off a horse and you get right back on again. That's called being a man but he'll never know what that is the way you're bringing him up."

Sadie ushered Daisy towards the stairs.

"He's not going on Saturday, Cyril, you can tell the headmaster whatever you like but William is not going."

She took the children up to bed and gathered up William from the landing, she laid a hand on his shoulder and guided him into the bedroom.

"Don't worry, I won't let him take you, get ready for bed and I'll come and talk to you, when I have got these two to sleep," she said.

Slowly, Sadie helped Charlie into his cot and Daisy into her bed. She tried to reassure them but her own anxiety made words of comfort hard to find. Eventually sleep overtook them and she was able to be with William. He looked so small in the bed that used to be Fred's. She reached down and laid her hand on his head, he didn't move. Exhaustion had got the better of him so she climbed in beside him fully clothed and spent a fitful night watching her son as he slept. She was woken, she did not know at what hour when she heard a crash and what sounded like breaking glass downstairs and then the sound of footsteps as Cyril stomped up the stairs to bed.

At first light, Sadie entered the kitchen to find that Cyril had thrown the sugar bowl at the wall. There were shards of broken pottery on the quarry tiles and the precious sugar was everywhere. She had placed the one remaining egg in the sugar bowl for safe keeping and it was smeared across the window. She set about cleaning up the mess and washing the congealed plates that were sitting, abandoned on the table. The letter from the Red Cross was open in the middle of the forsaken feast, Sadie put it in her pocket. Cyril came down to a clean kitchen, a bowl of porridge and silence. Sadie did not trust herself to speak. He behaved as he always did, got himself ready for work, breakfasted, fetched his coat from the hook on the door and quietly left.

"There's a meeting in the school hall at six o'clock about the rabbit cull," he said, "I'll be home late." In that moment, Sadie thought it might be hatred that she felt for her husband.

She went upstairs to see if William was awake. He was dressed and ready for school.

"You don't need to go to school today William," said his mother let's have some porridge together and talk. But William pushed past her and descended the stairs two at a time.

"I want to go," he said, "Tommy will be waiting for me, I don't want to talk…"

Sadie was at a loss as to how to handle his response. He was so agitated that she let William make the decision. They ate their porridge together but any talk was superficial and when her son hurried out through the front door Sadie wept.

TWENTY-FIVE
A Visit From Emma Moran

Frieda arrived early on the Friday afternoon, her shift at the factory had finished at lunch time, she got a tram to Carver Street. Sadie was glad to see her and they discussed the various possibilities that they had both been imagining with regard to what had happened to Fred. Had he been injured? Was he gassed? Was he in a camp? Was he working on a German farm? Sadie had put out her grandmother's tea set, four cups and saucers which had only survived the generations because they had been hidden away at the back of the kitchen cupboard. She washed the cups and saucers and laid them on the table. She was glad to see Gracie when she arrived with Ivy Rose. Gracie was looking more like her old self again and Ivy Rose was soon ensconced with her cousins who were playing with a rusty spinning top in the yard.

Emma Moran arrived just before two on a bicycle which she propped up against the windowsill. She took a leather satchel out of the basket. She introduced herself to Frieda and Gracie and she accepted a cup of tea which she said was very welcome before she opened the satchel and took out various letters and papers which she laid out on the table. Fred was in a prisoner of war camp in Alsace. Emma Moran spread a map on the table and showed the women the area where the camp was located which she had marked with a cross. Fred had been shot in the shoulder when the Germans took him but the wound was superficial and though it was far from adequate, another prisoner who had basic medical skills had tended the wound for him and it had healed. Most of the men in the camp were detailed to work in the fields but the Germans realised that Fred could speak and understand a few basic German phrases taught to him by Opa and they soon had him working in a large munitions factory in the town six kilometres from the camp. Six of the prisoners walked there every morning accompanied by a German soldier.

"Do you know how he is?" asked Frieda.

"Other than he's alive," replied Emma, "we don't really know. I'm afraid there is so little food in the camps that malnutrition is a problem. We send food parcels over but they don't always get to the prisoners, the local people are starving too so I think the treatment of allied prisoners is hostile to say the least. But as I say, he is alive and he has been told that you are being made aware that he is alive so that must relieve his anxiety. I think there's cause for hope, don't you?" She looked around at the faces of the three women and smiled.

Frieda let out a sob which made them all turn towards her.

"I'm sorry," she said, it's just the relief. What we need to do now is pray that this damned war is over soon and Fred gets home so that we can look after him."

"Amen to that," said Emma, "and there are signs that it is happening Frieda, I'm just glad to bring good news for a change, it's not always as rewarding as this."

With that, she gathered her papers and replaced them in the satchel. The women tried to thank her but she waved away their gratitude and said "it's my job and besides, it's brought me back in contact with Sadie and I have had the privilege of meeting the two of you."

Sadie showed her visitor out and watched as she cycled down Carver Street. Before she left, Emma Moran took Sadie's hands in hers and kissed her gently on the cheek.

"Keep going Sadie," she said, "I have a feeling the end is in sight, we'll all get through this."

Sadie was grateful for the encouragement.

Back in the kitchen, the kettle was once more on the boil, the children were drinking cups of milk and Frieda and Gracie were discussing what Emma had told them. It was noisy and animated and there was a feeling of hope bubbling up in the space. Sadie's spirits were lifted and when Gracie suggested an outing the following day she agreed without hesitating, grateful that this was the day that Cyril would be out on the rabbit shoot.

"Jack said the Tramways Committee has converted a tram to look like a military tank and they are touring it around the area to raise money," said Gracie. "He said it looks really impressive, they've parked it on Exchange Flags and there's a huge model of a Super-Dreadnought outside the Town Hall. Tomorrow is the last chance to see it, they are moving it to Manchester on Sunday. Why don't we take the children to see it tomorrow, I think they'll love it? Dilys wants to see it so I'll go to the dairy on my way home and see if she wants to come with us."

The three women made plans to meet the following day and when they parted it was with renewed hope. When William arrived home from school, Sadie told him the good news about Uncle Fred and he couldn't contain his joy. Sadie told him that by way of celebration they were planning an outing the following day and William's immediate response was to ask whether Tommy could tag along. Sadie was not about to deny her son his wishes and he tore out of the house and into next door where he passed on the invitation to his friend.

Saturday started grey with a mass of low cloud but it was dry and mild. Tommy and William walked on the pavement with Daisy between them. She giggled with delight when they swung her into the air as they headed for the tram. Sadie had a job to keep up the pace with Charlie in her arms. It was clear from the queue at the tram stop that lots of people had the same idea, there was a real feeling of enthusiasm in the air which Sadie hadn't felt for many months. It wasn't easy to spot the others on Exchange Flags, there were so many people milling around, but true to their arrangements, Gracie, Dilys and Ivy Rose were waiting near to Nelson's Monument. Sadie and the children joined them and William spotted Frieda and Henry approaching through the crowd.

There was excitement in the air, red white and blue bunting fluttered in the wind, hoardings had been brought in and were covered in posters encouraging people to dig deep and find a donation. Our boys were so near to winning this war, the posters said, all that was needed was a final push. Tommy, William and Daisy ran off in the direction of the tram-tank and Sadie called out to them to wait for the grown-ups. Everybody agreed that the Tramways Committee had done a spectacular job in re-modelling the tram to resemble a tank. It was very realistic. An official was just finishing a passionate speech from the top deck of the tram-tank, thanking the many businessmen who had bought national war bonds and raised massive amounts of money. Liverpool, he said, was at the top of the fundraising table, to which everyone cheered. The children ran around the tram-tank, Tommy and William pointing out its features. They each bought a pencil, printed with a picture of a union jack and from her bag, Dilys produced toffee that she had made and the children clamoured for their share. The toffee was pronounced the best they had ever tasted.

The little party walked to Dale Street to see the Dreadnought and it did not disappoint. The children were delighted, the model was enormous and a knowledgeable guide, sent from the Navy, was answering their questions about the battleship while the women queued for tea from a tea station in the back of a lorry. It was Dilys who brought the day to a close.

"I need to get back to the dairy for the afternoon milking," she said.

So, they said their farewells and started on their separate journeys home and the spirit of optimism that had been in the air all day went with them. Dilys, Gracie and Ivy Rose walked in the direction of the dairy where Jack was waiting for his wife and daughter after a long shift. Sadie, William, Tommy and the two little ones took the tram to Carver Street where Sadie was hoping for a peaceful evening. Cyril hadn't said whether he would be paying his usual Saturday night visit to his cousin Mary but Sadie was hopeful. Frieda and Henry set off for Netherfield Road where Frieda's mother had promised a rare fish pie. Sadly, Frieda's return to their rooms in the tenement did not bring the happy end to the day she was expecting.

TWENTY-SIX
Opa

When Frieda opened the front door, there was no smell of cooking and her mother looked strained and pale as if she had been crying. Her mother looked at her and glanced meaningfully at Henry.

"Go and play in the bedroom, Henry," said Frieda "while I get your tea ready."

When the boy was out of earshot, Frieda's mother explained that she had had a visit from the pastor's wife. Opa was gravely ill. He had had a chest infection which had turned to pneumonia, they weren't expecting him to make it through the next few days. The pastor and one of Opa's old friends were at his bedside, he was struggling for breath but wasn't complaining about pain.

"She said the kindest thing they could hope for was a quick passing," said Frieda's mother. The pastor has promised to stay with him and he'll send a telegram when there's any change."

The good news about Fred and the goodwill that Frieda had brought back from her day out now turned into anguish and anger. Her mother had lived with the news about Opa for most of the day and she needed now to feel the arms of her daughter around her but Frieda's pain was too raw for tenderness. She immersed herself in making the meal.

"Henry needs his tea, he hasn't really eaten all day, he's hungry," she said.

Quiet tears falling, her mother set the table while Frieda melted cheese and grated onion and spread a thin film of butter on potato bread hoping to disguise the taste. It wasn't until she stood watching her son from the bedroom doorway as he fell asleep that Frieda felt the full force of the sadness that was almost overwhelming. It was then that she hugged her mother.

TWENTY-SEVEN
Worry About Charlie

Sadie expected the two older boys to be exhausted by the time they reached home; it had been a tiring day out. On the contrary, as soon as Sadie and the children turned the corner into Carver Street, William and Tommy broke free and charged towards Tommy's house. His mother wasn't yet home but Sadie could hear the boys as they regaled Cate, his sister with details about the tram-tank and the battleship.

Sadie found her own house empty, Cyril's muddy boots were on the draining board next to the sink, there was no sign of his coat on the back of the door and Sadie, with some relief, assumed he had come home to get changed and had then left for Mary's house as was his recent habit on a Saturday evening. Just to be sure, she went upstairs to check that Cyril had not gone to bed and she took off her coat and scarf. She had cooked a bean stew which she now dished up into bowls, her hands were stained red by a beetroot that she had boiled and was now slicing. It was one that Cyril had grown on the school allotment, sliced thinly, it was enough to sweeten the stew. She saved a little for Cyril. Had Sadie known that Frieda and Henry were returning to the news of Opa's death, her mind would not have been on bean stew and beetroot. As it was, she got her three children into bed and was asleep herself before nine.

The following day, Sadie listened to Cyril for most of the morning with as much attention as she could muster. He was sharing the highlights of his day on the rabbit cull, how they had made a little competition of it, how they had had a small wager, how he had shot more rabbits than the headmaster, how the rabbits had been collected and sent straight to the distribution points, how the whole thing had been so efficiently organised, how the boy scouts had been invaluable, how William would have got so much from the experience. Sadie's patience was wearing thin, but she was still buoyant from the news that her brother was alive and Sunday passed with little friction.

It was Monday evening when Frieda arrived at Carver Street with Henry. She pushed the telegram which had arrived that afternoon into Sadie's hand.

"It's Opa," she said but Sadie had guessed the instant that she saw her sister-in-law's face as she walked into the room that her grandfather had died.

Eventually, Cyril left the women and the children in the kitchen and went to sit in the parlour. Frieda and Sadie told stories about Opa, the kind that made them laugh and cry at the same time. Henry had no memory of his great grandfather but he had been told many times about him, he knew that Opa was the German word for Granddad and he knew that he had been named Henry after him. William, on the other hand, remembered Opa, the funny voice, the smell of his pipe.

"He was kind," he said and left it at that. He and Henry went out into the yard to kick the ball.

"Take Daisy with you," said his mother and sensing the atmosphere, William didn't argue.

"I don't know what we would have done without the pastor," said Frieda. "I can't bear the thought that Opa might have died alone in that place, I'm not sure my mum would have ever got over it."

"Try not to think about that," said Sadie, "at least Opa was told the news about Fred before he died. You're right about your mum, she's going to need you now, she probably can't think straight. You couldn't blame her for feeling really angry could you? It's a good job she's got little Henry to keep her busy. Surely, it can't be long before this bloody war is over and our Fred's back with us again. There will be good times again Frieda, I'm sure of it."

"Actually, I've never understood why Mam isn't more angry than she is. Opa was never a threat to anyone and my mum is more English than the English. She won't have a word said against Lloyd George and she's always going on about the King and Queen Mary. She's only got two kids for God's sake, me and our Michael. I'm making bloody bombs for the war effort and our Mike's God knows where in the Royal Navy. How much more loyal to England do they want us to be?"

Frieda's frustration got the better of her and the two women stood and cried, leaning on one another in the gloomy kitchen with the sound of the children seeping through the wall and the steady rhythm of the heavy football drumming on the yard gate.

The visitors said a courteous goodbye to Cyril while Sadie stood in the doorway holding Charlie in her arms. She kept watch until Henry and Frieda got to the end of the street and disappeared.

"I don't know why you need to stand in the street like that Sadie with the door open," said Cyril, who had reinstated himself at his place in the kitchen. "You'll be wanting to put another shovel of coal on the fire next, you can see how low we're getting and there's no more to be had, you know that as well as I do."

Sadie nodded in her husband's direction but she had barely taken in what he was saying. Charlie had developed a bit of a cough and she was searching in the cupboard for medicine. She found a half empty bottle of cough mixture but decided to save the dose until Charlie's bedtime, hoping the cough wouldn't develop into anything worrying.

She ran the sticky bottle under the tap and without raising her head she said, "I'll be going to the German Church on Sunday morning, with Freida's family. I will take Daisy and William but you'll have to look after our Charlie for a couple of hours, I can't manage the three of them in the church."

She placed the cough mixture on the draining board and unsure what Cyril's silence meant, she glanced at her husband.

"They are doing a cup of tea back at Frieda's after the service but I won't go to that if you don't want me to."

Sadie waited for a response from Cyril on the off chance that he would give her permission to attend Opa's wake but she wasn't surprised when it never came.

Sadie couldn't help worrying about Charlie as she tucked him into bed. As soon as the little boy laid his head on the pillow, his cough worsened and his breathing seemed a little laboured. Sadie administered the cough mixture and tried to raise his head and chest with a second pillow. She wasn't sure if he had a fever. He seemed a bit hot but he wasn't kicking off his blankets. Her mother's words came to her, she could picture Mary

Jane standing in the doorway, "sure, you mark my words, big changes always come in threes," she was saying. Sadie couldn't help thinking that following the news about Fred and then Opa, Charlie's cough might turn out to be serious. She tried to push the thought out of her head, but she was recalling a conversation that she had had with Gracie.

There were stories circulating about a flu epidemic that had started in Spain, it was killing people, there had been a big outbreak in Ireland. They were saying that wounded soldiers had brought it back from France. Norah Price had said that there were cases in Liverpool and children were especially vulnerable. Everyone was calling it Spanish flu but Jack had said that no-one really knew where it had originated. It was just that in Spain, there was no embargo on the news because Spain wasn't at war. The Spanish newspapers were reporting deaths every day whereas the allies had a duty to bolster morale and our newspapers were not allowed to publish constant bad news about Spanish flu or any other flu.

"Jack said just because they don't report it, it doesn't mean it's not happening." Gracie had said.

Sadie slept with her son, comforting the toddler as best she could. In the morning, she decided to take him to Mr. Mills, the chemist for some advice. Charlie refused his breakfast and was fractious to say the least. "What's wrong with him?" asked Cyril

"I'm not sure," replied Sadie," I'm going to take him to see Mr. Mills and if he is worried I will get him to the doctor. It could just be a bit of a cold but there's that Spanish flu around so I don't want to take any chances."

"You don't want to believe all that stuff about the Spanish flu," retorted Cyril, "it's only in Spain, we haven't got it over here, it's just scaremongering."

"Jack said there has been an outbreak in Ireland," she replied, it's got into lots of countries, it might not even have started in Spain, they've just dubbed it Spanish flu."

"Oh well if Jack says so, it must be right, maybe you should take Charlie to see him instead of the doctor, he seems to have all the answers Sadie."

Sadie was too anxious about Charlie to retaliate and in any case, Cyril did not give her the opportunity. He was buttoning up his overcoat and exiting through the front door as he was finishing his sentence. She tried to clean her son's face but he fought off the facecloth so she placed him in the pram and helped Daisy on with her coat in preparation for the walk to the chemist. William looked concerned. He had witnessed the exchange between his mother and Cyril and was now worried about his brother.

"I tell you what, William," said Sadie, as they all left the house together, "when I have had a word with Mr. Mills at the chemist, I will walk down to school in time for your playtime. Stand by the railings and I will shout up to you from across the street and let you know what he says. I bet Charlie will be as right as rain by then."

With that, William spotted Tommy further up Carver Street and ran off at speed to catch him.

Sadie tried distracting Charlie, pointing out the cats and dogs, the children running to school, the sounds of the traffic but nothing worked. She was relieved to find that there was no-one waiting in the chemist. Mr. Mills knew Sadie well. He had been a great support when Mary Jane had been ill, giving advice and reassurance and Sadie had been touched when he had come to her mother's funeral quietly paying his respects at the graveside.

It was Mrs. Mills who stood behind the counter. "Sadie, how are you, it's a long time since we've seen you in here. Is everything alright?"

"It's Charlie," replied Sadie, "he's got a nasty cough and I think he may have a fever. I'm worried about this Spanish flu everyone is talking about."

"You're not the first one to come in worrying about that," said Mrs. Mills, "I'll just call my husband, he's in the back, he won't be long."

"Well, he hasn't got a fever, that's the first thing, so I doubt very much if it's anything to do with the Spanish flu. He does have a cough but I don't think it's on his chest, I think he might be teething though, is he cutting his back teeth do you think?"

Mr. Mills supplied some teething powders and cough mixture and with the help of Mrs. Mills, Sadie managed to get Charlie to swallow a powder dissolved in a spoon full of water sweetened by what the Chemist's wife called "a wee bit of sugar." At last Charlie settled in his pram and was lulled into a peaceful sleep. Sadie walked slowly towards the school, she felt her shoulders dropping and the throbbing in her right temple gradually ceased to bother her. She listened to Daisy chatting incessantly and the child was content to trot along beside her holding onto the pram. By the time they reached the Post Office, no-one would have guessed that the previous few hours had been so stressful. Sadie started to wonder if Cyril had been right after all, he was fond of telling her that she was too prone to court disaster, maybe she was. Perhaps she did need to regain some perspective. Perhaps all this talk of Spanish flu was scaremongering as her husband claimed, perhaps the disease was confined to Spain and it would never cross the channel.

Sadie's thoughts were interrupted when she bumped into her friend the seamstress.

"Sadie, I was just on my way to your house I wanted to have a chat, have you got time for a cup of tea?"

Eva Johnson was leaving the Post Office with a small parcel in the crook of her left arm. Sadie was glad to see her.

"That would be great," she replied but I need to walk to Bray Street, to the school to check on William on the way."

"Is he ok Sadie?"

As they walked along the pavement companionably, Daisy held Mrs. Johnson's hand and Sadie related the saga of the previous few hours.

"Well Charlie looks peaceful enough now," said Eva Johnson "that's the main thing, he'll probably be right as rain when he wakes up, you know how they bounce back at this age. It doesn't mean you weren't right to worry though Sadie, what kind of a mother would you be if you didn't?"

Eva Johnson and Sadie's friendship had begun when the two women had confided in one another after William was born. Sadie would never forget Eva's kindness at a time when the whole world seemed to be judging her. Since that first visit, the women had become firm friends. Eva was sorry that Sadie had chosen to marry Cyril, she had guessed from the start that Daisy was not his child but she had kept her suspicions entirely to herself and had never commented on Cyril or the marriage. Given her own secrets, to judge would have been hypocritical to say the least.

"What's in your parcel?" asked Daisy pointing at the box that Eva had now placed on the end of the pram.

"Guess," said Eva and a game began which kept the little girl occupied until they reached Bray Street.

They could hear the children's voices from the corner of the street and quickened their pace. They stopped on the pavement opposite the school and Sadie spotted William leaning on the playground railings on the perimeter of the school roof. He was shielding his eyes from the sunlight. Sadie waved and pointed to the sleeping Charlie.

"He's fine," she yelled and made a thumbs up gesture in the air. "It's nothing to worry about."

William waved and ran off towards a group of boys who were kicking a ball around and the women made their way to Carver Street.

"Sorry about all this mess Eva," Sadie apologised, "I didn't even have time to put the dishes in the sink this morning."

She cleared the table while her friend opened the box that she had collected from the Post Office. Inside were a dozen reels of satin and velvet ribbons, in every shade possible. Daisy was delighted when she was invited to choose two of them so that Eva could cut off lengths to make bows for her hair. She chose a baby pink and a lilac.

"Good choices Daisy," said Eva they will go nicely with your blonde hair. Go and fetch your hairbrush and we'll tie your curls up with the pink one."

"Actually, Sadie, I have got some news." Eva Johnson sounded a little hesitant as if she didn't quite know how Sadie would take what she was about to say. Sadie placed two cups of hot tea on the table and sat down.

"I'm leaving Liverpool to go back to Manchester," began Eva, "my father died a couple of months ago and my mother has written to me for the first time in all these years. She wants me to go home and live with her."

It was the last thing that Sadie was expecting. She was disappointed and she was aware of a strong sense of loss rising in her. She knew, of course that Eva Johnson owed her nothing but she had been a constant support and mentor ever since her first visit to Carver Street. In Eva, Sadie had found a kindred spirit and a bit of a heroine. Eva had survived the birth of her daughter out of wedlock, recovered from being rejected by her family and handled a move to a new city to start a new life with her baby. As well as this, she had managed to create a business and produce an income, sufficient to keep herself and Francesca in relative comfort.

"Why?" asked Sadie, "you've managed to keep the dressmaking and the haberdashery going all through the war, everyone's saying the war's nearly over, things are bound to pick up…"

"It's not that, Sadie, the business is doing fine. Our Francesca's a woman now, she's got a serious boyfriend. He's an officer in the Navy, he's older than she is, it won't be long before she comes to tell me that they are getting married, she's got her own life. My business is doing well but I can do even better in Manchester. All my suppliers are there, that's how I came to make contact with my mother. The company that sends me the ribbons is managed by a friend of my father, I've known him since I was a child. He put a note inside a box of ribbons to let me know that my father had passed on and when I heard, I wrote a letter to my mother. I wasn't sure if she would write back but she did, so I went to Manchester to see her."

"That must have been hard after all these years," offered Sadie with a slight shake of her head.

"It was, I didn't know what to expect. She's old Sadie and very frail, I suppose I feel like I owe her something after leaving her with my father all these years. Truth is he was a bully and she's had no life, trapped in that house with him. Nobody could have guessed how bad it was for her, it's a lovely big house with a garden and he bought her nice clothes, he had loads of friends in the fashion world. But she was a trophy on his arm. He controlled everything she did, he belittled everything she did. She was frightened to tell anyone; I think she blamed herself. Even now she won't have a word said against him. Top and bottom of it is, Sadie, I feel guilty that I left her with him all these years and there's not much time to make it up to her."

Daisy reappeared brandishing her mother's hairbrush.

"Can we put the other ribbon in my hair instead of the pink one, that's my favourite," urged the little girl.

"Of course we can Daisy, that's my favourite too," replied Mrs. Johnson and she sat Daisy on her knee and set to work.

Sadie was glad of the diversion, a million thoughts

dancing in her head. She knew about guilt and secrets, she had plenty of her own. She had plenty of questions too but despite the solid friendship they enjoyed, she knew that Eva would not thank her for questioning her decision.

"When are you leaving?" she asked, trying to sound positive.

Sadie had real doubts about Eva's intention to return to her roots but, clearly her friend had made her decision and it wasn't Sadie's place to interfere. She thought about her own decision to marry Cyril, pregnant as she was with another man's child. She would not have welcomed advice from anyone and Eva had not proffered any. Instead, she had supported her and now Sadie would return the gesture.

"This weekend," said Eva. The thing is, our Francesca is staying on in Liverpool. She's taking over the house. She doesn't think she'll get a job in Manchester and she's well thought of where she works. I'd rather she came with me but she's made her mind up. She's independent, I suppose that's my fault, and she wants to go back to being a florist after the war, that's her real passion. She says she has contacts here. So I will be up and down to Liverpool on the train to keep an eye on her."

"No doubt the boyfriend's got something to do with it too," smiled Sadie. "Daisy what do you say to Mrs. Johnson for brushing your hair and for your ribbons, you look like a Princess."

The little girl made her way upstairs to look at herself in the mirror on her mother's dressing table, careful not to make any sudden head movements which might disturb the new hairstyle.

"Do you need help to pack up your stuff?" asked

Sadie, "you are going to have to pack all your fabrics and patterns and all that haberdashery stuff aren't you, not to mention the two sewing machines?"

"Oh Sadie, I thought you would never ask," retorted her friend.

Sadie was glad to be able to do something for Eva Johnson, this was the first opportunity in all the years that they had known each other. She felt nothing but gratitude for their friendship but at the same time it was liberating to know that even her mentor had feet of clay.

As Eva left, her box of ribbons tucked under her arm, Charlie began to stir in the pram. Sadie felt his cheeks with the back of her hand, no sign of a temperature and with her son perched on her hip she lifted the lid on a pan that was simmering on the range hoping that he would take a little of the soup she had made. He managed a few spoons full before pushing away his mother's hand in frustration. Sadie watched as he drank a cup of warm milk to which she added a spoon full of sugar. She pushed all thoughts of Spanish flu to the back of her mind and settled both children on the floor where she could keep an eye on Charlie.

That night, Sadie took no chances. Daisy was delighted to share a bed with William, she lay at the foot of the bed, doing her best to stay awake until her brother was ready to join her but when William entered the room he could hear his sister snoring gently. Charlie had gone to bed without a struggle. Perhaps it was thanks to the second teething powder which Sadie administered. In any case, there was no sign of a fever and his sleep seemed peaceful enough. Nevertheless, Sadie lay next to her little boy in Daisy's bed and several times during the night she got up to check for any rise in temperature. In the morning, she woke to find the toddler lying next to her, happily playing with his mother's hair. From the next room she could hear Daisy trying to persuade William to get out of bed. A normal day! Sadie felt the tension in her shoulders evaporate.

"I told you there was nothing wrong with him," said Cyril. "Spanish flu, if there's any such thing it's in Spain. If you're not careful you are going to turn our Charlie into a little whinger like William."

Sadie contented herself with a mental retort, she was looking forward to spending the day with Eva and she was used to deflecting Cyril's barbs. Besides, even this early in the morning, the sun had broken through and apart from a few wispy clouds, the sky was a continuous blue. Summer had tried to make an appearance in April and again in May but neither attempts at an entrance had lasted, in the end, the wet Spring refused to let go. Today, however, the air was different, the day was promising. It was June and it felt like Summer had come to stay.

TWENTY-EIGHT
Eva Johnson's Story

Eva Johnson had arranged for Lilly, her neighbour's daughter to take Charlie and Daisy to the park for the day. Her daughter Francesca had cobbled together a picnic which Sadie placed at the foot of the pram. Sadie tried to give instructions to the girl but Lilly stopped her mid-flow.

"It's ok, I'm used to this, I'm the oldest," she said. "I've got my orders from Mrs. Johnson, I've to get William from school and I'll be back about five."

Sadie couldn't help smiling, the girl reminded her of her sister Gracie when she was fifteen.

Eva went into the kitchen to make tea leaving Sadie in her workshop which doubled as the parlour though you would have been hard pressed to find anywhere to sit or any surface free of clutter. It looked as if there had been a battle between lots of different fabrics and now they were all lolling around exhausted. Sadie had only been in Eva's house once or twice but she had been struck by the same thought each time. How was her friend able to turn out such exquisite creations working in such chaos? Sadie looked around, without the children's chatter the silence was a little unnerving. "We've got our work cut out to get this lot organised," she called out but Eva hadn't heard her and when she reappeared with a tray of tea, Sadie was examining a half finished scarlet dress held together with pins on a tailor's dummy. Eva had obviously been trying pearl trimmings up against the fabric.

"I can guess what you're thinking," said Eva, "where do they get the fabric and the finery when we can't even get hold of a pound of flour? You'd be surprised Sadie, if you've got money you can still get what you want not just what you need."

Sadie wasn't thinking about where the fabric had come from, she was wondering what it would be like to wear a dress as glamourous as this one. Of course, she knew she never would.

"Her husband's a judge, they live in Newsham Park," said Eva, nodding towards the dress.

Sadie wasn't sure what to do with this information, she wasn't used to it. Her conversations were about who had been evicted or who's poor son hadn't made it home from the Somme, so she made no reply.

"Her husband's the judge on that murder trial, you know where that poor man was stabbed in the neck by his wife, it's going on at the moment," Eva continued undeterred, " but it's not him with the money, it's her, she's part of the Stanley family."

Sadie looked blank.

"The Stanleys," Eva pressed on, "Lord Derby."

Tea break over, Eva opened the door to her kitchen to reveal dozens of boxes already fixed with luggage labels so that the myriad of bits and pieces which constituted her business could be organised, stored and transported with the aim of easy access when they arrived in Manchester. This was all in a day's work for Sadie, she delighted in bringing order to chaos. Methodically, she worked through the piles of paper patterns, matching sleeves to bodices and collars to yokes, she found boxes for needles and pins and colour matched swatches of fabric, she found containers for cottons and spools and identified the colours on the lids, she separated pearls from crystals and sequins from beads, she swaddled hundreds of ribbons in tissue paper to protect them and she created an odds and ends box of French chalk and scissors, thimbles and crochet hooks, embroidery rings and the all-important order book. She made careful inventories on the labels conscious that her friend would be unpacking all of this on her own.

The two women chatted amiably as they worked. Sadie watched Eva as she packed up the scarlet dress and two other unfinished pieces. She did it with such care and tenderness it was almost as if they were alive and had feelings. It occurred to Sadie that these creations were her children. Next, they got the two sewing machines into wooden crates and when Sadie took a moment to breathe and look around the room, she saw empty surfaces, two green armchairs which hadn't seen the light of day for many a year and a clock which had been buried under swatches of various coloured fabrics but hadn't been wound for months. On one of the little mahogany tables, Sadie spotted a candelabrum, it was silver and it had nine candle sticks.

"Oh, that's pretty," said Sadie. "I've seen one of those before, my mum used to clean for Mr. Goldbloom, he had the chemist shop near to William's school, she would take me with her to give her a hand, I must have been about twelve or thirteen. I remember I used to love cleaning all the little bottles. I saw the candlestick on his shelf in his rooms upstairs. Mr. Goldbloom told me all about it one day, he could see I was interested. It's

Jewish isn't it? I can't remember what it's called now."

Eva looked at the candelabrum and then at Sadie and then she drew in a deep breath. It was as if she had things to say but was wondering where to begin.

"It's called a menorah," said Eva, "we light them during Hanukkah, it's our New Year."

Sadie was confused, she had stumbled into an area of her friend's life of which she was unaware.

"I didn't know you were Jewish," she said, "I wouldn't have brought it up if I'd known."

"No, Sadie, you don't know because I have never mentioned it. It's partly why I'm going back. The reason I left Manchester all those years ago wasn't just that I was pregnant and not married, that was bad enough, but I think my dad might have come to terms with that if my boyfriend had been Jewish. The boy I was seeing wasn't a Jew, he was Catholic and the truth is my father couldn't get over the shame. My family is from Russia, my grandparents, Solomon and Sarah came over here when my dad was small. Solomon helped dozens of Russian refugees to get to Great Britain. He was a tailor but Solomon ended up importing fabrics, he left the business to my father and that's how I know so much about the rag trade. So, all in all, my family is in what they call very good standing in the Jewish community, everyone knows them, some people literally owe Solomon their lives. It's very hard to live up to," she said.

"What is?" asked Sadie.

"A family with that kind of reputation," Eva replied and then she stopped talking but Sadie could tell that Eva hadn't paused to invite comment or any other response, rather she was deciding how much to say.

"Anyway," Eva sighed, "I didn't live up to the

expectation. When I was young everything was fine. My parents seemed happy, dad wasn't home much but he was building up the business and mum and I got on well. I was about thirteen when he started drinking and the rows began. The more he had to drink the more nasty he was. I used to think it was my fault, I always thought he wanted a son and she couldn't give him one and I wasn't good enough. Then, I met Francis. I was working in the warehouse and he came in to pick up an order. He asked me to marry him but it was all too difficult, his family weren't any more supportive than mine. Well, the rest's history. When I came here to Liverpool, I was so hurt and angry I turned my back on the faith, the only thing I have is that menorah, the candlestick, my mother insisted I bring it with me. It's silver, believe me there have been many times when I have thought about selling it when business was slow, I pawned it a couple of times but it's still here, it needs a good clean doesn't it?" she laughed. "Francesca knows about her Jewish roots but I can't bring myself to tell her how my dad treated my mother, I don't know why but it seems disloyal somehow."

"Or shameful," thought Sadie. "Have you ever asked your mum why your dad suddenly changed?" she asked.

"It's her secret," answered her friend, "she's never spoken about it, she never will, she will take it to her grave."

Sadie asked herself if Eva was really talking about her mother's secret or her own. She also wondered whether William would be as understanding as Francesca if he discovered her own secret. The thought made her go cold.

"The thing is," continued Eva Johnson, "I have missed it. Maybe if I had met someone and had more children it would be different but I miss my past, I miss roots, I miss being Jewish. Now that my dad's not there and Francesca's got her own life, I've decided to go back. Maybe I can be who I was then at the same time as being who I am now. I'm not sure I'm making much sense Sadie. Anyway, that's the big secret. I didn't plan on saying any of that but you're a good listener."

Eva paused; she was pensive. "Now, those children will be back in half an hour and we deserve a last cup of tea while it's quiet," she said at last.

"Just one question," said Sadie who was conscious that her mouth had been open throughout Eva's revelations. "Johnson, your name, Eva Johnson?"

"You of all people should know how easy it is to change a name Sadie. My family name is Groisman. Evelyn Groisman became Eva Johnson. I'm going to use both of my names."

"Both?" questioned Sadie.

"Yes, I'm going to be both, plenty of people have a career name, why not, if it's good enough for Marie Lloyd it's good enough for me, you put the kettle on, while I rinse the cups."

The two women had a tussle as Sadie and the children were leaving. Eva had given William a little money to spend on treats and she handed Sadie a small lilac envelope which she said contained a fair day's pay. She couldn't have packed up her workshop without her help and what was in the envelope didn't seem enough for what Sadie had done for her. Sadie tried to refuse, Eva was a friend and it felt good to be able to give something back to her after all the help she had been to Sadie over the years. It was only when she got home and William was lifting his brother out of the pram that she noticed the envelope, slipped between the side of the pram and the sheet. Sadie shook her head and tutted, Eva was probably the most determined person she had ever known. She sliced open the envelope with a knife from the kitchen drawer and took out a five-pound note. To Sadie it was a fortune.

"My dear friend," the accompanying letter began. "You never know when you might have a rainy day, it's a gift, please don't insult me by trying to give it back."

"What's the matter Mam?" asked William seeing the tears in his mother's eyes.

Sadie wiped them away with the back of her hand. "I'm just a bit sad because Mrs. Johnson is moving away in a few days, she's a good friend," she said.

Spotting an opportunity in his mother's moment of weakness, William asked "can I go to the pictures with Tommy on Saturday, Mam, I can use the money that Mrs. Johnson gave me. Please Mam, everyone in my class is going, we'll come straight home after, honest."

Sadie's first instinct was to refuse her son on the grounds that he was too young but perhaps Cyril had a point when he said that she needed to let him grow up a little.

"I'm just going round to tell Tommy," he said, affording his mother no time to change her mind. With that William was out of the door like a greyhound from a trap. Sadie slid the envelope containing the money under the brown paper that she had used to line the top drawer of her mother's old dressing table. For the first time in her life, Sadie knew what it was like to have money which wasn't already spent. It would bring her a bit of security in a world that seldom felt safe.

TWENTY-NINE
The Americans

Not only had the summer arrived to stay but one beautiful day rolled gently into the next until the soggy spring was all but forgotten. The constant sun brought about a lift in peoples' spirits, dampened only by the fact that in June and early July the news from the front was mixed at best. Supplies of food for the troops and for people at home had dwindled from what they called "of serious concern" to what they started to describe as "a critical issue." The dry weather was not helping the vegetables growing on allotments in every park and garden and roadside in Liverpool. An appeal went out for an army of volunteers to bring water in tins, jugs, watering cans, jam jars, anything they could get their hands on in an effort to save the crops. Tommy, William and two of their friends filled old milk churns that Alun had provided, put them in the pram every evening after school and wheeled them to the park. Sadie was proud of the way that William stuck to his commitment. Cyril made no comment. The boys were so diligent they were given their own patch to tend. To a point, the plan worked and even Cyril recruited a few of the more sensible boys to water the crops in his raised beds at the school.

At the beginning of July, hundreds of American troops were making their way to Great Britain on a twelve-ship convoy from New Jersey. They zigzagged their way across the Atlantic to avoid the German U-boats. Three of the ships docked in Liverpool and the Lord Mayor made it his business to wring every drop of propaganda out of their arrival. The fourth of July was American Independence Day and fifty thousand people gathered outside St. Georges Hall to watch the American troops march through the streets. It seemed like everyone in the City had heard about the "Grand Review of American Troops" as it was advertised. Jack had a rare day off and was keen to go to see the spectacle.

"They are having a band to play the "Star-spangled Banner," Jack said, "and apparently the King has sent a message that they are going to read out. The powers that be are making the most of it alright but you can't blame them, we are getting close to the end Gracie, this American involvement will be what gives the Allies new heart, you wait and see, victory is in sight, I'm sure of it. Mind you, nobody seems to think it's odd that we are celebrating American Independence from Great Britain, everyone has forgotten they were our sworn enemies. It's a strange world alright!"

"I wish I could come with you," answered Gracie but I'm not taking any chances until this baby arrives safe and sound. I might go and see our Sadie and tell her I'm pregnant, I'm over the first three months so fingers crossed everything will be ok this time and in any case, I'm starting to show. She'll never forgive me if she guesses before I get chance to tell her."

Gently, Gracie placed her hand on her abdomen and then kissed the top of Ivy Rose's head as her daughter was pouring over a picture book at the table.

"If you are going to Carver Street, why don't you drop Ivy at the dairy, tell Mam I'll pick her up on my way back from St. George's Hall," said Jack as he left the house.

When Gracie arrived at her sister's house, Sadie was on her hands and knees scrubbing the step. Charlie and Daisy were perched on top of Maggie's step next door and Daisy was sobbing quietly. Gracie went straight to the little girl to comfort her but Sadie looked up and shook her head.

"What's been going on here?" asked Gracie.

Sadie sighed and replied "Daisy hit Charlie, they were fighting over the peg doll."

"So why is she the one that's crying?" answered Gracie.

"Because I've just told her off and she's feeling sorry for herself," Sadie said, finishing her work on the step.

"I suppose I'd better get used to this for when this baby comes along," said Gracie in a matter-of-fact voice. "I don't suppose my two will be any different."

Sadie dropped her scrubbing brush into the bucket creating a splash of soapsuds, wiped her hands on her apron and threw her arms around her sister's neck. The sudden movement put an end to Daisy's tears.

"That's great news Gracie, how do you feel? How far gone are you? When is it due?" The questions came so rapidly, Gracie had no time to reply to any of them until they were inside the house and seated at the table.

"Why don't you sit in Cyril's chair, it'll support your back better," said Sadie.

"Don't you start molly coddling me Sadie, I have enough of that from Jack, he's like a mother hen, I'm fine, I'm past the danger point and I've seen Doctor Grayson twice, he reckons I'm due about Christmas time," replied her sister.

"Where's Ivy Rose?" asked Daisy as she and Charlie made blankets out of newspaper for the peg doll with seemingly no repercussions from the skirmish on the step.

"She's with her Nan at the dairy," replied Gracie and Daisy's little face showed signs of crumbling.

"I tell you what Daisy," began her aunt, "how would you like to come to our house to sleep for a couple of nights and you can have a long play with Ivy Rose. We could even get Dilys to make you a new peg doll, she won't mind."

The little girl looked longingly at her mother, trying to cross her fingers like William had taught her to do.

"Are you sure you're up to it Gracie?" said Sadie, "you look a bit tired as it is."

"I feel fine, Sadie, she'll be good company for Ivy and anyway, I'd better start getting used to having two! I'll ask Ivy's granddad to bring you home on the milk cart Daisy," she added.

Meanwhile, Jack was watching the review from St. Georges Plateau, he was glad that Gracie had not joined him. The heat and the crowds where overwhelming. After the presentation and the speeches, Jack watched as over three thousand American soldiers marched to Wavertree Park.

"Where are they sending them now?" asked a woman standing near to Jack.

"The Corporation has laid on a dinner for them all in twenty marquees in the park," Jack informed her.

"What? And we've got to queue up for new ration books at the Walker Art Gallery next week, they'd better win us this bloody war, that's all I can say," responded the woman half smiling.

It was another month before the Allied advance to Victory became a slogan on everyone's lips. Mid-way through July, the Germans made their last great offensive on the Western Front but the French and the Americans drove them back to such a point that they were demoralised and fighting without conviction. Then in early August, there was an Anglo-French attack in Amiens which obliterated any hope of a German come-back. The newspapers and bulletins were full of stories about the Allied counter-attack, how the cowardly enemy turned tail and retreated to Germany. Now the talk in the queues was no longer whether there would be victory but when. And still the sun shone.

There was renewed optimism in the air but by late September the weather had cooled, there were very few miners to dig the coal from the pits so even stricter rations were in place and the winter was coming. The politicians seemed to be taking a lifetime to settle the armistice. In the meantime, men were being killed and maimed and anger was growing.

Gracie stood in the kitchen preparing Jack's "carry-out" or at least what "carry-out" she could cobble together.
"I notice they're not so keen to put up posters now," she commented. I can't believe our lads are still dying Jack, they told us two months ago that the victory had begun. And God only knows what's happening to our Fred over in Germany. Will he ever get home? I tell you if I didn't have this baby to keep me going I think I

would be losing heart."

Gracie looked tired but everything felt normal and there had been none of the bleeding that had devastated her other pregnancies, this felt much more like her pregnancy with Ivy Rose.

"It's the American troops that are getting the worst of it Gracie. The trouble is they are so young and they don't have any experience of fighting in wars, there are hundreds of them coming into the Docks every day, I see them, they're sending them back from the Front in droves. That new hospital they've made for them in Mossley Hill is already overcrowded. It's not just lads with wounds, a lot of them have got lung problems, some disease like pneumonia, but the word is the doctors are not sure what it is. I think it might be an idea if you and Ivy stay in the house as much as you can until the baby comes."

Gracie made no reply but she had heard the concern in Jack's voice and heeded his words. She nodded.

"You're right Jack, it must be awful for those boys, so far away from home," continued Gracie. "Our Sadie said that the men in the Rotary Club have been inviting some of the soldiers to their houses for a home cooked meal, she said that Mrs. Morris, from the bakery has had a few of them for tea. Sadie heard her telling the whole shop the other day. She'll be in her element, showing off her china cups. I bet she's had her poor husband making all kinds of cakes in that bakery. I notice she's able to put her hand on a supply of flour alright, it's more than the rest of us can do. Oh well I suppose it's a bit of home comfort for the Americans and Mr. Morris is a nice man, they'll enjoy his company, if he can get a word in edge-ways."

Gracie didn't suffer fools gladly and she certainly had not forgiven Mrs. Morris for the way she had treated Sadie when she had fallen pregnant with William. Her mother used to say that her younger daughter had a memory like an elephant.

THIRTY
William Is A Bastard

The sun was low in the sky, it was getting on for three in the afternoon. Sadie placed her hand over her eyes to get a better look. She thought she saw William leaning against the wall outside the house. She was at the top end of Carver Street and the first thing that had struck her was how much he resembled his father. For a second, she wondered whether it might even be William Tierney, after all he had appeared at her door in exactly this way before now. Then anxiety took over and Sadie began to run with the pram, poor Daisy doing her best to keep up. What was William doing home at this time, he was an hour early? She wondered if he had been feeling ill in school.

When her son came within earshot, she shouted "what's happened William, are you alright?" But William didn't reply, he turned to face the door and when she approached him, he refused to look at his mother, let alone talk to her. Once inside the house, William went upstairs to his bedroom and she heard the door slam. Sadie tried to get him to open the door but he made no reply. She tried pleading and shouting but nothing was working. Cyril was due home in a couple of hours and if he stepped into this scene there was no telling how he would be with William. Sadie had never seen her son so angry and it seemed to be directed at her. She got on with preparing the meal and settling her other two children in an attempt to bring some order to the turmoil.

At exactly quarter to five, William came down the stairs, walked through the kitchen and into the parlour, took down the wedding photograph of his mother, Frank and himself and stamped on it, shattering the glass. Sadie screamed at him to stop, Charlie and Daisy were too frightened to cry, they sat watching the drama unfold.

"What's happened?" asked Sadie. "Talk to me William, what's been going on?"

Just as the words left her lips, the door opened and Cyril walked into the house.

"I'll tell you what's been going on, shall I? Your son's been fighting in the playground, he's no better than the other tearaways round here, I've told you for years Sadie, he needs disciplining, he gets away with too much, you give in to him all the time and this is where it all leads."

Then he rounded on William, "and don't try and deny it because I saw you with my own eyes, you were in the middle of the ruckus. The Headmaster said you started it, I've never been so ashamed, all the years I've worked at that school and not a blemish on my record. And don't think you can pull the wool over my eyes either, you're not the little innocent your mother thinks you are. I've seen you in the entry behind the picture house smoking with the other little hooligans. You need a good hiding that'd sort you out."

William was too angry to worry about Cyril, it was as if he hadn't heard anything his stepfather had said. He wanted to escape back to his bedroom but he found himself hemmed in by Sadie and Cyril, as he stood in the doorway between the kitchen and the parlour surrounded by shards of glass.

When Sadie saw how William looked at her and how violently he had destroyed the photo, she started to put two and two together. The thing that she had dreaded since she had given birth to her son suddenly was happening. The secret that she thought she had buried so deeply had surfaced. It was time to pay for her mistakes. This was the day that she had always known would come, the child was being punished for the sins of his parents.

It had all started when William and some of the boys from his class were playing football in the playground. Tommy and he had been picked for opposing sides. Tommy scored and William disputed the goal. The same thing happened a hundred times a week but for reasons unknown to William, Tommy had been cool towards William for some time and this dispute had been coming for a while. After this fracas there would be no turning back.

"It was a goal, you liar," Tommy shouted with as much venom as he could muster.

"I'm not a liar," retaliated William, "it wasn't a goal" and he turned to the other boys for support.

"We know you're a liar," said Tommy. "You lied about your dad. Your dad didn't die in the war, he's not a hero, my mam said no-one even knows who your dad is, you're a bastard, that's what you are."

Poor William stood, rigid between the two makeshift goalposts trying desperately to make sense of the words that were coming at him like shrapnel. His mind went to the photo in the parlour, his mother's wedding photo, Frank, Sadie and himself. Glimmers of light started to flicker in his brain. He had called Frank dad, Sadie had always told him he was his father, he had never wondered until now how he could have been there, at their wedding. His mother had lied, he felt childish and stupid, he did not know who he was any more, he felt persecuted and Tommy had gone from being his best friend to his persecutor.

"William is a bastard, William is a bastard," the boys chanted over and over again. They were holding hands circling around him, baying like a pack of hungry wolves, vicious and vindictive and yet looking for all the world like innocents in a game of Ring O' Roses. William stood in the middle of their circle trapped, tears streaming down his face. It came to an end when Miss Wells grabbed two of the boys by the scruff of the neck and the rest fled. She marched the boys off to the headmaster's office and returned to deal with William but by that time his step-father had appeared in the playground and was dealing with the situation. Cyril was shaking William by the shoulders and Miss Wells tried to intervene suggesting that from what she had observed, it had not been William's fault but finally she returned to her class leaving step-father and son to sort out their differences.

Cyril returned to his work repairing a couple of window catches and that was when William fled the playground and ran home to Carver Street. His intention was to confront his mother but when he got home, the door was locked and the house was empty. Sadie had no idea how long he had stood there on the step.

William's face was ashen and his body was rigid, such was the anger he felt. He said nothing, but his silence spoke volumes. Sadie wanted to scoop him up and cradle him like she had when he was an infant but she knew better than to try.

"Cyril," she said, "I need to deal with this on my own. Your tea is going cold on the table."

"Here we go again, never mind what I think, let's all bend over backwards for the brat and that'll make everything alright, you're deluded Sadie, I'm telling you now, that lad's heading for the correction school if you don't come down on him hard," replied Cyril while Sadie held her breath.

Cyril took a few steps towards the kitchen, taking delight in standing on the photograph and hung up his coat on the door, all the time trying to provoke a response. Both Sadie and William remained motionless, resisting his game. Finally, he moved to the table and started to eat his vegetable stew demanding that Daisy should help Charlie with his meal.

Sadie tried to make eye contact with her son but he couldn't bring himself to look at her. He saw his escape, pushed passed her and made his way back to the safety of his bedroom. Sadie walked towards the table intending to help feed the children but Cyril rose from his chair and rounded on her.

"It's bad enough that everyone knows he's not mine and now they all know he's not even Frank's. Did you think that just by giving him your husband's name everyone would forget what you are? People are not fools Sadie. Christ, you can't fart round here without everyone knowing. And what names do you think they've been calling you all these years? You never listen to me, I'm just the poor sod who married you when you were desperate, that's all," he raged. "Don't run away with the idea that I believed all your lies, I wouldn't be the first man to fall for a pretty face and I won't be the last. Get this glass cleaned up before our Charlie cuts himself. Oh, I forgot, you're not worried about him just so long as your precious William gets what he wants. Maybe you should go and find his real father, let him feed and clothe him instead of muggins here. He shouldn't be too hard to find if he's a sailor, try the women on the Dock Road." With that, Cyril stormed from the house leaving Sadie on her hands and knees, head down picking up slithers of glass, silent tears coursing down her face.

When Cyril had left, Sadie felt a loosening of the painful vice that was crushing her temples. She tried to gather her thoughts. How much had William heard from upstairs, how much did her son understand? She returned to help the little ones finish their meals, neither of them made a sound. She could hear the rhythmic thumping of a football as it bounced off the wall, it felt comforting, familiar. It was Tommy, he was in the yard next door. Should she go out and question him to find out what exactly had happened? She resisted, she should hear it from her son. It was time to face him and to face her own demons. The one thing that kept haunting her was that Cyril had said that William's father was a sailor. How had he known that, was it simply a lucky guess? Had he made enquiries?

With the two younger children quiet in their beds, Sadie went into William's room. He was lying face down on his bed fully clothed. Half of her was hoping that he would feign sleep and she could postpone the confrontation but her son was awake and demanding the truth. What she wasn't prepared for was how she would feel when he called her a liar.

"William," she said, "are you awake?"

Her son sat up and pulled his knees towards his chest, hugging his legs, his jaw was set as if for a fight and his eyes flitted from the walls to the door, from his mother's face to the bedstead like a fly searching for a safe place to land.

"They all knew because Tommy told them," William began. "I was the only one who didn't know."

Sadie tried to compose herself and asked "what did the other boys know that you didn't?"

It struck her how young her son looked, there in his bed, hugging his knees like Charlie hugging his stuffed rabbit. Yet he was determined to hear the truth despite his pain, his bravery went far beyond his years. The last thing Sadie had wanted was for William to discover the truth about his father in this way. It was cruel.

"They said that no-one knows who my dad is, they called me a liar because I told everyone that Frank was my dad. They said Frank wasn't even a war hero. And they said that Tommy scored a goal and he didn't. I wasn't lying, I wasn't, but no-one would believe me. They said I was a bastard because I lied, but I wasn't lying. It's you who's the liar, not me."

The child's face crumpled into a series of violent sobs. Sadie reached out to wrap him in her arms but he batted her away before she could touch him. Her whole body trembled and she sat down on the end of her son's bed, suddenly exhausted and she waited. She wasn't sure what she was waiting for, a break in the sobbing, a flash of inspiration perhaps. Finally, the sobs subsided and

Sadie began to speak.

"I didn't mean to lie to you William," she explained. "I was trying to protect you, keep you safe but now I see that I should have told you the truth about your dad a long time ago. I would have told you years ago but Frank came into our lives and we got married and he wanted to be your dad more than anything. Remember the way he used to put you on his shoulders and how he took you to the games with Fred? Remember how he used to play football with you in the park and you used to show him your skills in the yard? Remember, we would sit by the fire and he would tell us all those great stories. He loved being your dad as much as I love being your mam. That's why he wanted you to be on the wedding photograph, he wanted everyone to know that he wanted to be your dad. But then the war came and he was a soldier, it was his job and he had to leave us. I've still got all his letters William, you can read them if you like, he talks about you in every letter and he writes to you on the end of every letter, just to you and he signs them Frank and Dad. Sometimes I think he loved you more than he loved me. Do you remember any of it?"

William's breathing slowed and he nodded in answer to his mother's question.

As Sadie talked, she could not hold back the tears, William appeared not to notice, she brushed them from her face with the back of her hand and continued.

"Frank was a hero, William, he died fighting for his country that's not a lie. You can see the letter that the army sent after he was killed. You weren't old enough to read when the letter came and I've never shown it to you since because you were so upset when we got the news that he wouldn't be coming home to us. I don't think I realised how grown up you've got and I should have talked to you about all of this before, I know that now."

"He's not my real dad though is he?" said William. Tommy's right. "So you did lie."

Sadie tried to steady her hands which were shaking, she took a deep breath and searched for the words which would satisfy her son.

"I didn't tell you about your real dad because he left before you were born, he never knew you and anyway Frank was a million times better than he was. It wasn't you he didn't want William, it was me, he didn't even know that you had been born. He was a sailor, he went to sea and the landlady where he lived told me he got married to someone else before I had you."

William's eyes grew wide, it was as if he forgot to breathe. Sadie took his hand and he was too absorbed in the information to reject her.

"Is he dead too?" the boy asked.

Sadie wasn't expecting that question.

"I don't think so, William," she said, "but so many soldiers and sailors have died it's possible. I have no idea where he is and anyway, I'm married to Cyril now."

"I hate him," William spat the words at his mother.

Sadie thought, at first that he was talking about his real father.

"I wish he was dead. When Uncle Fred gets home I'm going to ask him to shoot him with his rifle."

Momentarily, Sadie closed her eyes, she knew she should correct her son, tell him not to talk this way about his step-father but in all honesty, at this moment, she had nothing but contempt for her husband and she had had enough of her own hypocrisy. She knew better than to try to defend Cyril, there was no defence for the way he treated William. He was cruel. Neither did she try to justify why they stayed together. She had three children to raise. Her husband put food on the table and a roof over their heads, shoes on their feet. Without him, Sadie could only see a future in the workhouse or if not the workhouse, a return to the Courts. She knew from her childhood, what it was like to live in the Courts, two tiny rooms, sharing a lavatory with eight other families, a cess pool of disease outside your door. Cyril was the only thing which stood between their current life and poverty. She voiced none of this, William had ample to cope with, her mistakes had caused him enough pain. Cyril was a burden she must bear and now she must find better ways of shielding her son from his spite.

"Do I look like my real dad?" William asked quietly.

"You do," answered his mother, "he was handsome and he had blonde curly hair like you and blue eyes."

Sadie held her breath, she was dreading a question about Daisy, thankfully it never came.

"Was he any good at football?" continued the boy.

"I think you might get that from my family," smiled Sadie, "Uncle Fred's not a bad player is he?"

William looked as if he was thinking about how to answer that but there was no reply.

"What's his name?" asked the boy.

"It's William," his mother answered, "the same as yours, I named you after him."

"But what's his last name," he insisted.

"Tierney," she replied and William made no response.

"What do you think made Tommy turn on you like that, William?" asked Sadie, praying that William would not pursue his line of questioning.

William's eyes filled up again and Sadie wished she hadn't asked about Tommy.

"I don't know, he likes to be with the older boys now, the ones we went to the Picture House with, they're his new friends, it might be because he's a bit older than me." He looked sheepish and added "he's been calling me a baby ever since I tried to smoke a cigarette and it made me cough. He's been stealing his sister's cigarettes and they smoke them in the pictures. I don't think he likes playing with me anymore, he keeps hanging around with the other boys. He thinks he's grown up but he's not it's just because his mam's not there anymore and his sister lets him do what he likes so she can be with her boyfriend."

"How did Tommy know all this stuff about your real dad?" Sadie pressed.

"He heard his mam telling his sister and he asked her about it. I don't care, I'm much better at football than he is, he's rubbish. I'm the only one who ever picks him for the team. He was cheating when he said he scored that goal, he hit it wide. I wasn't lying."

Sadie ran her fingers through her son's hair, moved towards him gently and kissed the top of his head.

"Shall we get undressed and get some sleep?" she said. "It's getting really late."

"Do you think he'll come back?" asked William. Ever since Cyril had come into William's life he had refused to call him anything but he or him, no amount of encouragement from Sadie or scolding from his stepfather would change his mind.

"He's probably gone round to his cousin Mary's house, with any luck, he'll stay the night but I'm going to top and tail with you tonight, me and Aunty Gracie used to sleep like that all the time."

William fell asleep long before she did. Sadie woke every couple of hours anticipating Cyril's return, when she rose at seven there was no sign of him. It had occurred to her before that cousin Mary must have the patience of a saint to cope with his constant carping. Sadie wondered what Mary had been told about William and what she must be thinking about her. She heard echoes of Cyril's mother's voice, "Daisy looks just like William and nothing like Cyril…"

William heard his mother moving around the bedroom and lifted his head from the pillow.

"He's not in the house William," she said, "he'll probably go straight to school. Why don't you take the day off, I'll write a note tomorrow and say that you weren't feeling well."

William looked relieved and buried his head under his blanket. The other two children padded into the bedroom and she guided them down the stairs to start their day. William appeared in the kitchen an hour later, dressed for school and ready for breakfast.

"You've decided to go then?" asked his mother. "Are you sure?"

William nodded and ate his porridge in silence and Sadie had no idea what was going on in his mind. Was he hoping to patch things up with Tommy? Was he avoiding her? Was he trying to prove he was a big boy in order to defy Cyril? It wasn't prudent to ask him any of this but it was torture not to know what her son was thinking. It was then that Sadie realised that if she ever wanted William to trust her again, she would have to wait. It was no longer Sadie who would set the pace, it was her boy.

THIRTY-ONE
A New Beginning

The entire world seemed to be waiting. By October, Autumn had set in and the whole month was cold. Coal was like gold dust. Coats were thrown on top of beds once again and everyone said "God help us when the real winter sets in." Some of the schools had to be closed because Spanish flu was spreading and the advice was to avoid crowded places. Everyone waited to see where the next local outbreak would be. Waiting was a way of life. Men and women waited in queues for food, queues for ration cards, queues at the Post Office. Families waited for news of sons and brothers, husbands and fathers still fighting even though the enemy was all but defeated. When would they be sure if they would see their men alive again? The politicians waited for Kaiser Wilhelm to abdicate before they would agree to an armistice. The sick and the wounded who had arrived home, the so-called lucky ones, waited to see if life would be tolerable ever again. Everybody waited for news of the end and everybody longed for a new beginning.

When the end of the war came, it was sudden. The German Chancellor forced the hand of Kaiser Wilhelm and announced his abdication and two days later on November 11th Jack and Alun stood in Castle Street, looking up at the Town Hall Balcony where the Lord Mayor and the ex-Lord Mayor were confirming the news that an armistice had been signed that very morning. It had been signed, they were saying at five o'clock in the morning and at eleven o'clock firing had ceased.

Jack thought his ear drums might burst with the cacophony of noise that greeted the news. Not only did thousands of people in the waiting crowd shout and whoop and whistle but the bells of churches which had been silent for four years rang out all over the city, every craft on the river sounded its foghorn and locomotives pulling in and out of the station blew their whistles. All the clocks in the city chimed and chimed again.

In the afternoon, Sadie, William and Dilys met Frieda and her mother as they joined the crowds in Dale Street. When just about anything moved, everybody cheered. They cheered at soldiers arriving home on leave, they cheered as groups of American soldiers passing by, they cheered when they saw wounded soldiers, shaking their hands and patting their backs. Sadie and the others waited until dusk when, after a count-down that was worthy of New Year's Eve, the Town Hall was lit up. The symbolism wasn't lost on the crowd, everyone went eerily quiet as the lights came on. Even amidst this shared euphoria there was no escaping the sadness.

The celebrations continued well into the November night. The waiting was over, victory was theirs, their men were coming home, change was coming. Eventually, the crowds moved off from the Town Hall and drifted towards St. George's Plateau where, already, a sea of people had gathered to witness the illumination of the Hall and to listen to more speeches. William and the four women made their way up Church Street and on to Bold Street heading for the dairy where the younger children were waiting. As they walked, they were unusually quiet, lost in thought.

Naturally, Frieda's thoughts turned to Fred. Had he survived the last few months? Had the prison camp been liberated? Had he made it out of Germany? She pictured her husband's homecoming. How would he look? What had the war done to him? She had seen other husbands return from the front, changed so much their wives hardly recognised them. Would she know Fred when he appeared? Frieda could hardly wait for little Henry to meet his father. He could do so many things now, write his name and his numbers, kick a ball, sing a whole song, soon he would start school. She pictured the pride in Fred's face as their son showed off his skills. She tried to bury thoughts of what if, what if Henry was afraid of his father, after all, he didn't know him? What if Fred could no longer deal with a child? Surely, she thought, he would be home for Christmas.

Just as Frieda ached to see her husband, Frieda's mother longed for her son Michael to come home from sea. She had not seen him for thirteen months. He was serving on a Destroyer, somewhere in the Mediterranean and the last time he had docked in England the port had been too far away from Liverpool for him to get home on leave. She was immensely proud of Michael but she doubted that she would see a great deal of him in the future, his career in the Royal Navy had started well, he had been promoted to Petty Officer and she was sure he would sign up for long service. Besides, he had met an Irish girl called Kitty when his ship had docked in Southampton. Kitty featured several times in his letters and his mother was in no doubt that she was now his priority. None of this dampened her longing to see him and she couldn't help wondering if he might be granted leave at Christmas.

As for Dilys, her thoughts went to Gracie and Jack who were at the dairy, with the younger children, waiting for her to return. Her next grandchild would be born in peace time. It was what she had been praying for ever since Gracie announced she was pregnant. There was no reason why the birth shouldn't go well. Gracie's miscarriages were early in her previous pregnancies and there had been no complications when Ivy Rose was born. Dilys did her best to banish any negative thoughts. No, this would be a very special Christmas, a new life born into a new world, she allowed herself to believe that all would be well, this was a night of hope and optimism.

Sadie was wrapped in thoughts of Frank. She was picturing the day that she and William went to the station to meet him when he came home on leave. She smiled when she thought how William, had run away from her when he spotted Frank on the platform. They had walked home. She had never enjoyed a walk so much as that walk from the station to Carver Street. Would her son recollect it if she asked him? She doubted it and she doubted whether William would engage with her, she could not get him to talk about Frank. It was painful, it was like Frank had died a second time. She glanced at the back of her son as he strode ahead of the group. He was so young but war had robbed him of his childhood. He gave her few clues as to what he was thinking and ever since the incident at school, William had been reserved and quiet, polite rather than natural. There were plenty of pleases and thankyous but gone was the cheeky banter that used to be a feature of their relationship. As for William and his stepfather, they avoided one another. A routine had developed which enabled them to keep out of one another's way. William went to school on the last minute so that he could stay upstairs until Cyril had left. Apart from the occasional pass the salt, meals were a silent affair. Cyril had taken to sitting in the parlour in the evening and had brought home a small table from school on which he built his models in solitude. He sat with a blanket over his knees and complained about the lack of a fire. The nights had drawn in and William and Tommy no longer frequented one another's houses so William was confined to the kitchen but even though Sadie and he were thrown together every evening, William would not be drawn into confiding and his mother knew that since she had been the one to break the trust between them, she would need to let him come to her when he was ready. On this euphoric evening, spurred on by the bonhomie and the optimism, Sadie allowed herself a wish or a prayer, she didn't know what to call it. She wished more than anything that this renewed hope that accompanied the end of the war would reconcile her to her son. Nothing could bring back Frank. Cyril was the price she was paying for her own wrong choices. She could hear Mrs. Morris in her head, words she had spoken on the day that she left the bakery which would haunt her forever.

"You've made your bed, Sadie, now it's time to lie in it," but even though she blamed herself and had learned to live with the shame, to lose the confidence of her son was a cruel blow. Maybe by Christmas things would be different.

There was a warm fire burning in the dairy kitchen.

Alun had bought some logs from one of his customers, he had not asked questions but he suspected they had come from the docks. He never mentioned it to Jack. All four children were finishing bowls of custard, Henry was licking his bowl and Gracie was helping Charlie to scrape the remnants from his.

"No wonder they all love coming to the dairy," laughed Frieda's mother.

"We fed the horse," said Henry to his grandmother, "and the cows."

There followed a chorus of exciting things that they had been doing. All four children joined in, not to mention Llewy the dog, who had been woken from his reverie by the fire. It was pandemonium for a few minutes and it was enough to shake Sadie from her introspection.

While William ate his share of the pudding, the adults made a toast to a better world with a glass of sherry which Alun had kept for this very occasion.

"To absent family," said Alun and there was a moment of silence before the noise levels threatened to reach crescendo levels again. With the sweet sherry still warm in their throats, it was time to go their separate ways. Alun offered to get out the cart but Jack and the women wouldn't hear of it, much to the children's disappointment, they parted company and headed for their various trams.

The main roads were lit for the first time in years, the trams were packed with revelers, William and Daisy stood most of the way home and Sadie was too distracted by keeping Charlie amused to think about what kind of mood Cyril might be in when she reached home. She needn't have worried, the house was in darkness and she assumed Cyril was enjoying his own celebration in one of the pubs which all seemed to be heaving with people making merry. It occurred to Sadie that not many of them would be in work on time the following day but she knew that Cyril would not be one of them. Wherever he was, whether he arrived home that night or not, he would arrive at school, ready to start work at the allotted time the next morning, that much was certain.

THIRTY-TWO
Cyril

As it turned out, Sadie was wrong, Cyril didn't arrive at school the following morning. When Sadie woke, she was alone in their bed. She had given up wondering where her husband spent the nights when he didn't come home. It was feasible that he went to Mary's house but his absences were getting more frequent and Sadie suspected that there might be a less innocent explanation, she wondered whether he had found some friends and was playing cards. She found it easier not to address it and was even grateful for the times he was not at home because she and William did not need to tip-toe around him.

Sadie raked out the fire in the kitchen range and set about making the porridge before Daisy and Charlie woke. She shivered and decided to throw caution to the wind and use a little coal to light a fire before the children appeared. This was after all the end of the war. But she felt a cold breeze blowing through the house and opened the door to the parlour. Sure enough the front door had blown open and she guessed that one of the children had followed her inside and not closed it properly. She started into the parlour to shut the door and was stopped in her tracks at the sight of Cyril slumped in his armchair, the model he had been working on was smashed on the floor and the table upturned. She let out a scream, then got herself together enough to approach the armchair. At first she thought he might have been so drunk that he had passed out and was sleeping it off but that was not Cyril's style and as she got down on her knees she saw that he was a grey colour and was making a sort of clacking sound from a place deep in his throat. She felt his forehead and then his neck and his skin was cold and clammy, his face was distorted, it had dropped on the right side, she thought his breathing was laboured. Sadie opened Cyril's jacket and took off his collar and tie, she noticed his overcoat in a crumpled heap on the other side of the armchair and resisted the ridiculous impulse to hang it up in its rightful place on the door.

Sadie ran upstairs and woke William. "Quick," she said, "I need you to go next door and fetch Maggie, tell her Cyril has collapsed, ask her to go and fetch the doctor."

William started to dress but his mother stopped him "you don't have time to get dressed William, go in your pyjamas, tell her there's no time to waste it's very serious."

William hammered as hard as he could on Maggie's front door, it seemed like an age before she appeared, looking startled. William gave her the message and Tommy and his sister appeared behind their mother wanting to know the cause of the early morning commotion.

"It's William's dad," Maggie said, at which words William cringed, "he's collapsed, it sounds like he's had a stroke. Run to the doctors and ask him to come straightaway." Luckily her daughter was dressed in her coat and hat ready to leave for work and lost no time carrying out her mission.

Moments later, both William and Maggie arrived in the parlour and positioned themselves in front of Cyril.

"Our Cate's gone for the doctor, she'll be quicker than

me, hopefully he'll be there at this hour in the morning. Did you find him like this?"

Maggie looked flushed and nervous, she felt Cyril's forehead with the back of her hand and commented on his colour.

"Do you think it's a stroke?" she asked and Sadie could see fear in her eyes.

Tommy had crept in behind his mother and was standing next to William, the two of them watching proceedings without saying a word.

"Tommy, run up and fetch a pillow off William's bed and William, you go and check on your brother and sister, don't wake them up if they are still asleep," said Sadie.

She placed the pillow gently under Cyril's head. The clacking noise stopped momentarily and she took a step backwards afraid she had caused him to stop breathing.

It felt like time was standing still. Sadie paced the floor for fifteen minutes which seemed like fifty, Maggie was on her knees beside the armchair, occasionally she stroked the back of Cyril's hand in case he could feel her touch but there was no response. The doctor arrived and Maggie sent the two boys upstairs to keep Charlie and Daisy occupied until he had finished examining Cyril.

It was almost certainly a serious stroke and Cyril would need admitting to hospital. The doctor did not sound too optimistic about his chances of survival and he looked from Sadie to Maggie and stressed the point that even if Cyril did survive, the fact that he had been in this state for several hours would mean that probably he would have serious disabilities.

It was only when the ambulance had arrived and they were getting Cyril out of his chair and onto a stretcher that Sadie lost composure. Her husband was completely helpless, he was in some place between life and death, some place where no-one could be with him, he was totally alone. Despite their differences, Sadie was plainly distressed and Maggie must have felt it too because Sadie noticed that she was fighting back tears.

"I'll write a note to the headmaster," said Sadie, "do you think Tommy would give it to him when he gets to school? I need to drop the children off with Gracie and get to the hospital."

"I'll go into school with Tommy," replied her neighbour, "don't worry about the note, I'll go and tell him myself. Are you sending William to school?"

Upstairs, the two boys had helped Charlie and Daisy to dress and William was ready for school but given that Sadie's visit to the hospital might run into the evening, it was thought better for William to be placed with Gracie for the day. Sadie detected a look between William and Tommy which suggested a warming of relationships, for a second it lifted her spirits.

When she got to the hospital Sadie found her way to admissions and queued at the desk. She was told that Cyril had been with the doctors for two hours and that she would just have to wait. Three hours later she was directed to a ward, where, she was told, she could visit him. It struck her that everywhere was so quiet, she found it unnerving. Cyril didn't look much different from when she discovered him slumped in the chair but they had made him comfortable and they were giving him something through a tube, she wasn't sure what. She sat staring at Cyril, propped up on his pillow and her mind could hardly take in the enormity of the situation. His face was distorted, yet she couldn't help thinking that he was actually a handsome man, she wondered how it had never really struck her before. He was dribbling from the side of his mouth and she thought about putting her handkerchief under his chin to protect his neck but it seemed too intimate a thing to do, they had never really gone in for intimacy. Anyway, it felt like he was the property of the nurses and doctors now, that in this place, she had abandoned all rights to her husband. Sadie noticed Cyril's eye patch on the table beside the bed and she could not recollect ever seeing him when he wasn't wearing it. She mused how he would hate the idea that they had removed it. There were a thousand questions going around in Sadie's head. Where had he been? How long had he lay there before she found him? Could she have saved him from this? Had she somehow wished this on him, had the stresses of their relationship caused her husband to have a stroke? She couldn't pretend to herself that she liked Cyril, let alone loved him but she hated to watch him suffer. She had no idea how long she sat there, she had no awareness of other patients or nurses in the ward.

A doctor arrived. Sadie rose as he approached Cyril's bed. Her husband had had a major stroke and he was now being closely monitored. Only time would tell how badly he would be affected by the stroke but Sadie wasn't to expect a significant recovery even if her husband survived the next few days. How long Cyril would live after that would depend on the nature and severity of the stroke. When Sadie asked what he meant by that, the doctor sighed as if her question was a great imposition and he replied that it was possible to go on for years after this kind of stroke but more likely, Cyril would last a few months albeit in a much-reduced state of health. For now, he was in good hands and she must learn to take things one day at a time, what recovery there might be would be slow, she must manage her expectations accordingly.

As Sadie prepared to leave the hospital, a nurse put a brown paper parcel in her hands. The gesture made it feel like Cyril was already dead.

"Your husband's belongings," she said "and when you come in tomorrow for your visit, perhaps you could bring some nightwear and his shaving brush and razor?"

She gave Sadie a leaflet containing visiting times with some do's and don'ts printed on one side and carrying the parcel, Sadie walked through the hospital, across the grounds, past the lodge and out of the gates. The noise hit her like a steam train, people shouting greetings to one another, children playing, the screech of the seagulls, dogs scavenging, carts rattling along on the cobbles, motor cars, trams, the shrill of a policeman's whistle, the newspaper sellers yelling good news. There were swirling patches of fog blowing up from the Mersey but it was not enough to dampen the euphoria of yesterday, after four years of sacrifice, people were determined to celebrate and they were in no mood to bring the party to a close, there were people everywhere. Not so for Sadie, it was the end of the war but a new battle was beginning.

Sadie walked home. She walked quickly, as if the fog might swallow her up if she lingered. She expected to find the house in darkness but Alun's cart was in the street, he had drawn the curtains and lit the lamps, she could see the yellow glow of the gas lights. Once inside, Sadie braced herself for the cold but Alun had lit the fire and there was a scuttle full of coal in the hearth.

"I collected the children early from Gracie," said Alun, "in case the fog sets in. She said to tell you they've had their tea but it was early so they might need some porridge before you put them to bed."

"The coal…" murmured Sadie.

"Don't worry about that Sadie," said Alun, "the house was freezing when we came in, there's more coal down in the cellar, we can spare it, we've got all those logs to keep us going. Oh and Dilys has sent some mashed potatoes and onion gravy and a loaf and extra milk for the little ones. She said the loaf is only potato bread but she's sent some jam that she made and it's passable. Oh yes and Gracie said to be sure and tell you that young William has been a star. I'm not sure what she means, you'll have to ask him."

Sadie let go of the tears that had been welling up for hours. "I don't know what I would do without you and Dilys," she sobbed.

"We're family Sadie, that's what families do. Now, I need to get back to the dairy before this fog gets any worse, I don't want to spook Dragon, he's jittery enough in the dark let alone the fog. Don't let this fire get low, luv, you need to warm those bedrooms up."

Sadie gave Alun an update about her husband's condition and Alun promised to relay the news to Gracie and Freida. As she closed the door behind Alun, William appeared in the parlour and started to pick up the broken pieces of Cyril's model from the floor and place them on the table. Sadie scooped up his crumpled overcoat which she hung on the back of the door. It looked like Cyril might walk in any moment, sit in his armchair and take up where he left off, building his model.

"Gracie said you've been a star today," said Sadie.

"I'm going to help you Mam," William said earnestly. Their eyes connected in a way that they had not done since William had discovered the truth about his father, William Tierney. Sadie knew that she wasn't forgiven but her son was reaching out to her and it was enough for now.

Sadie had never been so grateful for the warmth of a fire. Children in bed, she sat as close to the grate as she could manage, she changed into her nightdress and wrapped her shawl tightly round her body, her head ached and she drooped with exhaustion. For a while, she lost herself in the flames as they danced, blue and yellow and in the noises the coal made as it sighed and wheezed. The last time she could remember a fire that really warmed her was when Frank was alive, Cyril would have plenty to say about this fire if he were here. Sadie threw on one more piece of coal. Tonight, she would be warm, tomorrow she would try to work out how she and her children were going to survive. Sitting there in the shadows, Sadie's thoughts went to the past. She tried to recall her father's face but she couldn't. Instead, what came to her was the touch of his hand on her shoulder. The relationship he had with her mother could not have been more different from her own with Cyril. Her mother had been truly devastated by his tragic death. As young as she was when he was killed, there was never any question of her marrying another man. Instead, she opted to work three jobs in order to keep her family together. The cost was her health. Sadie knew that Mary Jane could never quite forgive herself for the burden she laid on her eldest daughter. From her very early years, Sadie had been a mother to her siblings and a housekeeper to the family. She had never resented the responsibilities that were placed on her, raising Fred, caring for her mother, it was how life was, she counted herself as one of the lucky ones.

Sadie was comforted by her recollections and reluctant as she was to leave the warmth of the kitchen, she took herself off to bed just before midnight. The brown paper parcel containing Cyril's clothes was still sitting on the end of the bed where William had placed it. She ought to open it and hang up his jacket and trousers but she was too tired even to move it, she climbed into bed, still wearing her shawl, pulled the covers over her head and closed her eyes.

"Tomorrow is a different day," she sighed, "tomorrow is a different day."

THIRTY-THREE
A Different Day

William couldn't remember a day when he had woken before his mother. From his bed, he listened for familiar sounds but heard none. He padded bare foot into his mother's room and resisted the overwhelming urge to climb into the warm bed with her. Sadie's hair was splayed out like a fan on her pillow while the rest of her was hidden under bed clothes which moved gently up and down in time with her breathing. William slipped on a jumper and made his way down the stairs and into the kitchen. He set about raking out the ashes in the fire, shoveling the hot embers into the bucket as he had seen his mother do a thousand times. Later, when they cooled, he would take the bucket down the yard and tip the ashes into the big bin. He wasn't aware that Sadie was standing watching her son from the bottom of the stairs. He reminded her of her brother, he resembled his father physically, especially his blonde hair, blue eyes and stocky frame but he had none of William Tierney's bravado, he was much more of a gentle soul, trying in his own way, to make things better. It was that which was reminiscent of Fred. Sadie made a move to fill the kettle.

"You've made a good job of the fire William, I'll make us some tea."

"I said I'd help you Mam, and I will," replied her son. "I'll watch Daisy while you go to the hospital today, it'll be easier if you only have Charlie."

There was a rapping on the front door which Sadie hoped was Tommy to ask if William was ready for school. She glanced at William to ascertain if he was hoping for the same thing. Her son hesitated and they both headed for the door at the same time. It wasn't Tommy. A policeman was there, asking if Sadie was married to a Cyril Harmer. William was sheepish, he wondered if this could be about the smoking at the rear of the cinema. Sadie nodded and her knees buckled, the policeman stepped inside to stop her from falling. A pot of tea was brewing on the kitchen table.

"Have you got any sugar, son?" he asked.

William fetched down the sugar from the cupboard and the policeman heaped three spoons full into Sadie's tea. As he did so, the two younger children appeared from upstairs, they were still heavy with sleep and holding on to one another tightly. William led them to the table.

Cyril had taken a turn for the worse, the nurses had telephoned the police station and their advice was that Sadie should come to the hospital as soon as possible as her husband's condition was critical. The policeman's words were disjointed, his lips were moving but what he was saying wasn't making sense. What did critical mean? The doctor had said Cyril might last months, years even. Was he dying? Was critical the same as dying? The nurse had told her to come at visiting time, she had given Sadie the leaflet, it was in her bag. It wasn't even half past eight in the morning. What about the children? Could she bring the children?

"Mrs. Harmer," said the policeman, slowly and loudly. "The hospital wants you to go now, the nurse stressed it's very important you go straightaway."

Somehow, Sadie gained control of her thoughts, she

realized that Charlie and Daisy were sitting at the table and that William had given them cups of milk.

"I'll take the children to my sisters," she began but the policeman interrupted her.

"I don't think you have time for that," he said, "there's a porter's lodge at the hospital, your lad can look after the little ones while you go to the ward to see your husband." His voice was firm and commanding, it was enough to nudge Sadie into action.

Sadie wondered if she had been shown to the same ward, this one seemed longer and lighter, it wasn't quiet, anything but, there were men chatting and shouting to one another, nurses scurrying between beds with trays and instruments and all sorts of vessels and two doctors in suits, comparing written notes on a desk at the far end of the room. Cyril's bed was surrounded by pale green screens. He looked just as he had when Sadie had left him. Confused, Sadie turned to look at the nurse, she couldn't understand why they had sent for her so urgently. Then, she heard the rasping, the awful sound of her husband as he struggled for breath. The nurse put a kindly hand on Sadie's arm and pointed to a stool beside the bed. Obediently, Sadie sat, she felt hot but was afraid to take off her coat in case she disturbed her husband or knocked over the screens, in any case, she felt like this wasn't the time to concern herself with her own needs. She looked round to see if there was any indication on the nurse's face as to how long things would continue like this but the nurse had disappeared, leaving the couple together. Sadie had never felt so alone in her life as she sat listening to the sound of Cyril rasping. The time between breaths lengthened, Sadie was glad that Cyril's eyes were closed. She noticed that his eye patch was still on the table beside the bed, she wondered if she should put it on him, he would hate to think he wasn't wearing it, she thought, he didn't look like himself without it.

Her thoughts were interrupted by one of the doctors who appeared through a gap in the screens. He felt for Cyril's pulse, then he turned to Sadie and told her he was very sorry but her husband had gone.

"My children haven't had breakfast," she said quietly, "I've been here for ages."

"Only ten minutes, Mrs. Harmer," said the nurse as she opened up the screen to allow the doctor to exit. "Your children will be fine. I'll walk with you to the lodge."

The nurse started for the ward door but sensing that Sadie wasn't following, she turned to see her carefully reaching for the eye patch from the table and placing it over her husband's damaged eye. Now there was no mistaking who he was.

"The man gave us toast Mam," shouted Daisy from under a chair in the porter's lodge. Charlie was asleep on William's lap.

"There's a bit of paper-work to complete," explained the nurse but if you like you can come back tomorrow when you have someone to look after the children."

Sadie was grateful, all she wanted was to escape and get back to a world that was familiar. She intended to head for Carver Street but she found herself walking to the dairy in the hope that Gracie might be there. She was in luck, her sister and niece were expected a little later and in the meantime, there was scrambled egg and tea for everyone and Dilys was not taking no for an answer. Sadie could have stayed in the dairy forever, happy children, the food, the fire, the company of the women made her relax, that sense of foreboding that made her whole body ache was temporarily lifted. She laughed and cried in equal measure but mostly she enjoyed the feeling that nobody judged her and more importantly, safe in the dairy, she stopped judging herself.

"I wish you'd change your mind and let me come home with you Sadie," insisted Gracie. "I can leave Ivy Rose here, with Dilys," she added and Dilys nodded enthusiastically.

"No," replied Sadie, "I've got loads of things to sort out, I need to do this on my own. Anyway, you need to look after yourself and the baby, I don't want to worry about you as well as everything else. You need to rest Gracie, you won't get another chance, not when the baby's here. I've got William to help," she said, knowing that her son was in ear shot. "We'll be grand won't we William?" Sadie sounded so like their mother that Gracie knew she had lost the argument and Sadie and her children left for home.

Night was falling when they got to Carver Street. The lighting of streetlamps on the night the war had ended was short lived at least in the streets where the likes of Sadie lived. She froze when she spotted Norah Price coming out of her neighbour Maggie's house. Undoubtably, Norah was in receipt of all the facts about Cyril's stroke, and a few more. Sadie lingered on the pavement for a while, hoping that Norah would go into another house to spread the news and she could swerve the interrogation. She began to wish she had taken

Gracie up on her offer, her sister had a way of managing Norah Price. Sadie laughed to herself as she thought about the time, when they were children when Norah Price had come to the door asking to speak to their mother. Gracie had answered the door and shouted "Mam, Norah Priceless is here to see you." She had referred to the woman by her nickname ever since.

"Sadie," shouted Norah. "I thought it was you, have you heard about Mrs. Morris from the bakery?"

Sadie was baffled. She was expecting a barrage of questions about Cyril. It took her a few moments to realize that Norah didn't know about her husband's stay in hospital and Maggie hadn't seen fit to inform her. Norah was relishing the business of broadcasting some breaking news concerning Mrs. Morris.

"Only you know her well, what with working in the bakery all those years, so I thought you would want to know straight away. You were out when I came over, you've been out all day haven't you?"

Sadie's arms ached, Charlie had fallen asleep and she couldn't put him down. She knew from experience that Norah would not give up what she knew without something in return.

"We've been to see our Gracie," offered Sadie, "the baby's due before Christmas. You were saying about Mrs. Morris?"

"It's so sad, Sadie," came the reply. "She died this morning."

Norah went on at length with a detailed account of Mrs. Morris's demise and how she was a pillar of the community and how Mr. Morris would not be able to cope without her since she was the driving force and he was such a quiet man. By quiet man, Norah meant useless. Sadie was so shell shocked by the events of the day that she didn't hear half of what her neighbour was relaying. The bit of information that screamed at her like a siren was that Mrs. Morris had died of Spanish flu.

"They reckon she caught it off one of those American soldiers she's been inviting to her house for tea. They say there's quite a few of them got it in the camp. There she was, trying to do a good deed and this is what she gets for her trouble. Makes you think doesn't it? She was a lovely woman Sadie, a real lady, but you know that more than me…."

Charlie woke and started to fuss.

"I need to get him home, Norah," said Sadie, "he's hungry."

She made her escape and Norah, realising that time was limited before everyone would close their doors against the night, continued with her mission.

Sadie was reeling, the events of the day threatened to overwhelm her. She threw herself into familiar, domestic things, amongst which she felt safe. She boiled the potatoes and warmed up the gravy that Dilys had sent the day before, she put a match to the fire that William had laid and took out the ashes to the bin. She found a face cloth and washed the children's hands and faces, she sent William in search of their nightwear and they were ready for bed before the meal was on the table. No-one could have guessed what the day had thrown at her. There were no tears, she didn't feel sad, she didn't feel anything. Bizarrely, Sadie found herself feeling sympathy for Mr. Morris in his grief but needing no sympathy herself. When the house was quiet, she took a pencil and a scrap of paper and made a list of the things which she would have to do. Return to complete the paperwork at the hospital, go to the school to see the headmaster, go to Mary's to inform her of Cyril's death. The cousins had seen a lot of each other lately, Mary would be shocked.

Sadie knew that she must find out what sort of financial position she was facing, the rent was due, with that thought, the predictable sense of foreboding came flooding back. Wearily, she climbed the stairs and started to undress. There was the brown paper parcel still perched on the end of the bed. It was an easy task to slip off the string. Inside she found her husband's suit, his shirt, his shoes with his socks stuffed in the toes. She searched in the pockets of his jacket and trousers feeling like a thief in the night. Nothing. She found a large brown hospital envelope with Cyril's name on the front. She shook out the contents on the bed. A white handkerchief, still in its creases as when she had ironed it, some loose change, enough to buy tomorrow's meal, a penknife and a wallet containing enough to pay two week's rent. Sadie didn't realise that she had been holding her breath, suddenly, she took a sharp intake of air and felt a choking sensation, she was shaking. She scooped everything up from the bed and placed it on the nightstand. It struck her that Cyril would have hated this invasion of privacy. She noticed a piece of paper in Cyril's wallet, it was a note. Suddenly, Sadie's mouth was as dry as parchment. She felt Cyril's presence in the bedroom and shivered. She wished she had not refused Gracie's offer to stay with her for the night. She took a blanket and escaped to the kitchen, her domain, her safe place and drank a cup of cold water from the tap. She re-lit one of the lamps and in the dim light, Sadie read the note. It was obviously from Cyril's cousin Mary, she had signed herself M. It wasn't dated so Sadie had no way of telling how long the note had been in Cyril's wallet. Mary had written to Cyril to say that she was looking forward to meeting him the following day in the usual place. The usual place was probably the Hippodrome or one of the other theatres, Sadie recalled her husband saying that he and Mary had gone to more than one performance during the last few months.

Wrapped in the blanket, Sadie slumped into a chair in front of the dying embers of the fire, eventually falling into a fitful sleep. She woke with a start, her palms sweating, from a dream in which the house caught fire and, try as she may in the dream, she couldn't open the window. She hauled her aching limbs up the stairs and, despite the cold, slid the bedroom window open a couple of inches, finally crawling into bed. She prayed that whatever ghosts were lingering would escape into the night.

When Sadie woke in the daylight, she couldn't understand why the bedroom felt so cold, she could hear voices downstairs and the sound of crockery and cutlery chinking and clattering. The children were eating breakfast, the voice must be Maggie's. Perhaps she had misread her neighbour, been too harsh with her judgements. There had been times in the past when she and Maggie had needed to rely on one another, times when they had even shared the odd confidence. She had to admit that Maggie's life had been far from easy. George was absent in some far-flung country for months on end and Sadie had often wondered whether Maggie's husband preferred it that way.

The voice in the kitchen wasn't Maggie's voice, it was Frieda's mother. Alun had brought her. He had picked her up and then continued on his milk round and Henry had come too. He was eating porridge at the table with his cousins. The older woman wasn't given to displays of emotion but when she saw the gratitude and relief on Sadie's face she said nothing, instead she spread her arms, entreating Sadie to fall into them.

"Alun brought me," she said "Frieda said to tell you she'll be down as soon as she can get time off work. She can't afford to lose any money, all the women are getting finished up next month, just before Christmas, the factory is closing, they've had their penny's worth out of them, now it's back to skivvying for a pittance."

"Is there any news of....?" said Sadie

"Fred," continued Frieda's mother, "no, as far as we know he is still in France with his regiment. But, Sadie, no news is good news, we would have heard something by now if there was anything amiss."

Frieda's mother lowered her voice to a whisper. "There are a couple of schools in Bootle that have closed with this Spanish flu, Frieda's doesn't want to take any risks with our Henry. You know how his chest is in the winter."

Sadie gave Frieda's mother the news that Mrs. Morris had died of the flu.

Frieda's mother glanced at the children and quickly changed the subject.

"Anyway, we're all going to the park with the football while you get on with whatever you need to do today

Sadie. I've got all day and all night if you need me." She was determined to lighten the mood.

Taking her cue from the other woman, Sadie fished Cyril's key from his overcoat. "You're an absolute angel," she said as she gave her the key.

Sadie smartened up her appearance, did her best to smooth her unruly hair which really needed more than five minute's attention, put on her coat and hat and, armed with the list of things she had to do, left the house. She noticed that Frieda's mother had hung a brown, chenille tablecloth over the window in the parlour. She wondered if she kept it for just that purpose and how many windows it had graced. It was a macabre thought and a gesture which would certainly spark a flurry of excitement and activity in Norah Price's morning. Two unexpected deaths on the same day would be deemed extremely newsworthy and would require visits to every neighbour, with second and third attempts to make contact if they happened not to be at home. Sadie braced herself for an encounter as she made her way to the school but luck was on her side and Norah was nowhere to be seen.

THIRTY-FOUR
A Visit To Mary

The headmaster was gushing with sympathy for Sadie and heaped lavish praise on her husband. An absolute treasure in the place, saved the school from would be calamitous occurrences many a time, could turn his hand to anything, invaluable, to say they would miss him would be a gross understatement, he would go so far as to say irreplaceable, no idea how the school would find another caretaker, a charming man. The conversation turned to William and when he might return to school. The headmaster would ensure that William's teacher was completely au fait with the situation, her son must be devastated, he was so fond of his father, obviously a very good relationship. Sadie cringed and hoped that her feelings were not reflected in her face. She brought up the subject of outstanding money which might be owed to Cyril. The headmaster would make a telephone call and he would ask the appropriate person to write to her. She must not hesitate to come back if she had any queries after she received the letter, he was there to help.

"Will it take long?" asked Sadie.

The headmaster looked blank, he had ushered Sadie to the door and was watering his plant.

"The letter," said Sadie, "only I have bills to pay and Cyril's funeral to organise."

"I'll ask them to make it a matter of priority," he answered.

Sadie felt in desperate need of a friendly face so she made her way to the kitchens where she was sure of a warm welcome from Ada and Cora. They listened while she described how she had found Cyril slumped in his chair after his stroke, the visit to the hospital and how she had sat by his bedside as he took his last breaths.

"It was peaceful, really, she said, he didn't know I was there and I didn't realise he'd gone till the doctor told me. His mother had a massive stroke too, maybe there were signs and I didn't spot them."

Ada refused to listen to Sadie's self-deprecation. She lightened the mood.

"We saw him every day too, we didn't spot anything was wrong, he looked a picture of health to me. You look like you could do with a good meal Sadie, we'll put some stuff in a box for you and the children. It's cottage pie today, there's plenty, I'll put some in the box. Send William down about four o'clock to collect it, tell him to bring the pram and come to the kitchen door."

The women shared a pot of tea made by Cora who was no longer the skinny waif that Sadie had known at the start of the war. Sadie took her leave; she would make her way to the hospital to complete the paper work that would confirm her husband's death. Maybe then it would strike her that all this was actually happening.

With a letter from the doctor and a death certificate from the registrar securely in her bag, Sadie braced herself to break the sad news of Cyril's death to his cousin Mary. She knocked on her door. She was thrown into confusion when a small, neat, grey-haired woman in her mid-fifties stood smiling at her. Sadie didn't speak for a second or two.

"Hello, is there something I can do for you? I'm Jo, short for Josephine."

"I'm looking for Mary," said Sadie.

"Oh, please come in, she's in the back yard, we were mangling the sheets, it's a two-woman job! Who shall I say wants her?"

"I'm sorry," answered Sadie, "I'm Sadie, her cousin Cyril's wife."

The two of them walked down the dark hall and Jo opened the kitchen door. Mary came through the back door into the kitchen, drying her hands on her apron.

"Sadie," she said, "this is a surprise, sit down, I'll put the kettle on." It was Jo who put the kettle on and laid out the tea things, Mary sat beside Sadie at the table.

Mary took the news much more calmly than Sadie had expected.

"At least he was spared months of suffering," she said, "I know from looking after Cyril's mother how bad a stroke can be."

"I wanted to let you know before Saturday in case you were expecting him to come on his usual visit," explained Sadie. But it was clear that Mary knew nothing of Saturday afternoon visits and hadn't laid eyes on Cyril for months.

Jo joined them at the table, setting down steaming cups of tea in front of each of them, a glance passed between herself and Mary. Sadie noticed the glance.

"Jo and I have known each other for years, Sadie," began Mary, "we met on holiday in Skegness. She came to live with me here six months ago, it suits us both. It's so good to have company."

There was another exchange of glances and Mary's voice wobbled. Jo put a protective hand on her shoulder.

For some reason, the gesture brought tears to Sadie's eyes.

"To tell you the truth Sadie," continued Mary, "Cyril and I fell out a couple of years ago and we haven't really spoken since…"

Sadie felt the news like a blow to her chest.

"But he told me you were ill, I sent messages, he stayed the night because he was worried about you, he bought tickets and took you to the theatre," Sadie was baffled.

"I'm so sorry Sadie, I don't know what to say, I don't know how to help you," said Mary. She looked at Jo for inspiration but her only response was to sigh and shake her head.

Sadie was desperately trying to make sense of what she was hearing.

"What did you and Cyril fall out about?" she asked.

"Actually, it was about you," answered Mary hesitantly.

"I don't know if you ever knew how my aunt used to drip poison about you into Cyril's ear, it was horrible and unjustified. I tried a few times to tell him to stop listening to her nastiness but in the end he told me to mind my own business."

"I think I can guess what she used to say about me," said Sadie.

"Oh, it was all nonsense," explained Mary, "she used to go on about William, she persuaded Cyril that he had a right to know who William's father was, she even insinuated that you didn't know. Then when your little girl was born, she tormented Cyril with the idea that the baby wasn't his. She was like a dog with a bone she wouldn't rest until Cyril swallowed all her poison."

"So that's why he changed towards me and William," murmured Sadie.

"He was lucky to have you," Mary pressed on. "I told him so, I would have given anything for the chance to have a family like you gave him. I thought when Aunty died Cyril might change but she controlled him even from the grave."

Mary's voice wavered and finally gave way to tears. None of the women spoke. The silence was too much for Sadie to bear and suddenly she was embarrassed.

"There was a note in Cyril's pocket," she said, "I thought it was from you." She fished in her bag and produced the note, handing it to Mary.

"This isn't my writing, Sadie, I didn't write this, I would never sign myself M. Someone met my cousin in the usual place, wherever that was, but it wasn't me. I'm so sorry."

"I just assumed the usual place must have been the theatre," said Sadie, "you know how he loved to go to the Hippodrome." It was as if she might be able to persuade Mary that she had written the note if only she presented her with enough evidence.

Embarrassment got the better of Sadie. "There's obviously been some mix up, some mistake, I need to get home, Frieda's mother is minding the children, they've been to the park," she mumbled. "I'll let you know when the funeral is happening, they told me at the hospital that funerals are taking well over a week to arrange because of this Spanish flu."

"Did you know that there is room in Auntie's grave if you wanted to bury Cyril with his mother Sadie? It might keep the cost down, I certainly don't want to be buried there and there's no-one else to consider, no other family.

And if you want me to, I could ask the minister to call on you, that's if you are thinking of a service at the Methodist Church."

Until now, Sadie had given no thought to funeral arrangements, her mother's funeral had been straightforward, they were Irish Catholics, tradition took care of the details.

"Yes," she said, "that would be what Cyril would want, thanks Mary, it would really help."

Together, Jo and Mary showed her to the door.

"You've heard things you weren't expecting Sadie," said Jo kindly, "you've got a lot of stuff to think about. If there's anything we can do to help you, we'll be here, even if you just want to chat."

Mary nodded in agreement and as Sadie left, alone, she felt a slight pang of envy at the closeness these two shared. She longed to talk to Gracie and made her mind up to visit as soon as she could.

THIRTY-FIVE
M For Mystery

The cottage pie was delicious, Ada had smothered the top in cheese and Sadie browned it in the oven. There was just about enough for Sadie and the children and for Frieda's mother and Henry before they left for home. William had been delighted to be asked to collect the food from the school kitchen, especially pleased to be told to knock on the back door like a secret spy and even more pleased when Tommy agreed to accompany him on his mission. Sadie watched the two of them as they made their way down the entry pushing Charlie's empty pram in which they would carry home their spoils. It struck Sadie that only forty-eight hours ago William had been her biggest worry. Now, she was a widow whose husband seemed to have been living some sort of double life. How easy it was for things to turn on a sixpence. It was time to face the truth.

As quietly as she could, so that she would not wake the children, Sadie stood on a chair to reach the top of the wardrobe. It took some effort to pull down a leather bag that she vaguely remembered Cyril fetching home from his mother's house the day she had died. It had seen better days, straps and buckle missing, the bag had been well used. It looked as if it was empty, she could feel nothing as she picked it up. Safely back on the bedroom floor, Sadie knelt beside the bed, opened the bag and shook it. Apart from brown flakes of dried leather, nothing fell onto the bed. The light in the bedroom was dim, Sadie fished around inside the bag. The silk lining had rotted and only remnants had survived, creating loose flaps inside the bag. She pulled out a handful of papers along with some scraps of silk and lay them on the bed then fished around a second time. More papers. She rose quickly, staring at the little heap on the bed, her knees protested at the sudden movement. She gathered up what she had found and took the pile of papers and the bag down into the kitchen then laid everything on the table. Next she fetched a lamp that hadn't been used for months. The sudden smell from the oil lamp as it came to life made her throat hurt. She held the bag close to the lamp until she was satisfied that she had retrieved all of its contents then she began to sort through the heap of papers on the table.

Bills, invoices, receipts, ticket stubs, a page from a theatre programme, a bank book from the Post Office in Monument Place containing one pound three shillings, a Bank of Liverpool business card, all sizes and shapes, some folded neatly, others crumpled as if Cyril had thrown them into the bag in a hurry. Sadie set about sorting the papers in date order in the hope that a trail would yield clues as to Cyril's movements over the last few months. The bills and invoices were from hotels and restaurants in town, he had been to the cinema and the theatre, there were tram tickets and there was a receipt for a ring that he had purchased. At first, Sadie thought the ring might have been bought by his mother but the date on the receipt was clear, Cyril had bought it the day the war ended, eleventh of November, the day he had had his stroke. Sadie shook the bag again and searched inside for the ring, there was nothing. She carried the lamp up the stairs, opened the wardrobe and felt through the pockets in Cyril's clothes. There was nothing. Next, she tipped everything out of his drawer onto the floor but found nothing but clothes she had washed and ironed a hundred times. Sadie's mind was racing, she felt like her head might explode. Who was this man she had married? She felt as if the shadows in the room were mocking her. How had she not seen this coming? She could no longer trust her own judgement. For months Sadie had been ridiculed and judged by Cyril. For months, she had stayed quiet while he belittled her. She had been afraid to mention that William's shoes were a size too small because if she asked her husband for the money to replace them, Cyril would respond with a tirade of complaints about the boy. And all the time, all the time, what? All the time he had been living like a king, buying jewellery in shops she would never dare to enter, staying in hotels and eating in fancy restaurants where Sadie could only aspire to the kitchens.

Where had the money come from to pay for the lifestyle reflected in that little pile of papers on the kitchen table? She didn't know if she had the strength of mind to calculate how much had been spent but count it, she must. Intuitively, she moved towards her own drawer, opened it and felt for the lilac envelope that she had hidden under the brown paper liner. She was sweating, for a moment she could feel nothing. She panicked. Had Cyril discovered it and taken it? She held her breath. Then she found what she was searching for at the back of the drawer exactly where she had hidden it. She opened the envelope and confirmed that the five-pound note that Eva Johnson had given her was safe. Sadie's rainy-day money was safe. She must be rational, she must not give in to wild imaginings, she must search out the truth in a logical way.

Sadie looked in on each of her children and stood watching them breath, it anchored her and the floor beneath her feet gradually stopped moving. She would not attempt to sleep tonight, she re-kindled the fire, took pencil and paper and set about some calculations. It became clear that Cyril had had the post office savings book for years. There were regular small deposits and withdrawals. Sadie spotted a couple of withdrawals around the time of their wedding when Cyril had paid for a few things. Had it all been doomed from the start? Whoever M was, had she been part of his life back then? In the last few weeks, Cyril had spent so much time away from the house, he had stayed out at night, presumably with M, he had stopped trying to explain his absences and Sadie had allowed it, in truth, she had preferred it that way. Still, Sadie had not suspected an affair, she had not reckoned on another woman. Was this her own fault? Was she a drudge? Hard to love? How was it possible that despite the clues, Sadie had not seen what was going on under her nose?

Gracie arrived at nine thirty to find that her sister had not been to bed. She reached out to hug her but Sadie froze and then backed away. It startled the children so Gracie encouraged them into the parlour and distracted them with dominoes and some blocks that she had brought. To Sadie's surprise, when William had woken, he had asked if he could return to school. Sadie was puzzled until she saw that Tommy was waiting for him on the opposite side of the street. Her heart missed a beat as she watched the two boys, arms on one another's shoulders, zig-zagging across the cobbles. Her eyes filled up and she rushed back to her kitchen as quickly as she could, she was in no mood for her neighbours. Then Gracie and Ivy Rose had appeared as if by magic. Sadie had intended to go to Gracie's house but she was having trouble doing simple tasks. She had black circles under her eyes and her face was red and puffy. Gracie thought she might have been crying half the night. When Sadie rejected her hug, Gracie felt hurt but the pain and confusion in her sister's face told her that something more had happened.

"The wife's always the last to know Sadie," said Gracie quietly "that's what they say and it's always the quiet ones, not the ones you would expect."

Gracie had always been a doer rather than a listener but everybody recognised that in a crisis, she was the perfect ally. She sifted through the papers with her sister and drew the same conclusions. Then, in typical Gracie fashion, she decided there were three areas that cried out for action.

"I'll go to the jewellers tomorrow," she said "give me the receipt for the ring and I'll find out who he bought it for, I'll find out if it's this M person, don't worry I know exactly how to talk to shop assistants."

Sadie looked aghast at the idea of an interrogation at the jewellers but she had little strength to argue with her sister.

"You've got to let people help you Sadie, why don't you go back to his cousin Mary and get her and her friend to give you a hand with the funeral. It sounds like they want to be useful and we don't know anything about the

Methodist Church, is it a proper church?"

Sadie seemed mildly receptive to the idea.

"And I'll ask Jack to go to the Bank of Liverpool in Water Street, he's bound to know someone there, he can ask whether there's a bank account in Cyril's name."

"It'll be Charlie's trust money," replied Sadie, "remember, his mother left instructions in her will. She left all her money to Charlie for when he is twenty-one and none to the other children."

"I know, how could I forget, vindictive old cow!" said Gracie. Now go and get into bed and I'll tidy this lot away and see to the children. It won't be long before they are fighting."

Sadie picked up her sewing box and passed it to her sister.

"Keep the papers in here," she said and "put the receipt for the ring in your bag."

Obediently, Gracie took the box and smiled. She was the one who made grand gestures and had big ideas but her sister was the one who made sure they worked. It had always been that way.

Dressed in her best coat which, though it would not fasten, was very attractive on her, Gracie rang the brass bell on the shop door. She had made sure that the assistant, a blonde in her forties, had noticed her browsing in front of the window display. A commissionaire in uniform let her into the jewellers and Miss Baillis acknowledged Gracie with a practiced smile. How could she help today?

"I'm looking for a gift," said Gracie "it's for my sister-in-law. I think you may have met her a few days ago, you may remember because it was the eleventh, the day they announced the end of the war. I suppose we'll all remember that day for the rest of our lives."

"Is your sister-in-law a client of ours Madam?" asked Miss Baillis.

"She is," replied Gracie producing the receipt for the ring from her bag. "She came in with her husband and they bought a lovely ring. Your name is on the receipt, look."

"I remember her well," said the shop assistant, a lovely couple, obviously devoted to one another, he wore an eye patch, that's the right couple isn't it?"

Encouraged by this, Gracie pressed on with her performance.

"My sister-in-law has a birthday coming up and I want to buy her a necklace, something a bit special," she said.

Miss Baillis immediately unlocked a glass case on the wall behind her and took out two emerald pendants.

"Oh," said Gracie, I thought you might show me a sapphire to match the ring."

"Not with your sister in law's colouring," responded Miss Baillis, "next to that auburn hair. I'd go for emeralds every time. We have necklaces but pendants are the height of fashion at the moment. We can alter the length of the chain of course but if I remember her rightly, the lady in question is tall and slim and I think that chain will be exactly right for her. They make a very handsome couple don't they?"

Gracie stood pretending to examine the pendant, all the time longing to tell Miss Baillis how wrong she was about the devoted, handsome couple. Then she reminded herself how many times, she had used similar shallow tactics in the pursuit of a sale when she worked at

Bunnies. It went with the job. The women said their goodbyes and Gracie promised to return when she had made her decision. She hadn't had as much fun since her days in the lady's department. She couldn't wait to tell Sadie what she had learned.

Sadie had followed her sister's advice and gone to visit Mary who hadn't expected Sadie to return so soon nevertheless, she and Jo didn't hesitate when she asked for help. Did Sadie want them to speak to the Reverend? Mary had a little put by, could she contribute to the funeral costs? Was she planning to have a tea after the burial, could they make refreshments?

Sadie hesitated. Humiliation was burning in her face. She told the two women about the ring and how she was almost certain that Cyril was having an affair while he was claiming to be visiting Mary. Quiet tears fell and Jo retrieved a handkerchief from the ironing basket and pressed it into Sadie's hand.

"The thing is," said Sadie, "Cyril's body is still in the hospital mortuary and they are short of space because there are so many deaths from this horrible Spanish flu so they said I must bring him home until the funeral. I can't afford to put him in the funeral parlour and in any case, I believe they are short of space too."

"And you don't want to bring him to your home," said Jo. "Perfectly understandable, under the circumstances."

"Well, I think William would hate it and I won't rest until I know the truth," said Sadie. The idea that he is lying in the parlour while I'm going through his things in the kitchen…." Sadie shuddered and she never finished the sentence.

"We'll bring him here," said Mary. He can rest in the

parlour until we can bury him, it's the least I can do and if he's looking down on us maybe he'll realize that he hasn't won." She was obviously very happy with her little triumph.

"Do you think the neighbours will think it's strange when I don't bring Cyril home, they might start asking questions," said Sadie.

Jo tried to hide her exasperation. "If there's one thing I've learned Sadie it's to ignore what the neighbours think. Besides, there are so many broken men arriving home and so many disappointed women being forced out of jobs that no-one has time for anyone but themselves anymore. Anyway, everyone is hiding something."

Mary would make the appointment with the minister, Sadie would instruct the undertaker to bring Cyril's body to Mary's house and Jo offered to put together a fitting funeral service. Sadie and Mary were unsure how tongue in cheek Jo's offer was, they all knew she had a low opinion of Cyril but when Mary asked if she was sure she wanted to write the eulogy she laughed and said "trust me I'm a librarian." And so they did trust her. Sadie returned home feeling reassured that all would be well.

After tea, Jack and Gracie arrived at Carver Street, both brimming with news. Naturally, Gracie went first, recounting, in great detail, her experience at the jewellers. They laughed as she described how she had duped poor Miss Baillis who was probably busy spending her commission as they were speaking. Sadie hoped that Maggie couldn't hear the laughter through the wall, she was, after all in mourning.

Gracie was glad to see that remnants of the old Sadie were still there, it had been a long time since she had seen her laugh, not since she had married Cyril. It was as if she had forgotten how to play.

"So we know that she's tall and slim and has auburn hair Sadie. It could almost be a description of Maggie next door, don't you think?"

Sadie laughed out loud but then she looked at her sister's face and realized that she wasn't joking.

"That's ridiculous," exclaimed Sadie, "Cyril had no time for Maggie, he used to complain whenever she came in, and I'm pretty sure the feeling was mutual. Anyway, she's got two jobs, she didn't even have time for her children I don't see how she'd have the time to be meeting Cyril, never mind the energy!"

"For what it's worth, Sadie, I agree with you," said Jack. "I think it's very easy to add two and two and make six. It's much more likely this woman is someone from Cyril's past, or even someone he's met in connection with his work." He shot a look at his wife and added "Gracie isn't exactly known for holding back."

"I'm not saying it's certain," said Gracie, defensively, "but keep an open mind, her name does begin with M that's all I'm saying."

Jack's face was sceptical, Sadie looked thoughtful, it was the best that Gracie could hope for.

"Now, my bit of detective work," said Jack. "Cyril does indeed have an active account at the Bank of Liverpool, they wouldn't give me details, they said that you must go and see them for details of the account but they will allow me to go with you if that's what you want Sadie. Oh and they need to see a death certificate."

Sadie threw him a grateful nod.

"And Charlie's trust fund?" she asked.

"Ah," said Jack, that's a mystery. They knew nothing about any trust fund. It's possible it was set up somewhere else. They are holding a copy of Cyril's mother's will though and obviously they will give you that at your appointment. I told them we would call in tomorrow at eleven, I hope that's ok."

"Dilys said to drop the children off at the dairy and before you object, she's glad to help," added Gracie raising her hand so that Sadie wouldn't protest. "Now where's that pot of tea you offered us half an hour ago?"

The following day, Sadie was glad to have Jack at her side. The bank was huge, designed to be imposing and oozing power. She was totally intimidated. The man who dealt with her queries could not have been more charming, he shook hands with Jack, ushered them both into comfortable seats and offered them tea which they declined. He opened a huge ledger on his desk. He also produced a copy of Cyril's mother's will folded neatly into three in a crisp white envelope. One hundred and twenty-eight pounds had been deposited into the account at the time of her death. There had been no activity on the account until five months ago since when there had been weekly withdrawals amounting to seventy pounds, all made by Mr. Harmer and always on a Saturday. He was absolutely satisfied it was all above board. If Sadie would hand over the death certificate, the account could easily be transferred into her name.

Sadie searched in her bag for the certificate, unable to speak.

"Did you look into the matter of the Trust Fund for Mrs. Harmer's son Charlie?" asked Jack.

"We did, but we found nothing, it would be very easy to locate if Mr. Harmer had asked us to set one up, there is none. But I took the liberty of glancing at Mr. Harmer's mother's will because you said that it contained instructions referring to establishing the Trust Fund. I'm afraid you were mistaken about that, there is no reference to any such fund in the will. I see that the executor was the Referend Sharp, a local Methodist minister. If he hasn't moved away, I know Methodist clergy move quite frequently, it might be worth asking him about the Trust Fund. Perhaps he can remember the details."

Jack and Sadie parted company outside the bank. He walked down to his office, she started the trek up the hill to the dairy. She wasn't aware of putting one foot in front of the other but somehow she reached the dairy. Gracie was there, waiting for news.

"I know Mam used to tell us not to speak ill of the dead Sadie but the man was a pig."

Sadie showed no resistance. She had scrimped and scraped, darned and mended, she had gone to bed hungry so that Cyril and the children could eat, she had felt shabby and joyless and in a few short months her husband had frittered away seventy pounds that she did not know existed on some floozy he'd met God knows where, probably the pub. She was ablaze with anger. The anger was like food, it gave her energy and purpose. She accomplished all she needed to do with the undertaker in minutes. She batted away his condolences and agreed on a funeral date in four days' time then she arranged for Cyril's body to be transported to Mary's house.

"I don't have the money for any trimmings," she

stated, "just the basic coffin is fine."

When William arrived home from school, Sadie got him to throw Cyril's half-finished model on the fire. The little sticks of wood exploded into a myriad of colours and noises, delighting the children.

"What's happened Mam?" asked William

"I've woken up son," replied his mother, "I've woken up."

The following morning, William had left the house to go to school so the front door was ajar as it normally was. But Mary and Jo were not used to walking in unannounced so they knocked and shouted through the crack in the door. Daisy got there first, Sadie heard voices she didn't recognise.

"Hello, you must be Daisy, is your mummy in?"

"Who are you?" said Daisy just as Sadie arrived to rescue the women.

"The Reverend has a free hour this morning Sadie," said Mary "and Jo is going to look after the children while we slip round to the church to see him. I came to tell you yesterday but you were out. Is that ok?"

"I can't claim to have had a lot of experience with little ones," explained Jo "but I've dug out some of my old story books and I thought we could read them together. What do you say Daisy?"

Daisy slipped her hand into Jo's and led her to the table where Charlie was finishing his breakfast. The three of them were so engrossed in a story that none of them noticed when Mary and Sadie left.

Reverend Sharp was expecting them. Date and time, numbers and an order of service were all agreed after which Mary was surprised to hear Sadie ask a question about a Trust Fund. Had the Reverend any recollection of an instruction by Cyril's mother as to the setting up of a Trust Fund for her son Charles when he was twenty-one. The Minister insisted on addressing the answer to Mary. Sadie found it slightly annoying but said nothing.

"I do hope everything was in order when I distributed Mrs. Harmer's will Mary. I assure you I carried out her wishes to the letter. She left a modest sum to the church which went towards the roof repair if I recollect rightly, there was the thirty pounds left to you Mary and the rest went to Mrs. Harmer's husband. But there was nothing in the will about a Trust Fund, perhaps she asked Cyril to use the legacy in that way but I wouldn't know that, of course. There was certainly no written instruction as far as I know. Did she ever mention it to you Mary?"

Mary shook her head and the women took their leave.

On the walk home, Sadie disclosed the whole sorry tale to her husband's cousin. As they approached St. Georges Church, a funeral cortege was entering the church grounds. Mourners collected around the church doors which were wide open and as the hearse arrived with the principal mourners following, a hush fell over the whole gathering. The funeral was lavish by Sadie's standards, the mourners well-heeled and for a moment, Sadie questioned her decision not to give her husband a better send-off. She recognised Mr. Morris, walking directly behind the hearse. He looked smart, she thought, in a black coat and bowler hat. She was used to seeing him in his white overalls which Mrs. Morris claimed to boil and starch three times a week. Everybody knew she sent them round to Gertie Woodward for laundering. She thought he looked sad but dignified, surrounded by his fellow Rotarians and their wives. Sadie spotted Councillor Braxton having a discreet word with his friend the undertaker. Out of respect, she and Mary stopped for a second or two at the church gates and her heart went out to Mr. Morris.

The few days leading up to Cyril's funeral seemed interminable. The anger that was fueling Sadie was superseded by a feeling of anxiety. She found it hard to be convinced that she had no need to worry about money, Sadie kept thinking that at any moment someone would tell her that the money in Cyril's bank account was not hers to keep. She managed to access the small amount of savings from Cyril's post office account and with it, she enjoyed watching the surprise on the rent man's face as she handed over a week's payment in advance. She also bought William a new pair of boots. Then, she worried that she had been foolhardy. She had yet to find the money to pay for the funeral. She had received a letter from the Education Department expressing their condolences and praising the years of dedicated service that her husband had given to the school and they were pleased to tell her that his outstanding wages and other renumerations would be dealt with by the City Treasury in due course. Due course, what did that mean? Sadie calmed herself with the thought that upstairs lay her rainy day five-pound note. As soon as the funeral was over, she planned to search for a cleaning job. Daisy was due to start school after the Christmas holiday and she could take Charlie to work with her, after all, she had done it before. There were hundreds of women looking for employment, she knew that, but she had the letter of recommendation that Emma Moran had furnished all those years ago and Emma Moran might even be able to facilitate an introduction. For the sake of her pride, Sadie didn't want to ask for favours but she was painfully aware that beggars could not be choosers.

Thought after thought bounced around Sadie's head, batting them away was exhausting. Other ideas insinuated themselves, creeping up on her and clinging to her like fog on the river. Who was Cyril's other woman? Would she be so brazen as to turn up at his funeral? What was she like? Was it just sex? Did he love her? These were the thoughts which threatened to defeat her, the thoughts she could not bat away. She longed to be alone but three children and a stream of well-meaning visitors ensured that she was not. Though she was not relishing having to face the funeral, Sadie was glad when finally, the day came.

THIRTY-SIX
The Funeral

When Frieda and her mother arrived to take care of Charlie and Daisy and prepare cups of tea for the wake, Sadie was perched on a chair taking down the chenille tablecloth from the window.

"We can do that for you when you are at the funeral," offered Frieda.

"I need to let the daylight in," Sadie murmured. It was a blue-sky day, rare in November and it caught her by surprise, momentarily lifting her mood. She checked, one last time, that William was still determined to attend the funeral and the two of them left for Mary's house. As they got there, the undertaker was collecting Cyril's body. Alarmed, William took his mother's hand. Mary and Jo tried to distract him with questions about school but he struggled to answer and all four were relieved when they were making their way to the church in the fresh air where the silences felt more natural.

Along with Dilys and Alun and Gracie and Jack, they followed the coffin to the front of the church and Sadie scanned the dozen or so people who had gathered at the doors, she saw no tall, auburn-haired stranger. The headmaster was there, William looked away when he saw him, afraid he might speak to him. He needn't have worried; the headmaster was deep in conversation with an official looking gentleman who turned out to be representing the Education Committee. A distant cousin of her husband was in the little group, Sadie recognised him from Cyril's mother's funeral and Mary asked him to join them at the front of the church. When Sadie spotted Eva Johnson, they were both moved to tears. She reached out and took her friend's hand, drawing her close into her body taking strength from Eva's presence. The rest were neighbours, Norah Price of course, Maggie and a few of the other women.

There were no surprises. Reverend Sharp spoke more about Cyril's mother than about Cyril, he had known her well and Sadie had not been particularly forthcoming with stories about her husband that he could re-tell. It was Jo who had supplied the detail for the eulogy, not that Reverend Sharp used much of it. The burial was swift and seamless and as the mourners walked the short distance to Carver Street, a heavy cloud lifted from Sadie and she felt lighter than she had for weeks.

Once inside, William retreated to his bedroom. Platitudes about Cyril were bandied around, he was a rare family man, dignified, private but always said hello in the street, the boys in the school looked up to him, that kind of thing. Until at last, it was over and Sadie was alone again with the children. It was then that Daisy asked her if her dad would be coming back.

"No," said Sadie, "he won't be coming home."

"Where has he gone?" asked the little girl.

She lay on the bed next to Daisy and talked to her about heaven and angels. Sadie didn't believe a word of what she was saying but had no idea how else to explain Cyril's death to Daisy who seemed happy enough with the story until they both fell asleep, completely worn out.

"A nice wake…" shouted Norah Price from across the

street as Sadie was seeing William off to school. "You did your fella proud, Sadie, he wouldn't have wanted anything showy would he?"

Sadie smiled and hurried inside making sure the door was closed behind her. She had buried her husband but she knew that she could not begin to move on until she discovered the truth about him.

THIRTY-SEVEN
Moving On

Eva Johnson had a few hours before her train back to Manchester was due. Sadie was making the most of her friend.

"It sounds to me like Cyril has met this M woman and she has enticed him into parting with his money. Well it's not hard to see how is it? Nobody could accuse him of being a spendthrift, he never touched the bank account before she came along. And you say she was with him on the night he fell ill?"

"It was the night of the celebrations, half of Liverpool was out till all hours, Eva. So I just went to sleep, I assumed he must be in the pub. When I came down in the morning, he was slumped in the chair. I can't get the picture out of my mind. It was only when I found the note and Mary said she hadn't laid eyes on him for months, that I put two and two together. It all points to an affair, but I can't rest until I find out who she is."

"Well, Gracie managed to wheedle a good description out of the assistant at the jewellers, remind me to hire her next time I need a private detective," smiled Eva.

The time together passed too quickly for both women but Eva insisted that Sadie should bring the children for a visit to Manchester as soon as she felt able.

"My mother would love to see the children," said Eva, "she's enjoying her life now, she's far from well but she doesn't complain, a bit like your own mother Sadie."

Promises were made, hugs exchanged and Eva departed.

It was nearly a week before the letter from the City Treasury came. Would Mrs. Harmer pay a visit to the offices in Sir Thomas Street to collect three week's wages owed to Cyril and a small gratuity to help with her husband's funeral expenses? Any day, Monday to Friday nine thirty until four thirty. She would find the address at the top of the letter. Sadie was relieved and she paid a visit to the coalman, the thought of a decent fire lifted her spirits. Though it wasn't too cold for mid-December, the weather could turn nasty at any point. Like everyone, Sadie worried that a cold house was a good breeding ground for the flu and Spanish flu was no stranger in Carver Street. Since Mrs. Morris had succumbed, there had been another two deaths.

Since Cyril's funeral, Sadie had been enquiring about cleaning jobs and two people had told her to come back after the Christmas holiday. She was optimistic but she felt guilty competing with the girls from the shell factories, especially since she now had a savings account. Frieda's job was about to come to an end, they had already laid off the night shift. Frieda had managed to save some money but it would only tide her little family over until Christmas and then only if she was frugal. Her brother had his navy pay and sent money home to their mother now and again which eked out the meagre wages she got from her early morning cleaning job but they were by no means comfortable.

"We're better off than a lot of people Sadie," insisted Frieda. Lloyd George reckons our lads are coming home to a land fit for heroes, don't make me laugh, most of them can't afford a square meal. I don't know about fighting the Germans, they're fighting each other now over jobs. Mam says she's glad our Michael is staying in the navy. I never thought I'd ever hear her say that!"

"Take this Frieda," insisted Sadie, "you never know when you'll have a rainy day."

Sadie pushed a five-pound note in a lilac envelope into Frieda's palm saying "you would do it for me and anyway, our Fred won't speak to me when he gets home if I don't help out! It's just to tide you over."

Sadie waved away Frieda's protestations and changed the subject.

"What do you make of women voting in the election on Saturday? Times are changing Frieda, people aren't going to stand for the things they put up with before the war, once this country gets back on its feet and the men get home, you'll see, things will get better. They reckon they are going to build loads of new homes, 'homes for heroes,' they're calling them. You and our Fred might get out of that tenement, you never know they might give you a new house. If our Fred's not one of the heroes I don't know who is!"

"I don't believe anything any of them say, Sadie," responded Frieda, "not after the way they treated Opa. I hope you're right but I don't think things will change for the likes of us anytime soon, you've only got to listen to the girls at the factory to see that."

Frieda looked at her sister-in-law and was sorry she had dampened her attempt to lighten the mood.

"Don't mind me Sadie, after all you've gone through you don't want to listen to me moaning, I'll be fine when I have worked my notice and found another job. I hate all this waiting. I keep thinking Fred will walk through the door any day. I've sent a letter but he hasn't written back. Maybe the letter arrived after he'd already left for home. It's the not knowing that's driving me crazy."

Frieda wasn't the only one waiting for news. There were stories like Fred's on every street. Families expected a speedy return of prisoners and of the sick and injured but demobilization was frustratingly slow and chaotic. It was impossible to get accurate news of loved ones, everyone hoped that their missing soldier would turn up alive and that their injured son would make a full recovery, of course they did, but the reality turned out to be nothing like that. Train after train arrived at Lime Street Station disgorging hundreds of men, many of them wounded or suffering from the effects of poison gas, or just ill. Some were unable to continue on their journey until someone informed their families that they were there and help arrived. It was natural for families to hold to the hope that missing loved ones could walk in at any moment but in reality there was only bad news or no news for most of them. The nearer it got to Christmas, the more men in khaki could be seen clogging up the station. Jack kept trying to point out that though the war in Europe had ended, fighting was continuing in other places. But no-one wanted to listen, people needed to believe it was over.

Lord Derby made the decision to bring home essential workers as soon as the war ended, they had been the last to be conscripted and the first to be de-mobbed so the wives and mothers of soldiers who had sacrificed the whole four years and were still waiting for their demobilisation papers were naturally aggrieved. They didn't hold back with their complaints and the banter at the greengrocers and the post office turned nasty. Sadie did her best to avoid the queues. Nobody pretended it was going to be a Christmas with all the trimmings, rationing had put paid to that, but despite the deprivation and emotional turmoil, people found hope in the idea of new beginnings. It seemed the electorate was desperate to believe in this land fit for heroes that the government had promised. Christmas would mark a turning point and when the newspapers started talking about the holiday as the 'Peace Christmas,' suddenly the phrase was on everybody's lips. The atmosphere was one of cautious optimism.

Sadie couldn't seem to rest and however busy she made herself, unresolved questions nagged at her like gulls pecking at dead fish. She needed to know who had written the note. She needed to know who was wearing the ring her husband had bought. She needed details of the affair, who, why, where, when? Sadie was well aware it would be better for her to leave all these questions unanswered, but she couldn't, she just couldn't. Late in the evening, she would fetch the pile of papers still stored in her sewing box and sift through them to check for clues. Nothing changed, the same restaurants and hotels, the same tram tickets, the same theatre programme and the same receipt from the jewellers stared back at her as she spread them neatly across the table. She had learned them by heart, the amounts, the names, the addresses, the dark blue sapphire ring with two small diamonds on a twisted shaft. No amount of staring at the papers elicited any more clues as to the identity of M. Even Gracie suggested that it might be better to let sleeping dogs lie, she needed to focus on other things. Gracie had hoped that the baby would have arrived before Christmas but here they were, the day before Christmas Eve and no sign yet of her labour starting.

"If I hadn't been so near to having this baby, Sadie, I would have gone and asked questions at the hotels and restaurants to see if I could get any more information about whatever her name is, Maude, Mildred, Martha. I don't care what she's called, she's a home wrecking bitch! You could go yourself Sadie, nobody's going to take me seriously, I'm the size of a house."

But they both knew that her sister had neither the stomach nor the talent for this kind of chicanery.

Recent Christmases had been halfhearted affairs but despite the turmoil that was going on inside her Sadie was determined to make this one count. She bought a small Christmas tree from a group of youngsters who were selling them on the pavement in front of the butchers and she and the children cut out paper streamers for decorations. Sadie made three Christmas stockings from one of Cyril's nightshirts and she placed little surprises in them for the children. Ada and Cora had paid her a visit bearing gifts. They had brought potatoes and carrots and onions, rhubarb and apples and a precious bag of flour from the school and Ada had bought William, Charlie and Daisy each a chocolate coin. When Sadie tried to thank her friends Ada said that it was her Cyril who had grown them and it was only right she should get her share, anyway, school had closed for a week so no-one was going to enquire after them. She tapped the side of her nose and Sadie knew not to press the matter any further. With the rations she had managed to acquire, the treasure trove courtesy of the school and a contribution from the dairy, this was set to be a Christmas to relish. Sadie dived into the preparations, determined to throw off her compulsion to discover the truth until after her children had enjoyed their Christmas.

It certainly wasn't unusual to hear raised voices coming from next door, Maggie and her daughter Cate had been at each other's throats for months. It was usually sparked by the amount of time Maggie was spending away from the house and the fact that Cate was often left to look after Tommy. Sadie was making stars out of left-over pastry and Daisy was putting a tiny dot of plumb jam in the middle like a jewel. A rhubarb pie was just out of the oven and smelled delicious. It was making them all feel hungry. The boys were making hats out of newspapers, Charlie had streaks of black ink all over his face. Tommy was there.

"Mam," yelled Cate, "it's bloody Christmas Eve, which mother walks out on her child on Christmas Eve? What's the matter does our Tommy get in the way of you going dancing?"

"I'll be back to fetch him when I get settled in, I've told him that," retorted Maggie.

"When Mam? When your fancy man runs out of money?"

A silence fell on Sadie's kitchen. It was shattered only when Tommy stood, too quickly and his chair clattered onto the quarry tiles. His face was scarlet, Sadie could see panic and shame on the boy's face. He rushed to the door and out of the house. Sadie followed him in case his intention was to run away down Carver Street. He kicked open his own front door which stood ajar and more raised voices bled through the wall into Sadie's kitchen. Poor Tommy pleaded with his mother. "Please Mam, don't go, stay here with us…."

Charlie started to cry, the ink from the newsprint ran down his face and neck. He looked like a clown. William was trembling, he had reached out to comfort Tommy when the chair fell but Tommy had pushed him away, the rejection had hurt. Finally, there was the sound of a door slamming and Sadie ran upstairs to the bedroom to watch Maggie walk to the top of the street with purpose and determination carrying a suitcase. She never looked back.

Sadie tried to reassure William that it was all a storm in a teacup, that Maggie would be back in no time but neither of them really believed it. In Sadie's view, no woman would leave her family on Christmas Eve unless she was serious.

"Do you think she'll come back for Tommy Mam?" asked William when things had calmed down.

"I don't know luv, but Cate's a good girl, she won't leave him. He won't be on his own." Sadie hoped she sounded convincing. She knew that Cate was soon to marry her boyfriend and that she was planning to live with his family. It would be a big ask to bring her little brother with her.

"Can Tommy still come and play tomorrow?"

"I tell you what, we've got plenty of food," answered Sadie, "why don't you go next door and ask Tommy and his sister if they want to come and have their Christmas dinner in our house tomorrow?"

Despite the fact that he was afraid of another rejection, William carried the message the few yards to his friend's house. Cate answered the door, William saw that she had been crying, he was embarrassed and he hesitated.

"Tommy's not playing out just now William," she said, but when she eventually understood William's garbled message and the nature of the invitation, Cate nodded and said "tell your mam thanks, we'll see you tomorrow."

THIRTY-EIGHT
Christmas

Sadie brought up buckets of coal and lit fires in both rooms, she thought of the Christmas she spent with Frank and it gave her comfort. There had been a fall of snow overnight, entirely unexpected. Sadie thought how much cleaner and calmer the street looked as if nothing bad could be happening under those snowy white roofs. The children were making the most of it, building a snowman and throwing snowballs. William and Daisy joined them but when Tommy didn't appear, they soon returned to the warmth of the kitchen, their hands and feet stinging from the cold. As the day wore on, Sadie wondered if Cate and Tommy would appear for dinner, there was no noise from next door. At one o'clock, they both arrived, Tommy was carrying a box under his arm. "Look what me Dad's sent me for Christmas," he said proudly. It was Meccano, William had to control his jealousy, he said nothing.

The two boys dragged Cyril's model table into the middle of the parlour and were soon engrossed in the plan for the two-storey house they were about to build.

"Keep an eye on the fire in there you two," shouted Sadie, "don't let it go out."

Cate and Daisy helped Sadie to put the finishing touches to the meal.

"How did you manage to get all this food Sadie?" asked Cate, "you must have used up all your rations for a month."

"No," answered Sadie, "people have been very kind since Cyril died. That's a great present your dad sent for Tommy, it'll keep those two occupied for days."

"Yeah," said Cate, "he's always been good with the gifts, he never did come home empty handed, just a pity he didn't bother to come home more often. You might as well know Sadie, he's living with some woman in Bristol. He's been on leave for a couple of weeks now, there was a letter in the parcel for Mam. He's not coming back. He's as bad as she is if you ask me."

"Is that why Maggie's gone?" asked Sadie stirring gravy with one hand and dishing up carrots with the other.

"I think it might have put the top hat on it, but she's been seeing this fella for months, he's a doctor in Southport, he's fifteen years older than her, his wife left him last week, she must have had enough. My mam's gone to be his housekeeper as if anyone falls for that one! I don't know what she sees in him, except he doesn't mind spending his money on her, I'm surprised you haven't seen all the jewellery and the new outfits."

Sadie could hardly take in what she was hearing, she hoped she was responding with appropriate sympathy but the foremost thought in her head was that Gracie had been half right about Maggie, she was having an affair, but it was not with Cyril.

They ate like kings and queens, every tasty morsel was consumed. The rhubarb pie was judged to be the best bit of the meal, the fires were stoked, the children delved into their Christmas stockings, squealing with delight at each little surprise and for a short time the turmoil that was blighting each of their lives vanished.

"I can't remember a Christmas like this one Sadie," said Cate, "if Dad was home there was usually a row and if he wasn't, Mam was miserable."

"Do you think she'll come back for Tommy?" asked Sadie as the two women stood at the sink washing a mountain of plates and pans.

"I don't know Sadie," replied Cate, "maybe if her fancy man runs out of money, but I can't stay here waiting for that to happen. I can't afford the rent, not on my own. We were only just managing as it was. Me and Jimmy are getting married in February and his mam and dad have said that we can live with them but I don't know if they will take our Tommy in as well, it's a lot to expect isn't it?"

Sadie agreed that it was a great deal to ask but Cate told her that Jimmy's family rented a farm in Giddygate Lane in Melling. Sadie had never been to Melling but it sounded quaint and idyllic. Thankfully, Jimmy had been spared the war. When he was old enough to enlist, his job on the farm was deemed to be essential and a few months later it was all over. Sadie thought about the young land army women who had been recruited to the farms to keep the country fed, now surplus to requirements but she said nothing. Jimmy had lost his oldest brother at Ypres. Sadness was everywhere even in Giddygate Lane.

"It could be the making of our Tommy," said Sadie, "he might even end up with a farm of his own. It might be the best thing for him to get away from here." As the words left her mouth, Sadie knew that William's heart would break at the loss of his friend.

"Sometimes I think Mam's done this just to spite me Sadie. It's like she can't abide it when I'm happy, when I've got something that she hasn't got. I think she might be jealous because she thinks she's old and I'm young and I'm only just starting out. To be honest, I used to think she was jealous of you sometimes. Jimmy's a really nice lad, he's good to me but she's done nothing but criticize him since I brought him home. And I daren't mention the farm or his Mam and Dad, she just goes off in a mood if I even try and talk about them. I'm sorry about all that stuff in school between William and Tommy," Cate continued. "I know how it all started."

Sadie listened intently to what Cate was telling her.

"I had plans to go out with Jimmy but Mam wanted me to look after Tommy, and I made the mistake of saying that you took better care of our Tommy than she did and she flew off the handle. She was ranting on about how William's dad was some sailor and Daisy wasn't Cyril's child. Tommy overheard it all and repeated it to those lads he's been knocking round with. I was sorry after I'd said it all but it's true, you are a better mother to our Tommy than she is. Anyway, none of that matters now, I'm just sorry that's all. She's made her choice; she's gone and I'm all the family our Tommy's got."

Sadie's heart went out to the girl. Cate was old before her time like so many girls who grew up in those streets.

On New Year's Eve, Jimmy and his brother arrived with a cart. They took boxes of small items, a bed and some kitchen chairs from Maggie's house and piled them onto the cart. Tommy and William packed the completed Meccano house carefully into a wooden crate which

Jimmy had made specially. As Jimmy's brother turned the cart around, William ran to the top of Carver Street. He was determined to bid his friend farewell and he stood waving frantically until the cart melted into the distance and Cate ordered Tommy to sit down, fearing that he would be thrown out of the cart. William fought back tears of despair. Slowly, he started to walk home, head down and despondent. From her doorstep, Sadie had watched the whole scene and she felt her son's pain as if it was her own. A minute or so later, William heard the clip-clop of horse's hooves on the wet cobbles behind him. His heart leapt as he turned to look towards the sound, he thought his friend had come back but it was Dragon pulling Alun in the milk cart.

"Do you want a ride back to your house? Climb up William," shouted Alun, " I've got some good news."

Seconds later, they were outside the house and William was clambering down to stroke the horse. Alun was in full flow delivering the good news to Sadie and as fate would have it to Norah Price who was outside her house on the other side of the street.

"It's a boy Sadie, he's a smasher, they are both fine. Dilys is with them, everything went really well. They have sent me to tell you and Frieda. His name is Geraint David."

Sadie caught some of Alun's excitement, she was relieved and delighted for her sister. Tears started to flow. She didn't know if they were tears of joy or pain, everything had happened so quickly she could hardly take it in.

"Tell Gracie I'll be up to see the little fella as soon as the trams are running, is Dilys staying with them?"

"Wild horses wouldn't drag her away Sadie," he

answered. "I'll give her the message."

"Tell her I love the name, is it a name in Dilys' family or yours?"

"Neither," said Alun, "it's a new name for a new era, that's what they said. Your Gracie was adamant, this little fella is going to be his own man with his own name."

"With my sister for his mam Alun, I have no doubt he will be, have you?" replied Sadie.

Dragon nuzzled the side of William's neck with his nose and the boy was reluctant to let him go but Alun was in a hurry to get to Frieda's and back to the dairy in time for the cows. The boy slipped into the house unnoticed and left his mother to say her goodbyes but not before she had witnessed Norah Price scuttling from one neighbour to the next to broadcast her news.

THIRTY-NINE
Confrontation

It was the end of January before Maggie returned and it wasn't to reclaim her son, it was to collect some papers and a few trinkets that had been left in the empty house. She was lucky that the house had not been cleared and re-tenanted. The only reason that it hadn't was that every household on Sadie's side of Carver Street had received a letter informing them of the proposed electrification of their houses by the landlord. Surveys had been carried out and work was to start at the top end of the street in early February. There would be no charge to the tenant but naturally, a small increase in rent was envisaged.

"Naturally," muttered Sadie to herself when she read the letter.

Sadie hadn't seen Maggie arrive, but the house next door had been silent for weeks and when suddenly she heard noises through the wall, it sounded like footsteps on the stairs and drawers opening and closing, she went next door to investigate. Maggie was startled to see Sadie on the step.

"Oh, are you back Maggie?" asked Sadie, equally surprised.

"No, I'm just picking up some stuff, not that it's any of your business," retorted Maggie.

Sadie shook her head. She hadn't gone next door to argue with her neighbour, she hadn't even expected to see her there but something about Maggie's attitude raised her hackles.

"Maybe not, Maggie," she began "but if we are talking

about minding our own business, I tell you what was definitely none of your business, all that poison that you spouted to Tommy to turn him against William. Do you have any idea how much suffering that caused? William's just a boy for God's sake, he didn't ask for any of that and you didn't do your own son any favours either with your wild guesses."

"Don't you come over all holier than thou with me Sadie Harmer telling me how to bring up my own son. It would suit you better to look at the way you treated your husband. You've always thought you were better than me, Christ knows why, I've seen the way men look at you and your sister. I know your type. Cyril knew what you were. You've got some nerve, that man was tormented knowing that Daisy wasn't his, you lied to him and you lied to your precious son. So don't talk to me about wild guesses, I know for a fact it's all true. No wonder that poor man had his stroke…" Maggie stopped herself mid-sentence, her face burning with venom.

"That's rich, coming from the mother of the year who leaves her children to go to her fancy man on Christmas Eve. Have you even seen your Tommy since he went to live on the farm? How do you think he felt? I heard him begging you to stay, the whole street heard him. You're not interested in anyone but yourself Maggie, I hope this fella of yours has got plenty of money, he's going to need it, or have you got a replacement lined up? Some other poor sod you can move on to when the money dries up?"

Sadie was aware that she sounded vindictive, she tried to stop but she was feeling the need to defend herself which, coupled with a smarting sense of injustice, put her on the attack. It was like pouring fuel on to flames. Then it happened. The firestorm began and it would not be stopped. Standing squarely in front of Sadie and looking directly into her eyes Maggie said "well, it didn't take much to get your husband to open his wallet or his trousers and no wonder, the poor man was married to a drudge, I was the only bit of excitement in his life."

Sadie should have seen it coming, she should have been ready for the blow but until Maggie's confession hit her in the chest with full force, she really had not grasped that Maggie and Cyril had been lovers. Perhaps she had not wanted to believe it. She raged with humiliation and anger and out of nowhere, Sadie raised her hand and slapped Maggie across her right cheek. Maggie was stunned into silence, her eyes smarting with tears. She stood nursing her face and looking at Sadie. Sadie turned and walked out of the house, closing the door quietly behind her.

Gracie was nursing the baby in front of the fire in her kitchen.

"Don't you dare say I told you so," said Sadie "I feel foolish enough as it is I don't need you to rub it in."

"I wouldn't dream of it," laughed Gracie "but with that description I managed to wheedle out of the assistant in the jewellers who else could it be? You really slapped her across the face? I'm proud of you, sister, I never thought you had it in you."

"Well, things change and I've changed too," answered Sadie. "It's time I moved on Gracie, it's 1919, the war's over, I need to look to the future. Our Fred will be home soon, you've got Geraint. Daisy has started school. I worry about what's going to become of us. Everything is moving on, even the landlord, I've had a letter to say he's electrifying the house. I've made my mind up, I'm going to the pawn brokers tomorrow with Cyril's clothes and that bloody gun he loved so much. I'm getting rid of everything; things are changing and I need to change with them."

"That's the best thing I've heard you say in years but make sure you get a good price for that rifle, old Nichols won't do you any favours," said Gracie looking into her baby's eyes and smiling. "How about starting your new life by putting the kettle on, all this talk about changing everything is making me thirsty."

FORTY
Fred

Emma Moran must have been the busiest woman in Liverpool since the end of the war. She and the other women at the Red Cross offices in Gambier Terrace had been inundated with requests and enquiries about missing soldiers. The reality was that very few loved ones would ever be located and returning prisoners like Fred would come eventually to be talked of as miracles. Emma was feeling dispirited so when she heard that Fred was amongst a cohort of soldiers due to leave France in late February, she grasped the nettle and wrote encouraging letters to Frieda and Sadie. She could only give them an estimated date of arrival, things were chaotic at the ports and they should not read anything into the fact that Fred would probably be arriving on one of the hospital trains from Portsmouth. It was just that the army was using any form of transport they could get their hands on. It wasn't likely, Emma wrote, but should she hear anything more definite, she would, of course let Sadie and Frieda know. The news sent Sadie and Frieda into a spin, excitement was tinged with anxiety about Fred's state of health about which neither of them spoke.

In the meantime, life must go on and Sadie got William and Daisy off to school and then she climbed the stairs to the bedroom carrying a box that she had got from the greengrocer on her way home from Gracie's house the day before. She wasn't relishing the idea of packing up Cyril's things and she knew that if she put it off until later in the day she would lose her resolve. She opened the wardrobe and took out his suit and two good shirts and his well-polished shoes, folded the clothes carefully and placed them in the box. She tried not to dwell on thoughts of her husband with Maggie which had plagued her. Did they go dancing? What did Cyril tell her about their marriage, about William, about Daisy? She shuddered and opened his drawer, cautiously lifting out his collars and studs, his underwear, a silver- plated clothes brush and his shaving brush, bowl and razor. Images of Cyril lying helpless in his hospital bed sprang into Sadie's mind as she recollected the nurse asking her to bring in his razor. What if death had not come so swiftly? Would she ever have discovered the truth about Maggie? Sadie shook herself from her gloom, dragged the chair over to the wardrobe and reached up to bring down Cyril's rifle from the back of the high shelf, it was accompanied by a little box of ammunition. Once she was downstairs again, Sadie considered putting Cyril's overcoat in the box but she thought about Fred and the fact that returning soldiers were required to take back their army coats for which they were paid a pound. There was a depot at Lime Street Station. She found the thought of her brother having to relinquish his coat too painful to contemplate and decided to leave Cyril's coat hanging as it had always done on the back of the parlour door.

With Charlie settled at the top of the pram and the box balanced nicely at the other end, Sadie made her way to the pawnbrokers. She hurried as best she could, trying to avoid prying eyes and worse still, a collision with Norah Price. By the time she got as far as the bakery, she had relaxed a little and her thoughts went to Mr. Morris and how he was faring. She glanced into the bakery and thought how strange it seemed that Mrs. Morris was not in her usual look-out position in the shop window. She passed by but heard someone calling her name. It was Mr. Morris.

"Sadie, I have some currant buns for the children, it's good to see you. Hang on and I'll wrap up the buns." He disappeared into the shop, emerging again, paper bag in his hand, a few seconds later.

"Where are you off to with your big box?" said Mr. Morris.

Sadie could feel her cheeks burning, she considered lying but couldn't think quickly enough and Mr. Morris was always so well intentioned that lying to him seemed unfair.

"I'm on my way to Mr. Nichols at the pawnbrokers," she said, "I'm taking Cyril's things to sell."

"I'm sorry Sadie, I shouldn't have asked, it's none of my business," Mr. Morris was acutely embarrassed.

"It's fine Mr. Morris, actually I'm selling his rifle, I never did like it in the house, I think we've all had enough of guns and killing to last a life-time," Sadie ventured. "Actually, you might be able to advise me how much I should ask for, I have no idea." She lifted the lid on the box.

"I wouldn't know Sadie, but it looks like a good rifle to me I don't think old Nichols will give you what it's worth. I tell you what, I have a lot of friends who go shooting, they're always looking for firearms, some of them have collections. I've no idea why, but there you are. Why don't you leave the gun with me and I'll ask around and get you the best price?"

Sadie thanked him profusely, she was genuinely very

grateful and she handed over the rifle and the ammunition. When she tried to pay Mr. Morris for the fruit buns he wouldn't hear of it.

"They're a gift for the children Sadie, I'll be in touch when I have a buyer for the rifle."

It struck Sadie how much Mr. Morris had come out of his shell since he had lost his wife. The old Mr. Morris would not have been so bold as to offer his services or even to venture out of the comfort of his bakery. She came to a less than fair agreement with the pawnbroker, the haggling brought back memories of negotiating with the landlord at the Admiral for the sale of her pies. She was relieved to exit the shop and return to Charlie outside in his pram.

She stood browsing in the pawnshop window while she gathered her wits and there it was, for sale, a sapphire, flanked by two tiny diamonds on a twisted shank. There was no mistaking the ring. Sadie didn't know what to think. Seeing the ring on display in the window, nestled amongst the paraphernalia of other peoples' lives, made her sad. Maggie had parted with it so easily and Sadie had just sold her dead husband's belongings. She wondered if she and Maggie were so very different after all. It didn't mean she was no longer angry but seeing the ring sapped her of energy. Sadie knew that Gracie would say that it served Maggie right. Gracie was fond of the phrase "what goes around comes around" but Sadie just found it sad. She took a detour to the park where there were early signs of spring, snowdrops, the first daffodils, clumps of bright yellow celandine but she hardly noticed them because she was deep in thought. Was anybody's life what it seemed?

The musing was an indulgence which could not continue for long. Sadie made her way back to Carver Street to feed herself and Charlie and then to Mrs. Cleavers for an afternoon of cleaning. She never mentioned the ring to anyone, especially not to Gracie.

It wasn't difficult for Mr. Morris to dispose of the rifle, it was, as he thought a decent firearm and Cyril had kept it in pristine condition. He wasted no time in taking the money to Sadie.

"I think it's a fair price, Sadie, I hope it's what you had in mind," he said.

It was more than Sadie had expected and she made sure he knew she was grateful.

"Actually Sadie," Mr. Morris pressed on, "I have a proposal to put to you."

Sadie felt herself blush and made herself busy with making tea.

"Oh, no," mumbled Mr. Morris, "I'm not.....I didn't mean.....not that I wouldn't.....any man would be lucky to have you....no, someone like you....what I meant to say was I need someone I can trust to manage the shop while I'm in the bakery and you would be ideal. I'm offering you a job Sadie. You already know the ropes and with a bit more training, you would make a fine baker too."

Sadie was stunned. She had not been expecting this. Her first thought was Charlie. It wasn't like her current job, she couldn't take her son to the bakery.

"I would be happy to pay a girl to look after the little fellow while you're at work." Mr. Morris had anticipated the stumbling block. "Do you know anyone reliable you could employ?"

Sadie remembered the day she had spent at Eva Johnson's house helping her to pack up her dress making business. Eva's neighbour's daughter had looked after the children and proved more than competent. She could ask her; she might be interested. Her mind was racing.

On the other hand, perhaps Frieda's mother would agree to the challenge. Sadie was conscious that she sounded flustered, she wasn't used to being in demand and she wondered why Mr. Morris was giving her this chance. It never occurred to her that it might be because she was highly capable and just what he needed.

"I hope I haven't put you on the spot Sadie," he said, "I know you've run your own business and you might not want to go back to shop work but the thing is I know I can trust you and I haven't got time to train anyone else. We are getting busier now and I need to spend my time baking and anyway that's the part I enjoy. As you know it was always Mrs. Morris who managed the shop. I really haven't got much of a clue what goes on behind that counter. I'll understand if you say no, I know that my wife wasn't always kind to you, Sadie, I'm sorry for that, but that's not why I want you to come back, I really need you and don't worry I'll make it worth your while."

Sadie could hardly take in what she was hearing. She opened her mouth to answer several times but nothing came out. He mistook it for hesitancy. Eventually, she managed to tell Mr. Morris that she would make enquiries about child-care for Charlie. She made sure that he knew how grateful she was for the opportunity and for his kindness. As she was seeing Mr. Morris out, Snide arrived at the door to collect the rent. The idea flashed into Sadie's mind like a bolt out of the blue.

"Has the landlord let next door yet?" she enquired.

"No, not yet, we've had instructions to wait until the electrification is complete, we only received the keys back a few days ago. Why are you asking? The rent will be a bit higher you know when the electric lights are working." Snide replied.

"You remember Fred, my brother?" continued Sadie.

"Of course I remember Fred," retorted the rent man, "is he back, how is he?"

Sadie had no intention of going into detail but she replied that Fred had been demobbed and was making his way home. She was wondering if he and Frieda might be considered for the tenancy next door.

"We would need two week's rent up front," he said, "but if you're happy to vouch that they are good for future payments, I think they would be in with a chance."

Almost before she had said goodbye, Sadie had put on her hat and coat, got Charlie ready and was leaving for the tram. It was time to seize the day.

Frieda had taken a job cleaning in the wash house. She did the early and late shifts, scrubbing the baths, the floors and the tiled walls before opening and after closing. It was hard work and the pay did not compare with her wages in the munitions factory but there were so many women looking for work that she was grateful for the job. Her mother had started working as a char woman in the brewery which meant that one of them was always home to look after Henry. The latest report about the whereabouts of Fred had come, not through the Red Cross but from Jack. He had had sight of demobilisation lists which listed, not just battalions and squadrons but the names and ranks of soldiers too. There were two privates with the same name as Fred due to dock in Portsmouth on the last day of February, only one of them from Fred's regiment. It was hard to say how long he would need to wait for space on the Liverpool train but it was feasible that Fred might arrive home in the first few days of March. Frieda had been finding the uncertainty unbearable but this latest news had given her fresh hope and the beginning of March was only ten days away.

"So, what do you think Frieda?" asked Sadie, "Maggie's house has three bedrooms so Henry wouldn't have to sleep with you and Fred and the damp in this old place can't be doing him any good."

She had spent the journey between Carver Street and Netherfield Road thinking through the whole proposal. Frieda's mother would take care of Charlie, the other three children would be at school, Henry would be able to go to and from school with William and Daisy. Frieda could take the tram to her job at the wash house until she found something nearer, she might even be able to take over Sadie's current job if she put in a word for her and think how much easier it would be to help each other out if they lived next door to one another.

"Slow down Sadie," said Frieda," it all sounds too good to be true, I know this place isn't up to much but Mam's been here since she got married, she might not want to move. And when Fred gets home how will he know where we are?" Fred's homecoming was all she could manage to think about.

"Frieda, if your letters haven't reached him, our Fred will go to Opa's flat, he'll find it boarded up and then he'll work out that you have moved to your mothers so he'll come here."

"But then we won't be here Sadie, that's my point," interrupted Frieda.

Sadie persisted. "Your neighbours will tell him where you are and anyway, he's bound to head for my house isn't he? What if we go to Opa's old neighbours at the butchers and ask them if Fred turns up there, to tell him that you have moved to Carver Street. He's bound to ask around." She could see that her sister-in-law was mulling over her suggestions.

"I can't raise the money for two weeks rent up-front Sadie," argued Frieda, "I'm trying to eek out the bit of money I managed to save from the factory as it is, it goes nowhere, I need to put some by in case Henry needs medicine."

"Let me worry about the rent Frieda, this will be good for us all, let's grasp the nettle." Sadie would not be deflected.

Frieda's mother closed the door of her rooms in the tenement building for the last time and descended the stairs, it was easier for her to leave the old place than her daughter had anticipated. She wouldn't miss the peeling walls or the mice and besides, she was looking forward to her new role minding the children almost as much as Sadie was looking forward to her new job at the bakery. They turned Maggie's house into their own with the bits and pieces they had carted from the tenement and like everyone else in the street Frieda and her mother were delighted by the idea of lights which came on and went off with the flick of a switch. Frieda was excited to see what Fred would make of the electrification when he got home, the waiting was intolerable.

Sadie and the children got into the habit of going next door to Frieda's house each evening after tea. Charlie and Daisy would arrive first, followed by William and Sadie after they had cleared the table and washed the dishes. One such evening, the three women were sat around the table sharing gossip, Daisy and Charlie were cross legged on the floor under the stairs building a tower of dominoes which they balanced precariously on the seat of a wooden stool. The clatter and laughter every time the tower collapsed was noisy causing the women to raise their voices. William was in the yard with Henry, teaching him how to dribble the ball. The sound of the leather ball as the boys occasionally kicked it against the wall of the house was barely noticeable in the general din. Frieda sat in a chair with her back to the window while her mother and Sadie sat on the other side of the table, keeping an eye on the boys in the yard.

The women were laughing at something that had happened at the school gates. A man had turned up wearing a large overcoat and he had asked the waiting mothers if they were interested in buying some cuts of meat. He had opened his coat to reveal lamb and pork and even a couple of chickens tied around his body.

"Did anyone buy his meat?" asked Sadie?

"I don't think so," replied Frieda's mother, "it was probably contaminated and in any case two of the teachers ran out waving their canes at him and he shot off round the corner and headed up Vincent Street, he didn't half shift, I can tell you…."

As her mother was enjoying her moment in the spotlight, telling her tale, Frieda looked towards the children. Suddenly, she went white and gasped. She was staring as if she had seen an apparition. As she tried to get to her feet, her knees buckled. Sadie was the first to stand and turn and she let out a shrill squeal that frightened the children so that they huddled together, backs against the wall, under the stairs. As Charlie and Daisy moved, the domino tower crashed to the floor.

Fred was standing in the doorway between the parlour and the kitchen. He was wearing an ill-fitting suit, it looked like he had borrowed it for the occasion. He wasn't so much thin as gaunt, his collar gaped and his hair was all but gone but his eyes were unchanged, deep brown pools of gentleness. Sadie threw her arms around her brother and buried her head in his neck. They could both feel the warmth of her tears. There were no words even though Sadie had rehearsed this moment a thousand times. Freida, who had been gripping the table for fear of falling, approached and Sadie stood aside. Fred drew his wife's body into him kissing her face, her eyes, her mouth, both their bodies trembling.

It was the children who broke the silence.

"Who is he?" asked Daisy, still clutching Charlie's hand.

"It's your Uncle Fred," said Sadie, "he's come back to us from the war."

The children moved towards their mother, eyes fixed on this stranger, framed as he was in the doorway. Just then the back door flew open and William and Henry came crashing in from the yard. They had observed the scene through the kitchen window. William was overjoyed. His impulse was to launch himself at his uncle but something about how Fred looked made him stop, he was afraid that if he touched him he might break.

"Come here, lad," said Fred, "how's that tackling coming along?" and he held open his arms, wrapping them around his nephew. William was ecstatic.

Henry stood staring, he clasped his grandmother's hand and whispered "who is he?"

Frieda replied, "it's your dad Henry, he's home."

"But he's not a soldier," replied the little boy, confused. He hasn't got a uniform and a gun."

Everybody laughed.

"No," said Fred, "I don't need them anymore, I've left them behind, I've got you now, and your mam that's all I need."

Half clinging to his mother, Henry bravely reached out

and took his father's hand.

Fred had been convinced that he would never cry again, he had seen unimaginable suffering, he had just been informed about Opa's fate from his old neighbour, he was reuniting with his family, tears would not come. But the touch of his son's hand in his broke the dam and Frieda led her husband to the armchair where he cried and laughed, laughed and cried in equal measure. Sadie stoked the fire, gathered her brood and quietly left for home.

As she left, she heard her brother say "what does a man have to do to get a cup of tea around here, it's worse than the army?"

So began the long road to Fred's rehabilitation. His recovery was slow, malnutrition had left him with anaemia and for several weeks it was all he could manage to do to get up and dressed, on some days he didn't make it downstairs. Slowly, the story of his war emerged, a recollection here and a memory there. The remembrances often came out of nowhere, sometimes they were welcome and sometimes they were not. He was not alone, almost every house in Carver Street had someone trying to recover within its walls. Frieda had spoken to enough wives and mothers to know that she should not push Fred to talk, though it was hard, she was one of the lucky ones. Some men hardly spoke at all, some screamed in the night, some used their wives and children as punch bags. Fred was desperate to look for a job, ashamed that Frieda was forced to work so hard. She had continued her shifts at the wash house and had taken over Sadie's job at the cinema. She was often exhausted but when she got home to find Fred and Henry playing draughts or dominoes together her spirits lifted. Henry was a quiet child, happy with silence and he and Fred became companions, content with each other's company. The spring months passed slowly but bit by bit Fred's health returned. No one said so but everyone recognised that he was not strong enough to return to labouring at the docks. It was Frieda's mother who suggested he ought to try the brewery and as luck would have it, there was an opening. At the end of June, Fred found himself working as an assistant in the warehouse. The pay was inadequate but the job wasn't too physically demanding and Fred knew that he was fortunate to have any employment.

Outrage was growing, so many men who had been heralded as heroes were left on the scrapheap.

"Mark my words, Fred," said Jack as they stood in the yard smoking, "these men won't be kept in their places the way they were before the war. They have sacrificed too much to kowtow to bosses, they won't be treated like fools anymore."

"The dockers are talking about striking," said Fred.

"I heard the police are thinking of doing the same," replied Jack. "I don't blame them; their pay and conditions are a scandal but if they do I think there will be riots."

"Have you ever thought of going into local politics Jack?" asked Fred, "someone like you could make a difference."

"I would be lying if I said I had never thought about it" said Jack, "but now that I'm back in my job at the accountants and things have calmed down, I promised Gracie that I would be home with her and the children in the evenings. If you talk to any of these councillors they'll tell you that they are hardly ever home. Anyway, Gracie's got very interested in these Suffragettes since the election, she's all fired up, she reckons if women with businesses can vote she should be able to as well. You never know, it might be my wife who goes into politics, instead of me!"

"Well, our Gracie was never one to hold back," laughed Fred, " if anyone can get people to listen it's her. She's not a bit like our Sadie, I can't see her getting involved with the Suffragettes, the bakery is definitely more her style."

Sadie had already made a difference in the bakery. Mr. Morris had been totally amenable to changes. She had negotiated better prices with suppliers, customers had come flocking back as soon as raw ingredients became available, she recruited a school leaver called Nelly and taught her how to make customers feel special, remembering their names, asking after their families, that sort of thing, she produced a different bargain offer every week, sometimes it was a pie, other times a bun or a loaf and people would always buy something else as well as the bargain. Sales increased.

"People will always need bread," said Sadie.

Mr. Morris was well aware how good his new recruit was for business and moreover, though he would never admit it, he enjoyed her company. In contrast to his late wife, Sadie made him feel as though his opinion mattered. Consequently he became open to conversation, a new experience for him. People noticed. The Rotary club asked him to represent them on a fund-raising committee looking to build a war memorial in Everton. Earnest Morris would leave the bakery early every Tuesday to attend the meetings and those on the committee who knew him were surprised to hear him proffering his opinions and ideas. Caroline Hayes, who had been sent from the Council to act as secretary to the committee was impressed with his quiet enthusiasm and commitment.

"When you are the one taking the minutes," she said to

him one Tuesday, "you tend to notice the committee members who blow hot air and the ones who will do what they promise to do Mr. Morris." He nodded and they exchanged a conspiratorial smile.

Not only was the baker carving out a new image but the bakery was too. Rene Price, the landlady from the Crown came into the bakery every day for fifteen pies.

"They bring a few more lunch time customers in," she told Fred when he called in for a pint of beer after work, " but don't mention that to your other landladies, I could do without the competition."

It wasn't long before three other publicans appeared at the bakery to order pies.

"I'm going to see how they go on match days," said the landlord from the Swan. "I bet they'll go down a treat before the game."

It was the end of August, the nights were drawing in but summer was refusing to let go, days were still warm and pleasant. The much-awaited football season had begun. Fred called in at the bakery with William and Henry, they were on their way to the game. The first game of the season always generated huge excitement but this match was special. Supporters had been starved of football during the war but for the Blues there was something else. Everton had won the championship the season that war broke out and no-one had forgotten how close the one point victory over second place Oldham had been. It had been a long wait but now they were defending champions. The bakery was busy but Sadie managed to wish Fred and the boys good luck and wave them off as they joined the streams of men and boys passing the shop window on their way to Goodison, a new season, fresh hope was in the air.

When Sadie arrived home from work, a letter was waiting for her behind the door. The letter revealed surprising news. It was from her friend, Eva Johnson who had posted it in Scotland where she was on honeymoon. Eva Johnson or Eva Rosenberg as she was now called, apologised for not telling her friend that she was getting married but it had all happened in a bit of a hurry. She and her husband Isaac hadn't wanted to make a fuss, they had gone to the register office with a tiny group of people, enjoyed a lunch in the Midland Hotel and left by train for two weeks in Scotland. Eva's mother had not been thrilled about the register office nevertheless, she had attended the ceremony and given her blessing. Isaac was a widower with two sons a little older than Eva's daughter Francesca. He was a silversmith, he had a small jewellery shop in Piccadilly.

"He's a good man," Eva wrote, "we are both very happy."

Her own business was doing well and she had no plans to retire just because she was now a married woman.

Sadie had been half expecting news of a wedding but she thought it would be Eva's daughter, Francesca making an announcement. She was astounded to read that Eva had taken the plunge. As for Francesca, Eva's letter contained more news.

"Francesca's been offered a position with Cunard," the letter said, "it's what she's always dreamt of, designing and sourcing all the flower arrangements for the ships. She's postponed her plans to get married."

Sadie was shocked at the news. She was pleased for Eva and for Francesca. Eva's letter went on to say that she hoped that Sadie was still enjoying her work at the bakery and she hoped that Mr. Morris appreciated the new benefits she was bringing to the business. Eva was looking forward to catching up when she had a chance to come to Liverpool which she hoped to do in the next couple of months.

As Sadie was gathering her thoughts, the first trickle of supporters trudged past her door on their way up Carver Street. She could tell in an instant that their team had lost, gone was the bounce and the banter that was there before the game, the atmosphere was quiet and subdued. Sadie went next door to retrieve Charlie and Daisy from Frieda and her mother. Minutes later, Fred returned with Henry and William. Everyone expected Fred to be more disappointed than he was.

"We were unlucky," he said, "Chelsea are a good side, three-two is not a bad score and the last one was an own goal, just a defensive error, we'll get our revenge down there at the away match. Actually, Sadie, while we were standing there at half time, I had an idea."

The kitchen went quiet while Fred elaborated on his idea.

"A pie stall," he began, "inside the ground, pies at half time, imagine how many you would sell, they'd go like hot cakes. There are a couple of wooden stalls on the edge of the pitch, they would be ideal. The bakery could sell the pies to the club, just like you did at the Admiral but on a much larger scale obviously. You get paid for the pies, the club gets a profit. I can't see why they would refuse."

Sadie let out a sigh, "I don't know Fred, could we cope with an order like that? We'd need another baker unless I worked in the bakery and we got someone else to cover the shop." Sadie's mind was churning with questions and ideas and her head was still full of Eva's letter.

"We would have to deliver the pies," she continued.

"I thought of that," replied her brother, "I think I can get my hands on a second-hand cart from the brewery, it wants a bit of work doing to it but nothing I can't do.

"Can we get a horse Uncle Fred?" asked William.

"Well, not much use having the cart without the horse," said Fred, "but Alun will help us to buy a decent horse, and he can teach you two lads to be stable boys."

"I suppose we could keep him in the old stable at the undertakers," said Sadie, "it's never been used since Percy Baines joined up at the start of the war and his poor horse was requisitioned by the army, I don't think Mr. Freeman would want a great deal of rent, I could ask him."

In minutes, Fred's idea matured into a plan, everybody throwing in thoughts and opinions. They were all excited by the new possibilities.

"Talking of carts and horses," said Sadie eventually, "I think we're getting ahead of ourselves, we don't even know if Mr. Morris will like the idea and it is his business when all's said and done, he'll make the decision, not me. Let's not get too excited, not to mention that we need to sell the idea to the football club and we don't even know who to talk to."

When all was said and done, Mr. Morris did like the

idea and was confident that he knew someone who could initiate an introduction to the Secretary of the football club.

"His name's Tom McIntosh" said Mr. Morris, "I've met him a couple of times, you'll need to impress him Sadie."

He was fully aware that when it came to pitching an idea, Sadie was far more adept than he was and for her part, she was grateful that he was willing to give her the chance. So it was that the following week, Sadie and Mr. Morris walked together to the football ground. Sadie had borrowed a cream, high necked, lace blouse from Gracie. She had on a dark brown, woollen skirt which she had pressed on the kitchen table with a hot iron and a wet tea towel. She carried a small box containing one meat pie and a meat and potato pasty, her signature pastries. On Fred's advice, she had topped the pie with a tiny piece of pastry cut in the shape of the Everton club badge. Mr. Morris had declared it a stroke of genius.

They were ushered into a large room which the receptionist called the board room. Mr. McIntosh sat behind a large mahogany desk with a blue leather top, he was signing papers and signalled for them to sit on the two chairs waiting for them on the other side of the desk. He and Mr. Morris shook hands and when Sadie heard Mr. Morris introduce her as his partner in business, she was emboldened enough to stretch across the desk and claim her own handshake. Mr. McIntosh was taken aback but nevertheless, he shook her hand whilst taking in the situation.

Sadie noticed the array of silverware, cups, shields and

plates displayed on shelves on the wall behind the Secretary. "William would give his eye teeth to be here," she thought.

She pushed the box across the desk and Tom McIntosh was clearly impressed with the pie and the pasty, he did not hold back.

"It'll be good for us both," pitched Sadie, "think of the profit the club will make, the sky's the limit and we have worked it all out, we are confident we can supply enough pies and the deliveries are no problem. I promise you they'll all taste as good as the ones you've just eaten."

The deal was struck, contracts would follow and Mr. Morris and Sadie walked back to the bakery with grins on their faces.

"You did really well in there," said Mr. Morris to Sadie, "praise where praise is due."

"Mr. McIntosh was a pussy cat after the landlord at the Admiral," she replied.

Mr. Morris laughed out loud and took hold of Sadie's arms, squeezing her tightly. If either of them noticed, neither remarked on the gesture.

Two weeks later, Morris's bakery was the sole provider of pies to Everton Football Club, Sadie had used some of the money that Cyril had deposited with the bank to invest in the horse and cart, Frieda was managing the shop three days a week, Fred was in charge of deliveries and Sadie had become a second baker working alongside Mr. Morris. The only thing left to do was to fulfil the order! No-one bargained for the amount of hard work that it would take but when Saturday came, the pies were rolling out of the bakery as promised.

William handed the reins to Fred as his uncle jumped up into the driving seat, Henry and William were sitting beside him in the cart, muffled in their Everton Scarves. The cart sported newly painted signs advertising "Morris's Bakery Proud Providers of Pies to EFC." Blaze, so called because she had a white stripe down the middle of her face, pricked up her ears and started her trot from the bakery to the football ground. Alun, standing on the pavement, nodded his approval, satisfied with his choice of horse. The whole family had turned out to help load the trays of pies and to wave off the first of the morning's deliveries. Sadie felt proud as she watched the cart pulling away and Mr. Morris made it clear he was delighted. Sadie thought he seemed younger, enthusiasm suited him.

"Could you bring yourself to call me Earnest from now on Sadie?" he asked. Sadie promised to try.

"Don't be too long," Sadie shouted to her brother as the cart pulled away, "we've got another two loads at least."

"She definitely likes being the boss, your mam," said Fred to his nephew.

"I've been telling everyone that for ages," replied William rolling his eyes.

He's got too much to say for himself that son of mine, remarked Sadie, pretending to be offended.

Jack, who had been helping to load the cart, joined in the banter.

"I reckon this is just the start Sadie, your Fred has his heart set on an automobile you know. He reckons that if they start building all those 'houses for heroes' they keep promising and they move people out of town the women won't be able to get to the shops. He can see himself delivering bread door to door in one of those motorised vans. I don't know, maybe he's right."

"Well, I hope so," said Mr. Morris, "and let's not forget there is more than one football club in this city."

"Don't let our William hear you say that Earnest," responded Sadie.

Pleased that she had used his Christian name, Earnest Morris cajoled, "come on Sadie, back to work, these pies won't get themselves out of the oven will they?"

Sadie smiled, he had taken the words right out of her mouth.

FORTY-THREE
The Future.

The following months were hard work. There were times when Sadie returned to Carver Street too exhausted to do anything but sleep. But as the new decade was ushered in, things looked promising for the bakery. Frieda was managing the shop confidently and they were extending the bakery to make room for a second set of ovens and a third baker. Earnest Morris was teaching Sadie everything he knew and she was a quick learner. Fred invented a title for himself. He was now to be called "Head of Distribution" even though, as Frieda liked to remind him, he was the only person dealing with distribution.

Everton Football Club was so impressed with the success of the pies that they were building a series of kiosks to extend their catering service. Turnover at the bakery had tripled since Sadie had joined forces with Earnest Morris and Fred was delivering pies to more and more outlets. He had lost none of his enthusiasm to graduate from a horse and cart to a motor vehicle.

There was seldom time to stand around chatting but it was Saturday evening, the shelves in the shop were empty, pies had been distributed, Frieda had gone home. Sadie and Mr. Morris were standing behind the counter, carefully placing a wedding cake into a cardboard box. It was a chance to admire their work.

"It's lovely, Earnest," said Sadie, "I'll never be as

good as you at the decoration."

"Well, I know we've both been married before Sadie but I want our wedding to be really special," Cyril replied.

As he spoke, the bell clattered and the shop door opened letting in a rush of cold air. Sadie looked up and shouted greetings to Caroline Hayes as she walked into the shop. Caroline wasn't a frequent visitor to the bakery but Sadie had got to know and like her over the months that she and Earnest had been stepping out together. A mutual respect which had begun when they worked together on the War Memorial Committee had grown into something deeper and after a little prompting on her part, Earnest had finally asked Caroline to step out. As she entered the shop he quickly closed the lid on the cake box.

"Have you given it to her yet Earnest?" asked Caroline.

"No," he replied, "I was waiting for you to arrive."

"Honestly, Earnest, I don't know why you are so shy, Sadie isn't going to bite."

Sadie began to get a little nervous, she had no idea what Caroline meant. Earnest reached under the counter and produced an envelope on which he had written Sadie's name. He placed it in front of her and indicated that she should open it. Caroline smiled at them both. Inside the envelope was a share certificate, Sadie was now the proud owner of half the bakery. She was so stunned she was lost for words.

"It's only what's rightfully yours Sadie," said Earnest Morris. "You have built up the business, it's only what you've earned."

Sadie looked at Caroline.

"Earnest and I didn't want to get married next week knowing that you hadn't been repaid for what you've done. It's not like we have any children to pass this place on to Sadie and if you'll accept the shares we can go off to Cornwall and enjoy our honeymoon knowing the bakery is in good hands."

From the moment she had met Caroline, Sadie thought that she would be a good match for Earnest Morris. She was an encourager, she made him brave. The wedding would be a small affair but every detail would be attended to. Sadie and William were looking forward to being wedding guests.

Sadie was about to say thank you but Earnest walked towards the bakery and called from inside, "there's something else Sadie."

Moments later he reappeared carrying a thin wooden board which he laid on the top of the counter.

"I got the sign writer to cobble together a new design for the bakery," he said. "This is just a sample but If you like it, he'll make a new sign for over the shop."

"Morris and Settle Fine Bakers," read the sign and underneath in smaller letters, "Purveyors of Perfect Pies."

Earnest Morris searched Sadie's face for approval. "Do you like it Sadie?" he asked, "I took the liberty of using your maiden name since that's how our customers know you."

Sadie had been using her maiden name since Cyril had passed away. It came easily to her, there were very few people who didn't know her as Sadie Settle. The name change hadn't escaped the attention of Earnest Morris but he had said nothing.

"How could I not like it?" she replied tearfully, "and Settle will do just fine, that's who I want to be."

"Good, I was thinking black and gold, what do you think?" he continued.

"Oh I think black and gold is perfect Earnest," Sadie replied, "it's just perfect."

Sadie left the couple discussing the fact that Caroline had just heard that a site had been found for the war memorial and she started for the bakehouse to fetch her hat and coat. As she turned, she caught sight of William. Her son was mouthing something to her from outside the shop window. Was she ready to leave for home? She gestured for him to come into the shop and went in search of her coat. As Sadie re-entered the shop, William was coming through the door, the old bell clattering above his head. Not for the first time she found herself reflecting that William looked so much like his father. It wasn't just the blonde hair and stocky frame, it was the way he moved, the way he smiled, his hands, some of the things he said. In that moment, Sadie recollected her first encounter with William Tierney all those years ago and she found herself wondering whether he had made it safely through the war.

"I hope so," she said to herself, "I hope so…"

www.blossomspringpublishing.com